TOUGH LUCK L.A.

A native son of Los Angeles, **Murray Sinclair** lives there with his wife and two children. In addition to his crime novels, Mr. Sinclair writes screenplays. "There is no real Los Angeles," Sinclair claims. "L.A. will forever be a fiction, a glorious state of mind. Any writing of consequence about this town has a surreal quality to it—a blend of truth and fantasy which is absorbed from the past and present heritage of this illusory environment. This is the dream capital of the world, the place where people who believe in the impossible come to try to make their impossible dreams happen. And why not? After all, the California state flower is the poppy."

TOUGH LUCK L.A.

MURRAY SINCLAIR

Black Lizard Books
Berkeley • 1988

For Tootsie

Chapter One

I was hitting 60 when I heard the siren, heading west on Sunset, sweeping up around that long curve that overlooks UCLA and Westwood Village. A couple of jazzy Italian jobs had just passed me like I was standing still, so I didn't feel like I'd been breaking any speed records. I was in another world and wouldn't have bothered looking into the rearview mirror if Ellen hadn't casually mentioned something a moment before. She was past wanting to give a damn about me, and, looking back upon it now, I can't blame her. My lifestyle had plummeted to a nadir of dark brilliance, which is short for saying I had really become a pain to live with. The best thing she thought she could do was to leave me alone.

As I pulled over she didn't blink an eyelid. Her blank face was turned up toward the sun and her seat was tilted back against her typewriter, desk lamp, and the box with all the pots and pans. Her office clothes and reference books covered the top of the tonneau and there was a medium-sized carpet bag in the trunk. That's a full load for an MG. She'd moved everything else into her new apartment the day before. We'd just finished painting the kitchen in the morning. Then we had gone back to my place to get the rest of her things, and that's why, at this moment, she was sunbathing with seeming content to the accompaniment of a police siren. The tip of her tongue appeared, moistened her lips, then vanished from sight. Modestly, her hands rolled her sleeveless T-shirt back down over her belly, then she became inert again.

If I'm not careful, policemen have a way of overexciting me. Like a silly old mutt who would rather die than not go after the mailman or gardener, by the time I got out of my car and met the cop halfway, I was almost rabid. I went into my F. Lee Bailey act, ranting and raving and enjoying every second of it. Ellen had to give the guy my registration when I refused to let him see it. By that point, he had taken his nightstick out. He noted on the speeding ticket that I'd been uncooperative. And, in the end, with great audacity, I still swore I'd see him in court. Fortunately, the fellow had a well-developed sense of humor. He so much as told me so before he shook his grizzled head and walked away.

A petty thing. But I lacked civility and was bound and determined to make it all a big deal. I was feeling pretty righteous, and if a soothsayer had told me the truth then—that, in less than twenty-four hours, this very same wise-ass attitude was going to nosedive me straight into the clink on a trumped-up murder charge—I would have bellylaughed and recommended a couple of heaping spoonfuls of Geritol to pep up his flagging iron-poor spirits, then sent him on his way.

Ellen couldn't read tea leaves, but it wasn't hard for her to zero in between the lines. At first, as I resumed driving, she was so angry she just looked straight ahead at the road. Her voice shook as she spoke. My whole defense: two guys had been going faster than I had. Therefore, they were the culpable ones. Erroneous logic, so I was told. The conversation ended. We drove on in silence.

After a while, I asked, "Are you still angry?"

"Yes," quavered a little voice.

I looked over at her. She was holding her head up proudly and doing her best to conquer the tears that were streaming down her face.

"What's wrong?" asked the cretin.

"Everything, everything with you," she sobbed at me. Then, quickly, she stopped and got a grip on herself. She looked over at me. Her big brown eyes were hot and shiny. "If you would just stop and think sometimes."

"I know. I have a problem with authority."

"It's no joke, Ben."

"OK. So it's no joke."

We went on like that for some time, the gist of it all being that still lurking just beneath the venerable surface of thirty-two-year-old Ben Crandel was the angry little J.D. who distrusted, discredited, defied everyone and everything with or without reason—just to avoid responsibility.

2

I wasn't so sure she was right, but I was too much in love with her to make her cry again, so I told her she might have a point. After we got to her apartment and I helped her lug her stuff in, she lowered the axe.

"I'll pick you up about five, five-thirty," I told her.

"For what?"

"The Dodger game with Petey," I said.

"I forgot. But I don't think I should come."

"Why?"

"Because we aren't going to be a couple for at least awhile, and it's not fair to Petey to lead him on."

"That's crazy. He just likes you."

"Well, I like him too. Maybe I'll work out something to see him separately."

"You're talking like he's our child or something."

"Would that be so strange?"

A knife passed through my gut. All I could do was look at my feet.

Ellen went on: "He's very dependent on you, Ben."

"So?"

"Well, it seems like you're afraid to be alone with him. It doesn't seem like you've really talked to him for a long time."

"We talk all the time."

She wasn't listening. "It's like you've reached a certain point and you're not sure whether you want to go further."

"No."

"Then why haven't you told him about yourself?"

"You think he cares about all the morbid details of my life?"

"You don't think he'd be interested to know that you were also brought up in boys' homes?"

"Why should he?"

"You're afraid to get closer."

"That's nonsense."

I turned away and walked back down to the street. Ellen caught up with me, gave me a peck on the cheek, and told me to send her best to Petey. She also reminded me to hold to our promise. We were supposed to think about ourselves and our relationship. This was Ellen's idea, of course. I wasn't allowed to see her for six months. My only hope was that she'd change her mind.

Chapter Two

Afterward, I was edgy. It wasn't that I didn't want to be alone with the kid. I just felt like a deadbeat and I was afraid he'd start thinking it was something he'd done. At times he can be very sensitive. It's like a time bomb with a bad timer. You can guess but never know exactly when. So I called Vicky. I ran around with her before I met Ellen. Then we stayed buddies, which wasn't all that easy. She was only a kid, but in the time I'd known her, she'd been through hell and there was nothing anybody could do to help her. She had a stubborn streak a mile wide. But she'd come out OK. We had a decent, close relationship—like sister and brother—and I had no intention of using her as a shock absorber for easing my bumpy ride with Ellen. Just a good time at the ballgame for the kid and my peace of mind. But she was edgier than I was and didn't want to go.

"Kids can see right through us," she told me.

"See what?"

"You know," she said.

I couldn't see how the kid would possibly have any inkling that she'd once been a prostitute, but I wasn't about to argue with her. I asked her what she was so itchy about.

"Somebody's following me."

"Honey," I said calmly, "somebody is always following you."

"I know. It happens whenever I get upset."

"You become painfully self-conscious."

"But this time—"

"This time, what? It's always 'this time'."

"It's the same guy over and over."

"How many times?"

"A couple."

"He's smitten."

That got a laugh out of her. "I'm crazy," she said.

"Me too," I told her.

4

Even though her twenty-first birthday wasn't until the following week, she was going out of town, so we made plans for lunch the following afternoon. But I still couldn't talk her into the ballgame.

Chapter Three

"Is my check ready, Mr. Herbert?"

I could tell the fat old coot was going to play with me. His little pinhead eyes were dancing around, jiggling with his fat jowls while his big lips were scrunched up around his ever present, dog-eared, rancid, rum-soaked, five-cent Crook, moving it up and down, around his mouth. The cigar was what seemed to keep the whole engine of his face going. The cigar or food. I'd never seen him without either. Take away the mouth movement and he'd probably fall face down into his blotter, go into a coma.

"What do you think, son?" he whispered out of his throat. It didn't make him sound tough. It was like he was whining all the time. He puffed that saliva-darkened, fetid-looking thing, inhaled a little too much, and coughed the smoke toward my face. He was disgusting. His dress shirt was about five sizes too small, so he wore it open. Underneath, over the distended belly, his undershirt was pulled tighter than a dancer's leotard. You could see the great crater of his navel right through the stretched cotton.

"I don't know. Were there any problems in the manuscript?"

"Manuscript, ha!" he chortled. "Your *roman à clef.*"

"I thought it was just like the last one—except this time it was a schoolteacher instead of a housewife."

"Look at all this crap I've got to read. Do you think I like this?"

He looked at me demanding my approval, so I said, "I know."

"You know your last one stunk too—only I thought this one'd be better."

"Sir, I've been at this for years and—"

"Well, ya haven't been workin' for me, see." He said this

in his best Little Caesar imitation. Then he leaned over the desk and shoved a bunch of figure-smeared financial statements in my general direction. But before I could really look at them, he pulled the papers back toward his belly. "Look, now you're in the double distribution category. Know what that means? We pay more, we expect more. What'd you get for your first three—five hundred?"

I nodded.

"For seven-fifty, it's gotta be quality. What you gave me is artsy-fartsy."

"Maybe if you could pinpoint what you consider the difficulties."

"Do I have ta spell it out for ya? My other writers come to me, I tell 'em, 'Listen, this is no good.' They give a look of understanding lightning quick, immediately. 'More fucking and sucking?' 'That's it,' I tell them, and they go home and finish their work."

"So, that's the problem, as you see it."

"Look, you're new, relatively. I'll spell it out for ya: More come sequences. OK?"

"I've got an orgasm on every other page as is," I tried to explain.

"Well, there's your problem. Why go for every other when you can strive for completeness?"

"Sir, you've got to build up to something. It's much more erotic that way."

"Listen, who's working for who here?"

"OK, OK, I'll do it. But I've got to have half of the money now. My rent's due. I've got car payments. I—"

"That wasn't in our agreement, was it?"

"But can't you please try to—"

"After you're dependable, sometimes we give advances. Now, I can't. I simply can't."

"OK." I could see myself from afar, like I wasn't really doing this, but just imagined myself to be standing here on this asshole's threadbare carpet, listening attentively and looking sincerely into the beady little conniving eyes of a fat, pimping moron lecturing me on the art of writing pornography.

"All right then. But not just more sex. Remember."

"I'm not sure I understand."

"Kid, Jesus Christ! Have the teacher tell her kids to come on her face, over her tits, up her ass—you know, make it sloppy. Use your imagination, OK?"

I should have known better than to try to be logical, but the academician in me was foolishly demanding that context be balanced with content. "So you want me to change this thing from a rape story to a nymphomaniac piece."

With astonishing agility, Herbert bounced to his feet. "Fuck the goddamn story! This is the Pussy Prize, not the Pulitzer. More come, more sperm. Period."

He walked around from the back of his desk and I wasn't sure what he was going to do. I just prayed that whatever it might be, he wouldn't sit on me. He looked furious as he moved around me, bumping into my shoulder and practically sending me sprawling through the fourth story. Nice. I rubbed my shoulder to get rid of the cooties. Herbert turned around as he passed by, acknowledging that our paths had crossed accidentally on purpose. Then he continued on about his business as he sorted through stacks and stacks of porno strewn over a large side table. He waded through what he didn't want, discarding the cheap paperbacks to either side of his fat arms as they parted through the sea of desperate fantasies. Books toppled to the floor, but I wasn't about to help. I just stood and waited for my exit line.

Finally, he seemed to come across a few books that he'd been burrowing for. He perused these carefully for a second or so, flipping through pages and reading with his lips moving, cigar wagging. Then he grabbed three or four more at random and shoved the whole lot of these in my direction.

"Here. Read these. Dick Jones is one of our biggest penmen."

Golden rule: Keep quiet. Do not speak when you need money, and opening your mouth will not help you get it. Repeat: Keep mouth closed. Take orders with shit-eating grin. I looked around the room. Consistent with theme, posters from X-rated films adorned the walls, a couple out of the half dozen or so supposedly derived from Adult Press Books. Herbert had bragged to me about that before.

Herbert leaned over his desk and pounded a metal hotel

7

register bell in staccato bursts with his hammy palm. The sound was barely carrying because both of the large wire-meshed windows facing Hollywood Boulevard and Highland Avenue were open to a cacophony of street noise as cars, motorcycles, and large diesels either cruised slowly by rumbling their engines or downshifted as they accelerated up the gradual slope of Highland on their way toward the Hollywood Freeway. I was about to ask Herbert if he was trying to tell me something, when he knitted his brow into a straight line paralleling the creases formed over his wispy, receding hairline, and yelled out, "George, get your goddamn ass in here! George!"

Helen, Herbert's wife, came in calmly, taking all of this very much in stride. A beatific, almost idiotic smile showed her nice teeth. They were big and shiny, though not as brilliant as her platinum, lacquered mane.

"George went to get the car washed, honey."

"He was supposed to check with me." Herbert looked hurt. His cigar stump waggled downward.

"Hungry, honey?"

"Call Greenblatt's. Get me roast beef and turkey."

"Right away, hon." Helen said this affectionately. She turned around, and a noseful of perfume and powder wafted my way. She had enough layers on to put blush and color over the face of a baby elephant, and through it all you could still see the dark circles under her eyes. Her eyes contradicted her smile—they were glazed and rather lifeless. Prince Valium, horse tranquilizer, whatever it was she took, that's how this nice woman was able to manage. I couldn't blame her. After all, I didn't have to live with him.

"And wait a minute. I want some barley bean soup—not Greenblatt's, Canter's."

"Not on Wednesday, dear. They've just got split pea today."

"Then get me split pea," he blustered. "And pastry—whatever looks good. You know."

Helen walked over to the window. She put her hand above the old-fashioned iron-barred steam heater, then knelt down to turn it off. Her backside pressed up against the knitted woolen skirt, showing off a shapely bottom.

Herbert gazed down at the woman but didn't seem to notice or appreciate her. I could see that he was anxious for her to be on her way.

Helen straightened up and started back out again. At the door, she turned around. "When you have a minute, I'd like to talk to you about what we should do about the living room, Irv."

"Can't you see I'm in the middle of a very important conference?"

Helen's smile abandoned her, leaving deep lines around her mouth. She suddenly looked capable of sobbing.

Herbert belched almost demurely, patted his stomach, and said, "Pick out what you want."

Helen turned her toothy look back on. "Thanks, Irving."

She left, and Herbert frowned as he busied himself trying to find a match to rekindle his stogie. When he did, he settled back and puffed up his cheeks like a blowfish as he blew smoke and smirked and shook his head.

Chapter Four

Assuming that Herbert was finished turning his screws on me, I figured it was time to leave. But it was obvious he didn't want to let me out of his sight. He motioned for me to sit, then he started rummaging through another cluttered pile of porno books and papers on his desk. More reading samples? He shoved aside his paper weights: a big, icy hunk of polished quartz; your typically tasteless personified nut after the bolt, both with gangly wire-pronged arms and legs, mounted over a chunk of walnut; and to top it all off, a large plastic eight ball—you were supposed to ask it a question, then turn it over and your fortune floated up into an inky window across the bottom. I picked it up and kept turning the thing over and over to find out how many fortunes it had.

"Ask again later."

"You may rely on it."

I was being told that "It's doubtful" when Herbert found what he'd been looking for and held up a couple of best smellers with cheap color photographs on the front of a woman reclining over bed or sofa in an unmistakably compromising position.

"Look at that," he said.

Both poses were essentially the same—the typical frontal bit with the same enticing female. It was Vicky, sprawled out over a king-sized bed. The blankets and sheets were turned back, her legs were spread wide apart with both arms slightly hunched in from the shoulders, encircling her breasts and pushing them up and outward toward the titillated fantasist. On one book she was being mounted by a little teddy bear. On the other her delicate hands reached out upturned against the inside of her thighs.

Herbert saw me looking rather dumbstruck, so he handed me the books as he sat down at the desk and continued rummaging through a thick stack of papers. "You *have* seen her naked before, haven't you?"

I was not surprised at Vicky's nakedness. But she'd never said anything about working for Herbert. Of course, neither had I. I usually referred to him as "that schmuck" or "this asshole," and she'd never been curious to know more.

So I said, "Yeah. Have you?"

"That's for me to know and you to find out," Herbie answered childishly. He was studying my face, wanting to know if I really cared. "I heard from a friend of hers that you know her."

"From whom?"

"She shall remain nameless," he gleamed, then continued seriously, saying, "I got five days to bankroll a horny pic. Some people saw her pictures and they liked what they saw. You can vouch that she's no junkie?"

"Yeah. So what?"

"Kid, Ben, listen. We gotta have somebody that can read lines, act, be intelligent. This is sort of a class picture."

"You mean the penetration's off-camera."

"Yeah. So refresh your memory." He handed me a stack of eight-by-ten color glossies, all of Vicky.

"How old are these?"

"Year or so—why? Your girlfriend?"

I ignored that. "So call her up and talk to her yourself."

"Don't you think I have? I have! She don't want no part of it."

That made me smile. The old girl was finally coming to her senses—all by herself, just as she'd managed to get herself into a mess that way too. I really felt proud of her. "So what do you expect me to do about it?"

"Talk with her. Convince her. I've got connections could get her a spread in *Playboy* just like that." He tried to snap his fingers. Skin rubbed, but no pop.

"I see." I dropped my voice a little as I felt the need to be serious. "I think she's getting out of that, though, now."

"What do you mean?" He raised himself up by the arms of his chair, then dropped back down, his stomach swaying like a wave until it settled back into a mound of dough. He lowered his head, folded it into his chins, and talked at my chest. "She wants to be in show business, doesn't she?"

"I'm not really sure that she does anymore."

Herbert wasn't taking no for an answer. "How do you think Marilyn Chambers—Marilyn Monroe, for Christ sake—how did all of them begin their legitimate careers? Burlesque. Pornography. I'm getting out of these dirty books. You come by here in six months, this office won't even be here. I could use this girl. If you knew the backers I've got, the money—ugh! People are begging me to let them invest. See, the best way is to take this girl Vicky, start her in the sex films—then we can gradually make her a very, very big star. And I mean first class—no doormat. I'd like to talk to her about it." He stopped, then said, "Maybe you could help, you know—promote."

Nothing I could say would shut him up. So I looked through the pictures and didn't even listen. Some had Vicky lying on her side, finger in mouth, sucking; in a few, she was standing, caressing herself in the obvious areas; and a few were from behind with Vicky's face turned back over her shoulder, her mouth slightly slack, her eyes half-closed and dazed, the tan-lined cheeks of both buttocks glossy and firm. The pictures took me back to four years ago, on a rainy day, when I was standing in the Hollywood Wax Museum trying to figure out if anything about the place had story potential. After the auspicious reviews of my first two novels, I'd landed a cushy job teaching freshman English and creative writing at Penn State. I had loved it, but when one of my books came to the attention of a

11

big-name shyster producer, I had gone for an option deal hook, line and sinker and had come to California to do the screenplay. There had been very little on paper, but a couple of telegrams and a handful of smoothly orchestrated phone calls had made up my mind for me. Once I got a taste of California, I knew I wouldn't want to leave, and when my loyal shyster found a project he deemed "more contemporary" a few months hence, I hadn't had much choice. I'd been living hand to mouth, waiting for my script assignment to begin. But on this particular day, I remember I was sky high. I'd just sold my first porn. Three hundred fifty bucks for a week's work and, now, at least for a couple weeks, I could begin work on something that might interest me. I was eating and I had proved to myself that I could support my writing habit. Which was a real relief. I couldn't get my old job back, couldn't get a new one in teaching, and couldn't conceive of what else I might possibly do.

So I wandered around the Hollywood Wax Museum looking for a story. And from Washington to Nixon, Quasimodo to the Mummy, Garbo to Gleason, all I got was a conspiracy of glass eyeballs staring me down. A good image, really a metaphor not unlike the myopic eyes of Gatsby's Doctor T. J. Eckleburg looking down over America from a faded billboard. But these eyes had nothing to do with the heads they inhabited. They were supercilious, smug, and piercing. They made you feel that somebody else possessed something that you needed and wanted—the only problem being that it was impossible to know who had it or what it was, for that matter.

I was standing in the Chamber of Horrors, right in front of the Hitler-Mussolini display, when something hard bumped into the back of my legs. A girl's voice screamed and it fit in perfectly with the recorded soundtrack of eerie organ chords sighing forbodingly over hysterical cackles, ghostly winds, and creaking doors. I turned around and saw the whites of her eyes, her blouse, and kneesocks pulsating brightly under the blacklights.

I picked her up at the Yalta Conference. She was standing there scared and crying. She had a suitcase next to her that was almost as big as she was. Churchill, Stalin, and FDR didn't give a damn about it, but I did, so I took her for a sandwich. She had on what looked like a parochial school uniform: a sopping wet threadbare cashmere sweater matted down over a white blouse, short woolen skirt, kneesocks, and soggy penny loafers. Her waistlong damp blonde hair was tied back into a ponytail. She had a little narrow face and wide, startled amethyst blue eyes. She looked around eleven or twelve, but she was actually seventeen. She had run away from a pilloholic mother in Phoenix and, even though she was terrified, hell if she was going back.

Everything and yet nothing has changed since then. When Herbert grabbed the pictures from me and started leafing through them and commenting on how "she's good from any angle," I realized where I was and stood up and started for the door. It was clear that he wasn't finished, but I wasn't interested. "I'll see you tomorrow," I told him.

He stopped me, saying, "Maybe we *could* arrange advances for you. Would that give you more incentive?"

Sometimes lying doesn't hurt. "Umm, yeah. I guess so."

"You talk to her. See how she feels about things."

"I don't know if I'll be seeing her," I teased.

"If you could manage to run into her and tell her what I feel about her, uh, potential, I'd certainly do all I could for ya."

"I might see her next week."

"Wait a minute." Herbert pushed his chair back away from the desk to get his stomach out of the way so he could open a drawer. He took out a ledger and started writing a check, then handed it over. "Maybe this will help."

Seven hundred and fifty smackers. With my back rent and car payments and insurance, it was already spent. "I'll do whatever I can," I pronounced sanctimoniously.

"Today," said Herbert. "I gotta know by tomorrow."

"Do you still want the revisions?" I asked him.

He laughed obscenely. "Just do what you're supposed to."

"OK," I leered back at him.

"But I meant what I said before."

"More come sequences, sure," I told him on my way to the door.

13

Chapter Five

"Here he comes!"

"Well, whoopee do!"

"He's only the greatest switch hitter in history, that's all. Only gotten two hundred hits nine seasons out of fifteen. How many years do you think it took Ty Cobb to do that?"

"I don't care. He still stinks as far as I'm concerned."

"Twenty-three years."

"Ladies and gentlemen, leading off for Cincinnati playing third base, number fourteen, Pete Rose!"

An echoing of boos. Nearby, some eloquent cussing.

"Yea!"

"Pete, if you don't sit down, we're going to get lynched here."

"He's great."

"But if you had to choose a third baseman, you'd take the Penguin any day."

"Not me."

"You'd give up thirty homers, a hundred and ten RBI's?"

"Cey ain't got nothin' to him."

"Doesn't have anything in comparison to him, you mean."

"If you're gonna start correcting my English again, I'm leaving."

"Oh, calm down. You know it could stand some correcting."

"So could yours sometimes."

"Well, you should point it out to me then."

Wood on it. Rose sliced a low line drive through the hole to right.

"All right!"

"Sit down."

"Oh, shut up."

"You're a hypocrite, you know that? You can't root for the Dodgers and root for Rose at the same time. If your first

14

name weren't Pete, you wouldn't give a flying fuck who he was!"

"Bullshit! Watch your language too! I'm just a kid, you know."

"Don't remind me."

We traded smiles. It was therapeutic. Just me and the kid. I didn't want to think about whether or not Ellen was right, but I was enjoying myself and so was Petey and that was all that mattered.

So there I was at Dodger Stadium doing my usual irreverent impression of a conscientious dad on a bonus Big Brother night for an eleven-year-old juvenile delinquent from the Mar Vista Boys' Home. I'd been Pete Connelly's big brother for about a year now. I really liked the kid and I guess he had a good time with me too, although he'd never admit it, never say thank you when I dropped him off. He didn't have to see me and he could have dumped me and asked for somebody else, but he didn't. And he was the one who had asked me if I could get hold of some tickets for the game. So my guess was that he could put up with me. And even though I wasn't much of a father figure, I still thought the kid liked me for it. He seemed sort of relieved and appreciative that I didn't come on too hard-nosed and bossy. If I pulled the reins on him, I usually knew what I was doing. He could still do whatever he wanted within reason. I couldn't explain or define it, but we just had a good time together and he knew it. He also knew I didn't want to be his father. I just wanted to help him out, be his friend if I could, which is probably what a decent father does anyway. Not that I wanted to be one and not that the ideal works out when any kid and parent pursue that risky collision course on a full-time basis. I thought I could wait a while for that one. Maybe a lifetime.

The first day we got together, I let him drive my car and maul over the delicate transmission in a parking lot. I told the kid then that if he didn't like me or I didn't like him, we'd call it quits right away. Nobody was going to be anybody else's martyr. I had dumped a few other kids because I couldn't stand them, assuaging my guilt with the notion that perhaps someone else could be found who could establish a better rapport. I explained this to Petey the best I could and now that time had passed and we were still getting together, I thought he felt good about himself because he felt I really liked him, that I wasn't doing him some kind of begrudging favor. When he asked me one time why I did this sort of thing, I told him it gave me a break on my income tax. That shut him up, kind of pleased him, I think, that I wasn't out to save the world or anything.

I noticed that Petey was letting Stanley drink the whole large paper cup full of beer.

"That's enough."

"He likes it."

"Too much isn't good for him, Pete."

"Ah, what's it gonna do to him?"

"It'll make him dizzy. You don't want him to barf on your shoes, do you?"

The kid gave me a dirty look, took the beer away, and patted Stanley on the head. Stanley's a bit on the small side for a bassett hound. I sneak him into various events in this special duffle bag I've got. It was kind of a pain, but I knew that Petey liked it, so I brought Stanley along and let the kid carry the bag into the park. The ticket man knew we were up to something, but he was too busy to care. Which is what you count on.

The crowd was jumping. It was the first Dodger-Reds game of the season. Griffey, the Reds right-fielder, had walked, moving Rose to second, from where he went on to score after Bill Russell's wild throw to first base on the second leg of the double play. We were sitting in general admission on the third base side almost even with the bag, in the first row behind the railing. They weren't great seats but I still had had to get them two weeks ago. We were close enough to see Rose's familiar and repugnant hustle as he rounded third and came easily home. I almost expected him to slide in just for the hell of it, to impress upon us how hard he was trying to make everything look difficult and breathtaking.

Petey's eyes were locked onto the field. He jumped up out of his seat again, of course. He had one hand to his head holding a transistor tuned in to Vin Scully and Jerry Doggett; the other waved his mitt back and forth at the field. In any other situation, it would have looked like he was sending out a distress signal. His seldom smile was, for the moment, as wide as the Grand Canyon. So I didn't mind too much.

He sat down again and a paper airplane flew by us and through the railing. Stanley howled at it and started climbing out of his bag, so I had to push him back down and tell him to stay.

The Reds decided to let us go with only one more run and the first half of the inning ended, giving us time to concentrate on our hot dogs.

A vendor came by carrying a box load of souvenir paraphernalia. It wasn't enough that they had the concession stands all over next to the restrooms and food stands. They had to bring them to your seats too. The kid looked up at the old guy hunched over the pennants, autographed baseballs, balloon bats, and calendars. He showed he was interested by taking his radio away from his ear. When the vendor wiped his brow and started his slow trek up the stairs, Petey bent down and petted Stanley, mimicking a bassett look.

"All right, so what d'ya want?"

"Nothin' he's got."

"Oh."

"But I need to get me a windbreaker. I been pitchin' at school."

"So?"

"My arm gets sore if I don't keep it warm between the innings."

"Are you serious?"

He glared at me and said no with such bitterness as to defy a metaphor.

"Are you going to try out?"

"For Little League?" That pained him.

"Yeah. For Little League."

"I'm not gonna play with a bunch of babies."

"You could—"

"I don't care if I could be a first-string pitcher, make the All Stars, nothin'. I told you, Ben."

"How do you know you're that good?"

"Take my word for it."

"I think you're just afraid to find out. That's all."

He gave me the finger.

"That's nice. Very mature."

Some distinguished gentleman sitting in the row behind us leaned down toward my ear and spoke to me in a confidential tone. "I wouldn't let my kid get away with that if I were you."

I turned around. The guy was old enough to be my father. He had a long, loose, bronzed face, a funny-looking pencil-line moustache, thick, supple lips that were wet and smooth, oiled up from eating peanuts and probably ready to flap the breeze with anyone who came along. A real meddler wearing a yellow golf cap, red cardigan over a loud madras sports shirt with black on gray checked slacks. A man of distinctive taste. Petey had turned around too, having overheard him. "You gotta show 'em who's boss," he nodded sternly, looking sidelong at Petey.

I thought of all the charming turns of phrase I could send his way. Instead, I told him calmly, "If it doesn't bother me, I don't see why it should bother you." I asked Petey if he had been referring to the gentleman in question. He nodded no, and I said, "See?"

So the guy said, "If it don't bother you, something's wrong with you."

Petey told the man that he'd used bad grammar.

The man's bronze face turned crimson, like a sunset. A slight frail woman wearing a black wig regarded me disdainfully as she patted the man's arm with the back of her hand.

Petey looked at the man and curled his lip, sneering toughly. He put his mitt down and clinched his right hand into a fist. The other hand still held the radio.

I smiled at the man and did my best to act friendly. "I like your shirt," I said. "And thanks for the advice. If I need some more, I'll—"

I gave a vaudevillian turn of the hand, giving over the stage to my young protégé.

"—flush twice."

Petey smiled proudly. Then I put my hand on his shoulder as we turned around and laughed our heads off.

I could hear the man's wife saying, "Why, I never." Petey

laughed loud enough to make the dog start howling, and I heard the lady tell her husband something like, "Just ignore them."

Then we settled down to watch the Dodgers get their tails whipped. Morgan hit a double, went to third on a wild throw by Dusty Baker, then stole home. Three more runs for the Reds in the third. Petey yelled out things like: "You're givin' it away! Bums!" He gave the dog some more beer; and Stanley tipped the cup over, which solved all my problems—except that it spilled over Petey's sweatshirt.

"About that jacket," I said.

"Yeah?"

"If you try out, I got an offer for you."

"You're fuckin' bribin' me."

"Calm down."

"So what is it?"

"Forget it. I don't want you to think I'm bribing you."

"Oh, man."

"One promise, one pitcher's windbreaker."

"The kind with the snap buttons?"

I nodded yes. "If you play."

"Deal," he said.

We shook on it. I bought us two frozen Carnation chocolate malts. He grabbed for his, yanking it out of my hand. We ate our malts and watched Morgan hit his second double in the top of the fourth. Petey frowned and turned off his transistor. Then he turned to me and said, "I thought you were gonna ask Ellen."

"I didn't say that."

"Then why'd you have to sell that extra ticket?"

"You're prying into my personal affairs," I smiled.

The kid was serious. He really liked Ellen. In fact, my guess was that she was causing an almost volcanic prepubescent stirring inside his eleven-year-old body. "She dump you?"

"No, she didn't dump me."

"Sorry."

"We just decided not to see each other for awhile, that's all."

"Who decided first?"

"Nobody decided first. It was a mutual decision."

"Are you going to see her again?"

"Possibly. Probably. What makes you so interested?"

"You know."

"No, I don't. Why don't you fill me in?"

"Listen, if you wanta make me feel embarrassed, forget it."

"Jeez, I'm sorry. I forgot how experienced you are."

"Ben, you're really a jerk. You know that?"

"Tell me something interesting."

The kid laughed. "I could get a complex from you."

"Nah, you're complex enough already. I don't think I could make you more complex."

"Then why are ya tryin' to make me unconscious?"

"Self-conscious?"

"Yeah, that's right."

"Petey, I'm sorry. I didn't realize you were really serious." I paused, then started looking serious. "My mind's an open book. Ask me anything. Tell me anything."

He didn't say anything.

"Go ahead."

He laughed, then he yelled at me, "I don't have anything to say."

"You just wanted to know why Ellen wasn't here."

"Yeah."

"And I told you."

"Ben?"

"Pete?"

"Would you mind if I called Ellen?"

"Of course not."

"What would she think?"

"She'd be very flattered that you cared enough about her to want to call her."

"You think so, huh?"

"Yeah, sure."

"She's the only girl I ever met that knows anything."

"Like Pete Rose's lifetime batting average, for instance?"

Petey smiled. Then he turned pale. His freckles shined and seemed to multiply and pop out like measles. He swallowed first, then he said, "Some of the guys said it, so I'm not afraid to say that I think she's beautiful."

"Good for you, sport." I patted him on the back.

"Not that I'm gonna do it, but if I *was* gonna do it with anybody, I don't think it'd gross me out if I had to do it with her."

"That is, if you had to. If somebody made you like they do as part of the Chinese water torture."

Petey got mad and started to stand up, so I grabbed him by the sleeve which made him sit down again. "Hold it."

"I'm not gonna sit here and let you make fun of me."

"I'm not making fun of you. I'm just appreciating you."

He thought that over and either didn't understand it or didn't like it. He gave me a disapproving rise out of the side of his mouth.

"You're sensitive about certain things, and I understand that. And it makes me feel good that you talk to me about them."

"A lot of good it does me."

"OK, look. Try to see it from my point of view. You're at the point in your personal development where you probably never liked girls or hated them so much in your whole life—and to somebody who's been through it already, it's funny because I went through the same thing myself."

He looked at me with interest, appreciating the fact I was leveling with him. He petted Stanley and looked at him as we talked.

"I guess you feel that way until ya do it your first time."

I smiled hard and concentrated on not laughing. "Maybe," I agreed. "But there's lots of steps along the way before that."

"You mean like first base, second base, third?"

"Other things aside from sex."

"Like what?"

"Like talking to girls, getting to know them."

"That's disgusting."

"I know how you feel, partner."

"All I'm gonna do is do it with them, that's all. If they want me for anything else, they can just forget it."

"Some guys are like that all their lives."

"That's the way I'm gonna be."

"I doubt that."

"Why?"

"Because, oh, I can't explain it. You like talking to Ellen, though, don't you?"

"That's different."

"What do you mean it's different. She's a woman, isn't she?"

He hesitated, then admitted, "Yeah."

"See what I mean?"

Petey wrinkled his forehead, so I went on. "You're in the process of discovering things, finding out about yourself."

He was quiet for a moment, then he took his hand off of the dog and looked at me hard. "If you tell Ellen I talked to you about this stuff, I swear to God, I'll—"

I held up my hand. "I won't say a word."

"You better not if you know what's good for ya."

"OK, tough guy."

At the end of the sixth, it was eight to nothing Reds. I could tell Petey still had something on his mind, but I wasn't about to try to drag it out of him. And what's more, I probably couldn't have.

I let Stanley stick his nose in the cup and lick out what was left of my malt. Petey had turned his radio back on, but it was a boring no-contest game and nothing exciting seemed capable of happening.

Chapter Six

I left the kid with the dog and went up and got myself another beer. When I came back, it was the top of the seventh. We decided to wait for the Dodgers' next at bats and then leave if they didn't do anything significant. Cincinnati decided to take a rest in the top of the seventh, so when we stood up for the seventh-inning stretch, the score was still a mere eight to zero. I was halfway through the beer when I turned around and saw the peanut man coming down from the top of the stairs. I made up my mind to catch his eye by the time he worked his way down toward me. Petey and I were looking up at the Dodger scoreboard. Tonight we were welcoming the Los Angeles chapter of the Cystic Fibrosis Foundation, the Huntington Park Chamber of Commerce, etc. Then the baseball whiz quiz popped up there and asked us: "1. Who holds the major league record for consecutive steals? 2. Who holds the record for consecutive games played?" The answers would be forthcoming at the end of the inning.

"The second one's easy," Petey said. "Everybody knows that's Lou Gehrig. Two thousand and thirty-one."

"Thank God you love baseball. Otherwise, you probably never would have learned how to read."

"I like comics."

"Oh, that's right. I forgot that other aspect of your erudition."

"Irrigation?"

"Erudition. It means—"

Something slammed into me from behind. I was catapulted over the railing like a clown shot from a cannon. But my hand stayed clamped to the rail. I was hanging out over the reserved seats a hundred feet above the ground. The metal rail was wide and not exactly the easiest thing in the world to keep a good grip on when you've got close to two hundred pounds urging you to obey the law of gravity.

I heard Stanley howling in torment or sheer excitement. My neck was twisted around toward the overhead lights above home plate so I couldn't see anything. Then people's faces started coming out over the rail. I heard somebody tell me to hold on. So I held on.

Hands grabbed my shirt. More hands got me by the belt loops. Suddenly, I felt like Peter Pan, only without the strings. The next thing I knew I was standing back inside the railing on the concrete floor. Petey was standing in front of me, staring at me with his mouth open. Stanley was crawling around in between my legs and two or three people were apologizing to me.

"Gee, are you OK?"

"Yeah, I think so. What happened?"

There were three guys. One, an executive type who looked like he was born wearing charcoal grey pinstripes; another guy wearing a blue polyester leisure suit, yachting cap, and thick horn-rimmed glasses; and the peanut vendor, who looked and talked like a hardworking Chicano who'd probably been doing this since his freshman year in high school.

The executive took charge. "I was trying to get down the aisle to my seat. He was buying peanuts." He pointed to the man in the leisure suit, who looked on sympathetically, nodding. "The kid was leaning over to take his money. I bumped into him and he lost his balance."

I saw an empty aisle seat behind me and another one four or five past the blabbermouth and his wife. The leisure fellow saw me looking and pointed to the aisle seat. "That's my seat right here."

Then the peanut boy spoke to me. "Meester, I'm awful sorry."

I saw a few bags of peanuts on the ground and noticed that the vendor's shoulder-strapped red box was empty. "It's OK. It wasn't your fault," I told him.

He hung his head and looked terribly guilty. Then he turned away and hustled quickly back up the steps and away from all the commotion. My guess was that he felt bad enough in addition to losing most of his supply of peanuts. He'd probably have to pay for it.

Everybody settled down. People returned to their seats to watch the last half of the seventh, and I sat down again too, feeling strangely weightless, as if the people's hands were still on me, holding me up in the air. My heart felt like it was beating hard enough to burst through my chest. I looked over at Petey and he smiled. "You shoulda seen yourself," he said. Then he shook his head and laughed. I was still a little too scared to laugh yet, so I leaned down and petted the dog.

The Dodgers were hitless and remained scoreless, so, by the top of the eighth we, like thousands of other not-so-diehard fans, packed up and left.

On the way out, I stopped at the very last concession stand before our exit and bought Petey a Dodger warm-up jacket. The jacket was twenty-five dollars. I'd spent almost seven dollars on peanuts, hot dogs, frozen malts, cokes, and beer. I got jumpy again for a second. Then I remembered I had a half a tank of gas in the car. That was fortunate because, at this moment, since I hadn't had time to cash Herbert's check, I had a total of exactly twenty-seven cents in my pocket.

Petey put his jacket on and socked me on the arm. That

meant thanks a lot. It wasn't exactly the highest form of expressed appreciation, nonverbal, verbal, or otherwise; but for a kid who'd spent much of his life locked up in small rooms, all but forgotten by strangers the law had called parents, hell, my guess was that he was starting to do OK.

Chapter Seven

It was around eleven-thirty by the time I got home. The phone was ringing as Stanley and I came in the door. I picked it up and a raspy, unfamiliar voice cried in my ear, "He just left!"

"What? Who is this?"

"Vicky," the voice whispered huskily. "Somebody just almost killed me."

"I'll call an ambulance," I told her.

But she said not to. She was all right. The assailant had been the guy she suspected of following her. I walked Stanley into the bedroom, made him jump up onto his place at the foot of the bed, then I left the house and drove over.

I turned off of Santa Monica Boulevard onto Robertson, passing the small galleries and decorator shops, turned on to Vicky's street and pulled up in front of her bungalow court, parking across the street in front of a large highrise under construction. In the apartment adjoining Vicky's, people were having a small party. Their front door was propped open with a chair. Sweet smoke and disco music drifted out into the still air. Three guys stood on the small porch passing a joint, laughing, talking animatedly with their hands. Framed in the light of the center living room window, a few of the girls were dancing side by side, practicing a hustle step. They didn't seem to notice me as I went by.

A screen door creaked open from across the way.

"It had better git quiet or I'll be forced to take action!"

I looked over there. It was pitch black, but I'd know that harmless old chihuahua growl anywhere: Mrs. McGinty, the landlady.

One of the guys yelled back at her, "Up yours, mama!"

"Young derelicts," was her retort, and, at that, her screen slammed shut.

I went up the three steps and knocked on Vicky's door.

"Ben?" came from the back bedroom.

I tried the door. It was open, so I went right in, announcing myself loud and clear. She was sitting up in bed in the dark. I walked over to her, sat down, and held her. Then I turned on the little lamp on the nightstand. Her head was drooping. Long, thick, shaggy, permed blonde hair hung down over her face. I brushed the hair back behind her ears to find a strange face. It was a pale, muted mask streaked with blood, real only because of its terrible look of pain. The eyes were swollen shut, buried deep in shadow. They tried to open and one succeeded more than the other, glimpsed me for the briefest moment from underneath long lashes, then folded from the strain as the mouth contorted into a wide U, a clownish smile that was actually the most horrible and painful of grimaces.

I bit into my knuckles and looked away. When I looked at her again, I was all right. I wanted to take her to a hospital, but she wouldn't let me. So I helped her into the bathroom and cleaned her up. The injuries appeared to amount to: a cut lip, bruised nose, slight gash on the forehead, right eye swollen shut, a couple of bruised ribs, nail gouges over the throat and breasts, and other sundry scratches and bruises that all seemed amenable to quick healing. Her left eye was starting to open already. It wasn't as bad as it had looked.

After that I brought her into the kitchen and fed her a glass of wine. She had been strangled, her throat was bruised and tight. So it was hard for her to drink, and, after a few sips, she gave up. Then we talked for a long time. The story took a number of detours and alternate routes, but eventually centered on one basic chain of events. Late that afternoon, Herbert had appeared with George, his bodyguard, asking Vicky whether she'd reconsidered his offer. She said she hadn't changed her mind. He then offered her a few thousand dollars up front, plus some "shared percentages" in the projected profits of the film. Which didn't sway Vicky.

Herbert then played his trump card—my alleged approval of and potential involvement in the production. I supposedly had said it could be a good career move for Vicky. She didn't doubt the possibility that I might somehow be tied up in a Herbert extravaganza, but she did have doubts, very big ones, about my having condoned her involvement. She insisted that everyone who knew her—and most of all myself—would feel nothing other than embarrassment that she was going back to the same old thing. Herbert grumbled that she'd be sorry and left.

Then, five hours later, somebody knocked on the door saying he was a friend of mine. Vicky let him in. He was on medium height with dark skin, young, well dressed in a tight beige suit. He said I'd sent him over because Vicky was the greatest contortion act in town and wouldn't mind if things got a little nasty. She hadn't gone for that. Then he became exasperated because he thought Vicky was supposed to know who he was. She fought him tooth and nail until a late arrival at her neighbor's party knocked on the wrong door. Then he ran out the back.

Actually, the last part was told first and the first part was told last. The story only achieved its final reconstructed order when Vicky decided that Herbert had caused it all to happen.

"It was one of his hired pawns," Vicky said.

"I've never seen anybody but George," I told her. "Maybe a couple other guys, but they don't fit that description."

"But don't you see?"

"No."

"If I could be made to believe that friends would betray me, why would I care what anybody else thought of me? What would stop me from going back to the old grind?"

"You're willing to give Herbert that many points for subtlety?"

"I told him you were practically my best friend."

"And he believed he could get somewhere by destroying that 'illusion'," I said, making quote marks with my fingers.

We decided that the theory made sense. And, between lousy friends or suspicious mates, dumber schemes have been known to hit the jackpot. I stood up and moved toward the door. I could see my hands laced nicely around Herbert's neck, just like a bench vice. Vicky knew where I was going.

Chapter Eight

Months ago, on a weekend, I had dropped off my first dirty book there, on Hudson, near Wilshire Boulevard, in Hancock Park. There were bigger, more resplendent homes, but I remember being taken aback by someone as crass, thick-headed, and tedious as Herbert choosing to live in a quaint, rambling California version of the storybook gingerbread house: lots of lattice work over the windows; bits of bricks and large fake oaken beams artfully embedded in the plaster; a textured tar-shingle roof that sloped and waved across the top of the house like a wet thatch; then, rising high above the twin gabled upstairs windows, a tall cylindrical chimney with its bright red bricks angled in a swirling pattern. You could find exact copies of it only blocks away, but it did embody a certain elfish sense of fantasy and adventure. It was one A.M. and, as I drove past, the lights were out except for the front and side porch lights.

I parked around the corner and shut off my lights and engine. My only concern was Herbert's bodyguard George, who was usually close at hand. Herbert had a long list of enemies, or thought he did, and wanted his goon around at night; either that, or he slept with an arsenal of sophisticated weaponry.

I closed my car door quietly, turned the corner, and walked toward the house. I detoured around the Cadillac in the driveway and went through the back gate. The door on the service porch was locked. So was another door on the far side of the house. I climbed the two short steps to the narrow wooden porch that looked out over the back lawn. It was rickety and creaked with each step. I slowed down, lifting my feet like moonshoes as I approached the center panel of the French windows and pulled it outward by its small handles. It wouldn't budge. The house was sealed up tight.

I stood still for a moment and felt a quietness about the

28

place that mocked me to pieces. Hadn't Vicky and I forgotten that this supposed pawn of Herbert's had been putting a pretty obvious tail on her for two, three, maybe four days before he struck? Why in the world would Herbert have wanted her followed? To find out whether she was still hustling or feeding a daily drug habit? Possibly. But it still didn't seem right. Something about it didn't quite fit. And could Herbert have really been that desperate for a featured meat grinder? He had sought out Vicky as a matter of convenience, it seemed to me, but that didn't mean he couldn't easily find a million others who would jump to it at a moment's notice. The man was shrewd. I couldn't deny him that. He wanted to control risks or eliminate them if at all possible. Getting dependable personnel—especially for the tight budgets these sleazy shows always had—was crucial. But there was no reason to bludgeon or kill for it.

What sense was there in damaging the hot property one sought to acquire? It would be weeks before Vicky would be ready to go before the cruel eye of a camera with or without makeup. A little less lucky, and she might have needed plastic surgery. That wouldn't exactly be the way to go about organizing to meet an urgent deadline for beginning a production. Putting aside all doubts, what could I prove by busting into Herbert's house, then vilifying his lousy, sleepy face?

I looked up at the dark second-story windows. I stepped off the long porch, went back through the gate, and cut across the front lawn.

Chapter Nine

I was on the sidewalk beyond the front of the house, just around the corner from my car, when the tired hum of late night traffic a few blocks further up on Wilshire was broken by a car door slamming. Shock waves killed my legs, made them numb, and the whites of my eyes popped like the flash cubes on an Instamatic. It had come from around the corner—where my car was. I steeled myself and turned the corner.

There was only one person, a squat, square-figured man who had his driver's door wide open and was about to give it another throw. The door must have either fallen off its hinges or bounced back. I was getting ready to ask him if he was using some modern method to practice the shotput when I realized he was George, roaring homeward with enough of a buzz-on to fuel a jet. His legs were buckling under the strain. If you drink like that, you need pretty good landing gear. The door was swung back all the way, straining at its hinges, and George was draped over it with all of his weight. His arms were extended through the open window, and they hung limply at rest over the inside of the door.

I was hoping he'd find it a good place to catch some shuteye, when, suddenly, he leaned a little too far forward and swung toward the car with his feet dragging behind him. He saw me through the window on the passenger side as I walked by. Out of the side of my eye, I could see his hands waving toward me. He stood up straight and banged his back and shoulders against the inside of the car. The car rocked and he pulled his head out, straightened up, and staggered toward me, his arms jerking out in front of him, looking for something to hold onto.

"What you doin' here?" He was trying to look menacing, but gave that up as soon as he heard himself. Then he smiled at me like an old friend.

"Not much."

I could tell he was trying hard to focus on me. "You writin' somethin' for Herbert?"

"That's right."

He came over and stood by me and let his arms drop over my shoulders like a couple of steel girders. "Herbert, he'll give me hell if I get home any later 'n midnight. Gets scared if I'm not there to protect 'im. Used a gun, wouldn't even need me. That's what I told 'im. But he's afwraid—wittle fat 'fwraidy cat. Ha-ha-ha."

I tried to smile and look like I was enjoying this.

"Got some bourbon. Let's you and me go sit an' . . ."

Then his legs folded and I let him sink down to the sidewalk. He went down on his belly, eyes closed, and the side of his face flattened out against the cement, fixing his mouth into a goofy sneer.

"Helen and Herbie—you could write a story!"

This seemed to strike him as the funniest thing he'd ever said. I wasn't sure whether he was amused by the idea that someone might write about Herbert and Helen, or if it was the notion of writing itself that cracked him up. I left him there on the sidewalk, got in my car, and drove off.

Chapter Ten

I went back to Vicky's and we hashed over the situation one more time, then decided to make a police report in the morning. She was a wreck. I ran a bath for her, then I put her in bed and tucked her in like a little tot. I turned off the light and stood in the doorway for a moment and heard her start saying her prayers. Then I got an extra blanket out of the hall closet and spread out on the living room couch. We said goodnight and went to sleep.

I awoke around seven-thirty and remembered I had an appointment at nine with Bradford Bobby, the producer. My plan was to get him to renew his option on one of my old screenplays. It had just expired and I needed the money, so I didn't want to cancel the appointment. It might be worth a couple thousand dollars to me. I wrote Vicky a note and told her I'd pick her up at noon for lunch, went into the bedroom, and put it next to her pillow. Then I left.

A half-hour later, when I got down to Venice, I felt worried so I parked my car by Brad Bobby's office and walked down to the boardwalk to look for a pay phone. Kids were whizzing by on rented rollerskates—some crouched down like experts, leaning forward to reduce their wind resistance and gather speed; others clumping along, half-walking, sliding out of control, and flailing about with both arms in an effort to maintain balance. A juggler was practicing on the grass area fronting the beach, twirling four bowling pins as his German shepherd reared up on its hind legs, snapping at the air and trying to intercept them. I saw a phone over there.

Vicky had awakened as soon as I'd left and was on her

way out to have breakfast. I didn't want to scare her, but I felt relieved knowing she wasn't going to be hanging around there. She knew it and told me not to worry about it. We couldn't stop living, could we?

Chapter Eleven

"Hey, Benny, what's happening? So what d'ya think?"

"It's nice, Brad. Very comfy."

His new office building. BRADFORD BOBBY: MAVERICK MOGUL. Last year's *Time* cover close-up was perma-plaqued on the side wall by his desk. Our young and aggressive, brilliant, new and improved seventies-Irving Thalberg—only to top poor old Irving, Brad wasn't head of production for nobody. No siree. Bradford Bobby was a man without studio who had made his own coming from the outside. Independently. Just because he'd started with a piddling five million palmed off of his father's dress business—the kid had talent! So, hell, what's the diff? He looked like a matinee idol: dark, compact, and sleek, with gorgeous baby blue eyes. He knew all the right moves, but his mainstay was giving college kids a break, pumping them dry for ideas and material, then discarding them before they got reputations and became expensive. Bobby did this adeptly, subtly, and thus maintained a stance as a sort of social barometer of the current scene. But I was supposed to be on a privileged status because my agent was his brother-in-law and he never stopped letting me know about it.

Something was different about him. Bobby had taken on a new pose to go with the office. The gold chains and matching bracelets were *in absentia*. His Hong Kong tailor also seemed to have bitten the dust. And what had happened to the hand-tooled lizard skin Luchese's, those boots that had made me drip with envy? In mothballs. Now it was back to basics. T-shirts, jeans, and tennies. Aviator shades for a touch of mystery. The low-profile crawl away from the rat race so that the rat race might be resurrected in newer, less congested, and more expansive environs. Ten miles from Hollywood, at Venice Beach, mingling with the derelicts, winos, and complacent poor, here we sat: me, like Sisyphus, still pushing that goddamn rock; and another phony-baloney with a bank book for talent.

By way of greeting, Bobby tipped the sunglasses down to the end of his nose, revealing a decent shiner. "I'm getting rid of the motorcycle," he frowned at me.

I asked him what had happened and he said something about a wino in a '56 Chevy. It made him sick to think about it, so I asked him what else was new. He started getting happy when I told him I hadn't heard about the deal on Alex Freeman.

"You know," he said. "You gave me his script."

"Yeah. Did you read it?"

"Read it?! We're in preproduction at Paramount."

"You mean you're making it?"

"They are. They put up everything so they can do it. That's fine with me."

"How'd it happen?"

"I thought it looked good so I sent it over. And they loved it. They went bananas over it. I mean it."

That fucking sonofabitch Alex. He hadn't even called me to say thank you. "Good luck—for him."

"Envy, Ben?"

"No."

"Well, at least you're normal."

"What does that mean?"

Bobby let out a belly laugh that bounced off the walls. "Listen to this: I send him, Alex Freeman, over to Paramount for this very big meeting, you know?"

"Yeah."

"Well, in the middle of it, he's talking to Barry Diller, the chairman of the board or somebody, and he announces that he thinks they should know that he's a homosexual."

"What?"

"That's what he said. 'I think you should know I'm gay.' Something like that. Did you know?"

"That Alex is gay?"

Bobby nodded.

"Knowing Alex—how could I not know?"

Bobby let out another belly laugh. He was shaking his head. "Alvin Meyers calls me from there, asking me whether this guy's crazy. I tell him, 'Of course not. He's just eccentric.' So Alvin says, 'Oh, I see.' The faggot tried to blow it for himself, but he couldn't. They want that property."

"I guess he's sitting pretty."

"You betcha." Bobby tilted his cane backed rocker and swiveled around a hundred and eighty degrees. He pulled his Venetian blinds the rest of the way up and looked down into the bleached out, squalid street. "Ben, I'm tellin' ya. I really dig being in Venice."

"But how do you get any work done? I mean, don't you just feel like lying on the beach all day?"

He laughed. "Are you kidding? I'd probably get mugged. It's mellow, though, really," he seemed to feel he had to assure me. "Everybody's mobilizing to get on the council's tail. We're gonna make them clean up this shit hole."

"But where are all the bums gonna go once you've purified the environment?" I chuckled a little to make it evident I meant no harm.

"They can go to Beverly Hills for all I care," he smiled at me, taking it well. "Bring me any porno?"

"Nope."

"You know I love your porno," he snickered, punctuating our running joke with that fearless, self-satisfied smile. "Next time, make sure you bring me a dirty book, OK?"

Now it was time to get smug. "Sure. But I'm not going to be needing that. Did I tell you that I had lunch with Dino De Laurentis last week?"

A complete fabrication, but what else could I do? Let the script stand on its own merits? I knew it was not one of my better efforts. The only reason I'd done the thing in the first place was because I knew the jerk was a boxing fan. Bobby laughed.

"Well, keep laughing. But I think he's really into the woman boxer story."

He kept laughing. Then he threatened to check up on it. I called his bluff with a good shrug. And then he said he didn't care and didn't want to reoption. Bobby was cocky and told me he trusted his intuitions about the general marketplace. According to Brad, people now wanted to "get taken away on more of a head thing instead of a violent thing, unless the violence is really weird and horrifying." He paused for a moment, then he lit up and said, "Why don't you write a ghost story? People have been getting into that."

"For sure." I sat up in my chair and looked animated as I used my hands to conjure up some garbage on the spot. "OK. It's April twenty-first, 1978. Now, what if all the people who died on April twenty-first, 1900, come back on the same day they died—but seventy-eight years later—and look around for their homes and families. They aren't aware of the fact they're dead, and they can't understand the time lapse."

Bobby swiveled back around to his desk, then he got up and paced over the elegant Bokara covering the center of the wood floor. He stood under his folksy propeller fan, twirled it a few times, then pulled the chain that started the motor. He was seriously deliberating. "You mean that the people alive now don't know them, so they aren't aware that these people are dead either."

I put on an intent look. "That's right."

"How do they get back here on earth?"

"I don't know. But they'd come back in the costumes of their day. That's how people would start to suspect that something's strange."

Bobby looked pensive. He rubbed his chin, then slowly, "Good. Why don't you put it in a treatment?"

"On spec?"

"Listen, right now there's too little to go on. You know that, but you're being greedy anyway." He frowned and looked a trifle confused, then he laughed through his nose to let me know he was sure about what he'd just said.

I said I'd think about it. Then I stood up and we shook hands and said goodbye.

Bobby gloated knowingly. "Tell Dino I say hello."

Bastard!

I walked out into the street and looked back at Bobby's building. I remembered that I used to park my car here sometimes when I went to the beach. Bobby's building had been the neighborhood Pentecostal church before he bought it. Now, within just a few months, other producers and a few ritzy art galleries had opened up on the same block. The morning fog had thinned out and almost disappeared over the wide stretch of sand beyond the boardwalk. But it hadn't been sunny long enough to get warm. I took a breath of fresh air, looked out at the gray-blue water, then drove home.

Chapter Twelve

Ten-thirty.

"Stanley, I'm home!"

If Stanley was at all angry, at least he was putting on a charade of not showing it so I'd be quick to fix him his breakfast. The trash bag was intact, none of my stray socks or shirts had been chewed, and there was absolutely no foul odor of elimination. There was nothing with which to upbraid this noble guy, which meant he was really playing all his high trump cards right away. He just gave me a few wags of the tail, howled good naturedly, and waited by the door. I combed the cabinets above the sink. Fresh out of dog food. I opened the door, pushing him back with my foot, closed it, and started walking the short block down the hill to the Canyon Store on Laurel. But he took up with his "I am STRANDED" howl before I could get two feet; so I went back, put him on his leash, and walked him down there. The lady at the checkout counter was nice enough to hold onto him while I picked up some Kal-Kan ("Only the best—you're my man, Stan"). I bought myself a paper, then we headed back. I fed him on the front porch outside the door, and he somehow managed to keep his ears separated from the food long enough to get it all down.

I looked over my little lean-to. It was past the point of needing new paint. The wood was weathered and gray, getting soft and spongy like balsa wood. Paint wouldn't make much of a difference now. Still, it would have helped. But who had the time or the inclination? If I fixed it up any better, maybe the owner would get an offer on it and I'd be out on my ear. I remember when I'd rented originally, they'd been trying to sell with no comers. That still hadn't prevented them from telling me it had once been owned by Robert Taylor. Every piece of shit Hollywood apartment, house, or bungalow has been the coveted property of some illustrious has-been.

I brought Stanley back in the house, closed the door, and opened up the windows to let in some fresh air to go over my dirty dishes. And they certainly were none but my own. Ellen had taken all of hers. I allowed myself just one jigger of Jack Daniels. Then I applauded my steadiness with another. It didn't make the slightest difference, so I went into my bedroom and sat down at my desk. I could feel my Smith-Corona staring at me, so I reached into my big box of typing paper, took out a sheet, and shoved it into the machine. Nothing but wide open spaces. I opened up the paper, got out the sports section, and moved over to the bed.

Chapter Thirteen

I woke up to find two oily black pools pressed close to my face. Stanley was sitting over my chest, regarding me with what appeared to be a benign form of contempt. It seemed to me that he was wondering where his next six month supply of Kal-Kan was coming from. It seemed to me that he wanted to know why Ellen wasn't typing in the living room.

"None a your bee's wax!"

I pushed him off, then I had to pat him on the head. I sat up to look at the clock. Ten to twelve. I got up, washed my face, gave Stan a milkbone. Then I found my checkbook, made out a deposit slip, signed Herbert's check, stuck it in a stamped envelope from my bank. I wrote out a check to the leasing people for three out of five of the back months, stuck that in another envelope and wedged them both by the metal flag on my mailbox. Then I got in the car and drove down the hill.

At the corner of Crescent Heights and Sunset, I beeped my horn to the tune of "Shave and a Haircut" and waved across the street toward Elmo, the shoeshine man. He was wearing his English sports cap pulled down low over his forehead, and his mirror shades glinted off his dark face in the midday sun. He was carrying a couple of pairs of shoes into Schwab's, probably to a few middle-aged bullshitters eating Reubens as they drooled over the daily grosses in their grease-smeared *Hollywood Reporters*. Elmo heard me and waved in my direction with a pair of shoes.

I was reminded of one Sunday over breakfast at Schwab's counter when Vicky had pointed out an octogenarian who'd taken her to Puerto Vallarta. The old toad had been too senile to even remember who she was. He had looked right at her, no more than a foot away, as the three of us stood in line at the cash register. He hadn't had the slightest idea. Either that or he was a great card player. Lizard skin, long shaky hands, breath that smelled like formaldehyde, and a crooked pompadour toupee that bore a faint resemblance to Davy Crockett's coonskin cap. I had asked her how she could do it—that is, assuming that he could. And she had just said, "You lie there and think of the nice things you'll be able to do with the money; plus, you get off mentally on making somebody else happy."

Since then, she had changed, thank God. She had a little more respect for herself, at least.

"Asshole—*move!* Fuckin' shit!"

Christ. Reality at the stoplight. I had stopped traffic in the right-hand turn lane for, God knows, at least twenty seconds. A mortal sin, no doubt. I hung my head, barely catching the wrathful stare of a self-righteous hairy young potentate as he swerved around me in his silver gray Corniche. His car phone was under his chin. I had probably forced him to reschedule an appointment. His license plate read: I BOOGIE. A music mogul.

I crawled through the Strip with the bogging traffic. Like a cartoon exercise in mitosis, the eleven-foot visage of a contented Salem smoker was splitting down the middle right between the eyes, as a workman on high hooked a cable over one of the center panels and lowered it by crane down toward the installation truck. Another billboard was baled up on the ground, waiting to take its place.

When I pulled up to Vicky's, I gave my horn a TOOT-TOOTTOOTTOOTTOOTTOOTTOOT. Cute. Could she hear me all the way back there? The landlady sure had. She came toward the front of the court wearing a starched pink cotton housedress that hung down over her ankles like a wall of plaster. You wouldn't have even known her body existed if the waist hadn't been drawn in with a narrow belt that looked as snug as a hay bale. Her twiglike, sun-withered arms were warring with a tangled garden hose that trailed along behind her. The water was gushing out hard. From a distance, the hose looked more alive than she did. Like an aggressive viper that was winning its battle.

I got out of the car and walked down the court. The old woman somehow turned the water off. She mopped her brow against one of the short sleeves of her dress. Her shock of mousy white hair was wet in spots, matted down and slightly grayer over the top of her forehead and in the back where a few strands hung down.

"Afternoon, Mrs. McGinty."

She ignored me, of course, as usual. But that didn't mean she kept her nose out of my life. She eyed me with a sour look like it was all my fault, followed behind me as I walked, then clumped hurriedly ahead and cut across the short lawn toward Vicky's side of the court. I noticed her big feet. The Pinocchio syndrome: nose, feet, whatever. Some part of us gets thrown out of proportion as we get older. Just clomping around so hastily and angrily all day long would be bound to flatten your feet and lengthen them over time. I remember thinking that my face would shrink and my nose would grow into something children would want to play with. I'd get winded putting on my pants and walking to the mail box. And I'd hate punks like myself for not being kindly and considerate. I wouldn't be gracious. I'd hate not being young. This old bag was probably a queen in comparison to what I'd be. That is, if I got that far.

The old woman broke off my reflections when she went into Vicky's bungalow. I was still coming down the walk when I heard her screams from inside. Like a bird with clipped wings shrieking landward from a great height.

I ran toward Vicky's.

Chapter Fourteen

Before I could put my foot on the first step, the front door swung open and I was face to face with some lethal-looking metal.

"Hold it right there."

The gun was about three inches from my face and I felt like I was wearing bifocals as I looked up at the officer's face without taking my eyes off of what was in his hand. It was long and narrow, mournful looking, and the nose was small and bony and a little too turned up like it had been worked on. The cop's lips were sealed airtight; the jaws clamped down like iron. Little veins throbbed and danced along the sides of his temples. The eyes said nothing above freezing. I suddenly felt like I was already dead. I had to say something before he took a breath and blew my brains out.

"What's wrong?"

The guy turned his head a little without taking his eyes off me and motioned me into the house. Mrs. McGinty was still shrieking her lungs out. I was nervous, but I didn't know what the hell was going on. A younger uniformed cop came out of Vicky's bedroom, and the nice guy who had his gun trained on me spoke to him: "Shake him down."

The younger guy approached me, knelt down, and went over me from the feet up.

"He's clean."

Mrs. McGinty was babbling loudly now, and my friend with the gun looked like he'd like to plug her mouth up with one of his feet. He walked over to where the old lady was standing in the short hallway, took her firmly by an arm, and started moving her toward the door.

"Listen, ma'am, go back over to your house. We'll come over in a few minutes."

She pointed at me. Her hand was trembling, but the pointed forefinger shook most of all. "He did it. This man. I should have called you last night, but I thought it was the party. I saw him over there. I saw 'im. Didn't I tell ya?"

"You can tell us all about it."

He practically carried her out the door. Then he changed his mind and handed her over to the younger guy who escorted her out across the way.

I was alone now with the boss man. He put his gun on my face. Then he lowered it to his waist and motioned me away from the hall and toward the living room sofa.

"What are you here for?" he asked me.

"What am *I* here for? What are *you* here for? What's going on here?"

I was mad now, really mad, and I wasn't about to be intimidated by some fucking cop and his toy gun. I started walking toward Vicky's bedroom, but he stopped me with a hard arm that was like a toll gate. I tried to lift it up and over to the side. Then it came down across my face and the gun was waggling up toward me again.

"Right there. Just calm down now."

He pushed me back over toward the couch. But I didn't sit down. I rubbed my face. No blood.

"I'm here to see Vicky." My voice was straining to be calm. My whole body was shaking. I felt like I couldn't get the words out, but I still had to try. "I'm here to see Vicky. Her landlady's hysterical. I heard her screaming as I came down the walk. I come to the door and find two cops here, and now you won't let me go into her bedroom."

He moved over to the door and shouted across the way: "Hey, Bill!"

"Yeah."

"Get her account."

"OK."

My pal turned back into the room. He looked at me with professional concern. There was something in him that cared—I could tell that. But he wasn't going to let it get the best of him. Besides, he was really more curious than anything else. I thought he was trying to decide whether he liked me. Then he put on a totally blank expression and acknowledged me with a nod. "So what do you think happened?"

"What do you mean? I don't know what to think. That's

why I'm asking you." I sat down on the couch, put my hands down under my thighs and kept them there. "OK, look, goddamn it, is this your way of telling me . . . goddamn it!"

I was so mad I didn't even see the guy as I jumped up and tried to make it to the bedroom another time. When I looked up, somehow I'd ended up on the floor by the front door. The younger cop was back. He had both his gun and his nightstick out, and he was looking over toward his partner. His blond hair was combed to the side and flopped down across his face. In the back, it stood up on end in a few cowlicks, like "Our Gang's" Alfalfa. Without the worried look and thick moustache, he would have looked just like a teenage beach bum. His blue eyes were pretty, but wide and slightly glassy. They needed to be told what to do.

"He's real upset." The big boy sounded almost sad. Almost. "He wants to see his girl. What's the old lady say?"

I sat back against the door molding. The big boy still had his gun out, so Alfalfa put his back into the holster. He slapped his nightstick lightly against his palm. "She says she heard arguing and fighting while he was here last night. She was gonna call in except it started to quiet down. She saw him leave—"

"I can tell you what happened, officer."

My pal ignored me. "What else?"

"She saw him leave this morning. Then she came over later to ask her to close her windows because she was going to water. The radio was on like we found it. So when nobody answered the door, she decided to give a call."

I stood up. My head hurt from being pushed around, and I felt wheezy, slightly dizzy. My face must have been the color of pea soup because Alfalfa looked at me and said matter of factly, "I think he's gonna throw up."

And he was right. Because I suddenly felt my stomach taking on a will of its own. I started moving toward the kitchen sink and they didn't stop me. Alfalfa followed me and watched me puke my guts up. I only wished it were possible to puke your thoughts and memories too. I walked back into the dining area and sat down at the table where Vicky and I had sat and talked last night. It was easier if I kept my head down.

"I still haven't heard you say it." I heard my small voice. "How do you know it's her? Did the landlady say it was her? Did she actually clearly see her *before* she started screaming? For God's sake, won't you just let me make an identification?" My voice became shrill. It was ringing in my ears. I stood up and held onto the table. "Goddamn it! If you had any idea what we've been through—the things we did together—"

"Should we take him in?" asked junior.

"Don't get your prints on the table," the big boy admonished.

"Is she dead? Can you just answer my fucking question?"

"We better get him out of here," muttered Alfalfa.

"The girl in the bedroom is dead, friend," the big boy said slowly, carefully, making sure I got it.

"*Friend*, the girl in the bedroom is dead, *friend*. That's a nice way of putting it. What d'ya do for fun—watch 'Dragnet' reruns?"

The youngster started to get brassy. The smell of death seemed to give him a shot in the arm. "Hey, what else is there to say? You asked a question, you got an answer."

I turned to the big boy: "Now you're supposed to say, 'yeah, so what d'ya want—flowers?'."

"That's pretty good. You should be a writer or something," the asshole told me. Well, at least he was right on the button—enough so to make me want to upchuck another time. I didn't turn away. I just stood there and let it come and got nothing for my efforts but a few half-hearted sound effects.

Alfalfa winced. Getting paid for this didn't seem to help. He looked over at the big boy. That last retching spasm had made my stomach feel like a garbage disposal trying to digest a fork, and my legs felt about as substantial as confetti, so I started to sit down again. But before I could, my old pal pushed the chair away with his foot. "I just want to ask you something," he said.

"I don't feel so well. Would you mind if I sat down first?"

"Would you object to coming in with us to answer some questions?"

"Now?"

"Right."

"If you wanna tell me what this is all about."

"Questions, that's all."

"I'm in no mood, at this moment, to talk to you or anybody else for that matter."

He turned to his mate, saying, "That's just what I figured. Read him his rights."

Alfalfa told me a story, put me in cuffs, and we walked out with me in the middle, the boys on either side. My hands were behind my back. They each had an arm inside mine. It felt like I was floating away.

"Come on, walk, goddamn it," said one of them.

Vicky was lying there all alone. She hadn't had a chance. She hadn't even really gotten started on liking herself. It was unfair. It made me angry as hell. I cursed everything I could think of and got dragged along.

Halfway down the walk, I heard a door open, then slam. Then the old biddy's footsteps came clomping down behind us toward the street, and she hustled out in front, taking long, hard strides. The starched dress squeaked against her bony frame like the sound of a box boy filling a shopping bag. A cream-colored sedan pulled up and double parked in the middle of the street. Two men stepped out of the car. One, a long-limbed, giraffe-necked black in a wrinkled khaki suit short on all the cuffs; the other, a beer-bellied little man wearing a crew cut, loud print shirt, and white shoes. He had a large leather case strapped over his shoulder. They crossed over toward our side of the street. The black man approached big boy and they talked. They were polite and didn't seem to know each other. I overheard myself referred to as "a suspect."

Big boy turned to Mrs. McGinty. "Ma'am, would you show these men into the apartment?"

"I'll be happy to, officer," she answered in a pleasant sing-song. She looked excited. Like she was getting ready to watch Lawrence Welk. Having the time of her life, for sure. "Is there anything else?"

"Oh, just keep an eye out."

He might as well have asked her to continue breathing. Still, she was thrilled. Her lips were pursed and her mouth moved around like a bowl of mush. She had to make a sneering face to force her dentures back into place. Then, with all of that polished porcelain, she smiled wide enough to hurt your eyes. "I sure will." She looked meekly back and forth from the black plainclothes to big boy as she avoided my eyes.

Big boy opened the back door of his car, an unmarked brown Dodge, parked right in front. Alfie helped me down into the car and put his hand over my head so I wouldn't bump it. Good manners. Big boy closed the back door and walked around to the driver's side and opened his door.

The other men were waiting for her, but Mrs. McGinty stood on the strip of grass by the curb, waving at us as we drove away. "I hope he don't give you a hard time!"

Chapter Fifteen

It's amazing all the roving eyes and sycophants you're able to pick up when you're being officially escorted. The boys had their hats on and that was enough to spread the word. We hit four red lights and at each of them folks both young and old made with the double takes and craned their necks to get a good view of me sitting in the back seat.

We pulled in and parked at the back door of the Beverly Hills City Hall. At a glance, it looked like one of the old California Spanish missions. Alfalfa swung the door open then shoved me out. He was tired of being nice. We went through the police entrance on the bottom floor, took the little elevator upstairs, and came in past a bone-thin, pale wraith of a woman glued into asstight prefaded denims, knee-length buff-colored riding boots, and a royal blue, badge-laden Cub Scout shirt. Her hair was flaming red, cut very short.

"On Rodeo Drive—in the middle of the street!"

She was yelling, but her facelift was pulled so tight around the ears, it forced her face into the suggestion of a perpetual smile. The desk officer was nodding his head off with close-lipped, trained piety, mumbling back at her in a quiet voice I couldn't hear.

"In front of Hermes . . . I opened the door, he ran up and

grabbed it . . . I demand that you do something . . . but *plenty* of credit cards . . . I pay my taxes and if this is how you protect Beverly Hills . . . let me speak to your superior officer."

We passed the distraught shopper, went around the front desk, and into the work area behind it. Plainclothes with gun packs over their shirtsleeves were moving around together exercising their jaws. It looked like they'd just come out of a meeting. A droopy-eyed sergeant bent over the front of a desk. He looked up from a stack of cards he seemed to be alphabetizing, licking his thumb every second or so like a schoolmarm counting her pay stubs. He turned around and faced us with a weak chin sagging over his pinched collar. There was enough slack-reddened skin to supply a rooster's comb.

"Book 'im?"

He looked back down at the cards and fiddled with them, doubling a rubber band around the middle.

The big boy looked at me. "You're going to have to talk to us sooner or later. Why not make it now?"

"Maybe because I don't like the idea of being pushed around just when I've lost somebody close to me."

"So then you won't cooperate and answer a few questions?"

"Listen, I don't want to talk about it. Are you going to let me go home or what?"

"Book him then," says big boy. "Murder one on Victoria Swall."

The youngster stayed with me while I was mugged and printed, then finished his escort job by taking me down to my cell. I'd been informed that I could make a phone call. I had a few lawyer friends, but I didn't really feel like talking to them at the moment. They probably would have had to get back to me anyway. What's a distant acquaintance when you've got a hot PI case cooking on hold? Providence, though, came to my aid, and I realized that before I started getting chummy with my new cellmate, it might be a good idea if I informed someone of my whereabouts. About twelve feet square, and even if it's the Beverly Hills jail, the whole prospect of being locked in there was something I relished just about as much as death itself. And who else was there but Ellen? She was the only one who could listen and understand.

Another rookie cop was sitting in a chair by the corner, and Alfalfa told him to unlock my cell. The youngster had one of my cuffs off, but when I made my request, he reluctantly put them back on and led me back into the main office area. He sat me down at an empty desk, got me the number, handed me the phone. She wasn't home. Figured. But I thought she might be at that magazine where she worked on features. So I got the kid to call up information, get the number, and dial it for me again. His eyes weren't watery and faraway any more. They were hard and bright and small. He didn't look polite.

It was a case now. A serious responsibility. I was being charged with murder—Vicky's murder. A surge of blind panic shot up through my stomach and chest, bit into the back of my neck, and flooded me with adrenalin. I could hear myself speaking into the phone, asking to talk with Ellen Brockhurst. I was afraid of my own voice saying it was very important. The receptionist asked me what my name was and told me to please hold.

There was a long pause. Alfalfa had a cigarette going. He was sucking on it like a milkshake, tapping his fingers on the side of the desk, getting very impatient. The same voice came back on the line. "Ms. Brockhurst is tied up now. She can't take any calls."

My face was twitching. The PBX, teletypes, and typewriters, loud talk, and clamoring footsteps were shutting out my thoughts. The overhead fluorescent lights suddenly seemed like heat lamps bright enough to burn through my skin. I couldn't gather my thoughts.

"Yes? Hello?"

"Yeah. Listen, what it's about is—I mean, tell her this is Ben Crandel."

"She knows who it is, sir."

"Yeah, that's right! OK, try this: I'm in jail." I realized that what I was saying, the way I was saying it sounded like a ruse, one of my stupid schemes. "Wait, that's not it. Tell her that my friend Vicky, she's been murdered, and they've got me here at the Beverly Hills police station."

"Your friend Vicky's been murdered and they've got you

there at the Beverly Hills police station. Is that right?"

"Yeah."

"OK. Hold on, please."

I held on for another moment or so before Ellen came on. "One minute. I've got to get on another extension."

"OK." She put me on hold again before my first syllable went through.

"You finished?" asked Alfalfa.

"No, I'm not. I haven't even talked to her yet."

She came on again breathing fire. "All right, Ben. If you're that desperate, I don't mind talking, but you didn't have to fib to the whole office, did you?"

"I wasn't fibbing."

"What do you mean?"

"I went over to pick up Vicky today for lunch, and there were two cops there. They arrested me when I wouldn't come in for questioning, and they told me that Vicky's dead."

"Are you serious?" She was listening now. Her voice was still hostile, but not quite as strident.

"Yes."

"If this is another one of your—"

"Listen, it isn't, OK? I wish it were."

"Let me talk to somebody there."

I turned to Alf. "She wants to talk to somebody."

"What?" He put out the cigarette, shoved a stick of gum in his mouth, and started chewing it hard. His cheeks crinkled up disdainfully around his eyes.

"She doesn't believe me. So she wants to hear it from somebody else."

"Who is it?"

"Girl I know."

"Figures." He snatched the phone out of my cupped hands.

My hands turned into fists, and my wrists rubbed against the edges of the cuffs. "What?"

He just ignored me and talked into the phone. "Officer Galbraith. Yes, this is a police station . . . Beverly Hills . . . He's charged with murder in the first degree . . . We'll have to see . . . No, I'm afraid there's no one else you can talk to at the moment . . . Take my word for it."

He hung up. I looked toward him for an explanation. "She hung up," he told me.

Then he took me back down the same corridor, unlocked the cuffs, and put me inside my cell. After he locked me in, he just stood there. His eyes addressed my chest as he said, "Sorry 'bout that remark."

"What remark?"

He looked at me and said "Good luck" in a way that made me think I was really going to need it. Then he walked away.

Chapter Sixteen

My roomie was a lean black guy dressed to kill in a heavy, green-brown, three-piece tweed with wide lapels and a black shirt open at the collar. His shoes were new on the bottom. He had a full beard and smelled like violets. We didn't talk. A couple of minutes after I laid myself down, I turned around and faced the wall. He left me a few hours in the afternoon. When I was all alone, I fell asleep and dreamed that I was stabbing Vicky. That was my guilt having a good workout on the old psyche.

Then somebody came and opened my door. I sat up. It was another young cop.

"Come on with me."

He took me out, handcuffed me, and walked solemnly by my side. He was fairly big and soft looking—seemed to be insulated with a layer of baby fat. Not fat, really, but plump and cherubic looking. I imagined that he lived in a big incubator, had his wife burp him after meals, and never sat in the sun. Our feet made loud martial sounds over the cement floor. We got in the elevator, went up a floor, and got out. We stopped halfway down the hall and he knocked at a door that answered us from its other side, so he shook hands with it and we went in.

It was a small office with matted, blue carpet. The thick, husky trunk of a big palm stood a yard away from the one window facing Rexford Drive and the public library and centered the view as it continued climbing up out of the frame. It was still late afternoon, but there didn't seem to be much sun out. From where I was standing, all I could see was a gray white sort of haze. Smog and fog and clouds. There was one chewed-up, short, stubby wood desk that came with the building. Behind it sat, or rather perched, a cop who frightened me. First of all, he was wearing his shoulder holster which, oddly enough, was empty; second, he was the smallest cop I'd seen all day; but third, he was by far the meanest looking. And my guess was that he hadn't managed it by looking after the chic affairs of high-strung, aging clothes horses. He was the sort of guy who landed in the golden ghetto by way of promotion, the kind they bring in hoping to tighten up the slack. The general appearance was that in dealing with assholes day to day, year in and year out, this man's niceties and social graces had been worn flat, smooth, and hard like the surface of the best rocks for skimming over water. He was sitting there, his shoulders hunched forward over his elbows, which were planted almost halfway across the desk; his chair was tilted forward with the back legs off the floor to help him make the reach. The face was dark and smooth and hard with regular though small and scaled-down features—fer-retlike: his design and biological aim to sniff out, then squeeze into small, unseen places in order to force wary thoughts, motives, uncertain intentions up out of hiding. He had a few papers spread out over an open manila file and didn't look up.

"Take off his cuffs."

Baby Hughie snapped the cuffs off. They'd only been on for about two minutes, but having them removed was like taking off uncomfortable shoes after a long hot day of pounding the pavement. I felt almost too free, like I had already been getting used to confinement.

My new escort waited a second or so wondering whether there was anything else that needed to be said; then he smiled rather sheepishly and walked out of the room, closing the door behind him. He had seemed like he was anxious to get out.

The Ferret Face looked up with the typically inscrutable eyes I had assumed would go along with the rest of it—no lids and all pupil, black. Then came a quick, close-lipped smile that worked ironically off his brows. The brows curved down as the lips curved slightly up. It was as if they were both speaking to me.

Lips: *How are ya? Nice ta meet ya.*

Brows: *Are you kidding? I'm gonna tear you apart. If I can. If you'll let me.*

Both gestures cancelled each other, leaving me empty, adding to my confusion. He pulled back his elbows and pressed his hands against the edge of the desk, improvising a graceful pushup that suddenly sprung him onto his feet.

"George Steifer, investigative detective."

He sounded much nicer, more cordial than I would have thought. He offered his hand. I shook it, saying, "Ben Crandel."

Both of our hands were limp, almost falling over each other like rubbery pasta. He came out from behind his desk, walked across the room, and fetched me back a chair. He told me to have a seat, then went back behind his desk and sat down. In a moment or so, he was leaning toward me with his chair half off the ground. I was afraid if I opened my mouth, he'd scurry down my throat; but I still thought that if I were the first to launch into things, I might have a little more control over the ensuing discussion.

So I blurted out, "OK. You guys make up your minds yet?"

His mouth opened wide with interest. "What about?"

"Whether I'm the Hillside Strangler or just a common murderer."

He laughed so quietly and quickly I wasn't sure I heard it.

"Well, I'm paranoid. First they tell me she's dead—" I stopped myself. I had heard my voice rising, and hadn't known where either the sound of it or my sentence had been going.

He looked concerned, like a friend "Why'd you stop? I want you to tell me what you think happened."

"How can I tell you if I don't know? They wouldn't even let me see her."

"You look like an intelligent young man. What do you do?"

"I'm a writer."

"For the movies and television?"

51

"Yeah."

"Well, don't you ever use police procedure in your writing?"

"I don't know."

"Even if you don't, I'm sure you know that when there's a murder, they can't let you run around and smear up all the prints."

"But when somebody that you're . . . I just wanted to—"

"You couldn't believe it unless you saw it. Isn't that what you're saying?" His voice was casual, quite tame, except the black blots of his eyes were fastened on me like leeches.

I tried to pull in the reins on my emotions. "If you want to put it that way—I guess."

"If it was just seeing, though, that would be OK. But then you probably would have fallen apart."

"What does that mean?"

"It means that you would have then touched things you weren't supposed to." He gave me a pause. I didn't answer it. So he went on. "Your arresting officers said you were emotionally torn apart. You were recalcitrant when Officer Morgan ordered you to stay out of the bedroom. It says here in his report that he was made to use force two times. Then, when you were asked to cooperate and come in for questioning, you refused to comply with the request."

"If it was a request, why was it necessary that I should have to comply with it?"

"We're talking about murder, Mister Crandel. I don't care how lily white you may be—when murder happens and there's the slightest shred of a suggestion linking you to it, then we have to ask you to cooperate. We're ignorant, we don't know a damn thing about your involvement or non-involvement until you tell us about it. We're not mind readers, so the only thing we can ask you to do is talk to us. Besides, if someone close to me were hurt, I would want to do all I possibly could to help. I think that makes sense, don't you?"

"Listen, sir, when somebody close to you is suddenly no more, you don't feel like talking, discussing it with nobody—at least for a little while. I could think of better places to be than even the Beverly Hills Police Station at this moment."

"Mr. Crandel—"

52

"Besides, wait a minute. When two supposedly intelligent police officers are sitting around and listening to a gossipy, attention-starved old lady talk about me as if I'm a fucking murderer, then I feel even more sick."

"OK, now you listen to me for a second, all right? The woman said she saw you at the girl's apartment last night. You didn't deny it. The woman said there was arguing. She said she almost called the police. She had heard lots of arguing there on other occasions before—which may or may not be connected to you. But the issue is last night. There was arguing last night. The next morning the girl is dead. You saw her last night and, for all intents and purposes, you were the last one to see her alive. Don't you think it's logical that we'd like to chat PDQ?"

"Don't you think it's logical that I wouldn't feel like talking right away?"

"Yes, I do."

"Then why didn't you at least let me go home for awhile, then come in?"

"There's only one problem with that."

"What's that?"

"If you had really killed her, then you might just disappear."

"Why the hell would I have left and then come back if I killed her?"

"Well, that depends on how long she was dead, your finesse as a murderer—a lot of things. One, most murderers are amateurs at it. They don't kill for a living. They do it in a fit of passion. It's an emotional thing, so they're not completely aware of what they're doing when they're committing the act. You, for instance, might have been coming back to remove a trace of evidence you thought you left: a coat or a tie, or maybe your watch fell off. Two, if you knew you'd be implicated in any way, maybe you had some cockeyed idea that you were creating an alibi for yourself by coming back in plain daylight and letting people, including the police, see you be surprised and taken aback by what you were supposedly getting wind of for the first time."

Without thinking about it: "Jesus Christ, you make me sick."

Ferret Face remained unruffled. He put on a show of how

sensitive he was. "I know it's hard. But we can't always be concerned about your personal feelings. We'd like to, but we couldn't operate like that."

"You'd like me to say I killed her, that's what I think. Then you could file away all the little papers and close it up. It would make life a lot easier."

"You know, for a writer you're a pretty stupid guy." He leaned over even farther, giving me that bewitching brow and lip smile. He didn't show it with his voice, but his lips had gotten thin and tight. I realized he was close to boiling, and I wondered what he did then. Probably smiled continually, then let his leechy eyeballs loose on your skin. You'd never get them off, and they'd multiply as they fed on you. "If we convict the wrong guy, then the real murderer is still out there running around and killing more people. Do you think we want that to happen?"

"I don't know. Do you?"

He shook his head and leaned back in the chair, tilting the two front legs off the floor as he planted his back up against the wall. He rolled up the sleeves of his shirt, did it carefully and made sure the cuffs were flat and even on both arms up past the elbows. He blew air through his nostrils in a poor imitation of laughter which, I guess, was supposed to mean I was funny.

"It doesn't reflect well on us either when they do find the right guy. Of course you wouldn't think about that. You're too busy thinking about the terrible injustices we're heaping on your head."

"OK. So cops are really just a bunch of princes. Your intentions are only the highest. I apologize. So drop the charge and let me go home."

"I'd like to. But as long as you're here already, I think we should wait and see how the autopsy turns out."

Chapter Seventeen

Mentioning the autopsy made me think that if they could find out what I thought they could, it was time for me to say something informative. Even if they couldn't, and I told them later, it would seem like a lame try on my part to rearrange the facts. So: "I don't know what you find in autopsies, but I should tell you a few things now so I won't have to tell them later and sound like I'm defending myself."

"Go ahead." He was too casual, the way people are when they think you'll spill the beans if you're made to feel relaxed.

I held back, heard myself saying, "I don't know how she was killed."

He looked at me a little uncertainly, then decided he could say, "Shot. In the back of the head from what appears to be fairly close range."

I swallowed hard and closed my eyes for a few seconds. The room started spinning. I popped them back open and forced myself to concentrate. "That's pretty hard to take."

Ferret Face didn't say anything. His face was cast into a benign mask. He seemed to be hoping that I'd forget he was there. He was waiting, encouraging me to be myself and tell my story. That expression would never change. He'd always be my friend. Just a sympathetic ear, a good listener. At least that's what the dark carved stone of his face was saying.

I talked to it only because I knew I had to. "OK. If they can separate the gunshot from the other wounds or bruises, they'll find a discrepancy of time there." My voice was slow and heavy, working to be placid, to bury the emotions for the time being.

I had thought that he'd ask a question, but all he did was vaguely knit his brows and nod agreeably, encouraging me to continue.

"What I mean is that I don't know what else aside from the gunshot was done to Vicky at the time of the second assault; but when I came over to see her last night, she had already been beaten."

He gave me the double smile. "Any names?"

"Whoever it was said they were a friend of mine."

He worked on the skeptical curve in his brows, made it into a straight line, enlarged the smile, then froze it again. It was the smile of a dutiful nurse for a dying patient. "Did you have any idea who it might be?"

"It wasn't a friend."

"Who was it?"

I told him about Herbert. Everything I knew. It probably took me a good fifteen minutes to trot it all out. I felt winded like I'd been running as I finished, and the little man's face was no longer a mask. It was moving around with lots of expressions, all of which looked slightly displeased. The brows went crooked and sarcastic again. The little eyes seemed to come alive. They narrowed in on me and studied me with a mixture of contempt and disbelief.

"I think you're holding something back." He tried to say it nice, but it came out hard like a kick under the table.

"I'm not."

He scratched the side of his small nose. He was thinking. Then he said, "I think we've done enough talking for now. You better think over what you said. As far as I'm concerned, it doesn't make much sense. If you explain away the two sets of bruises, you're only trying to give yourself an alibi for being there last night. How do we know that you didn't beat her up last night, then kill her some time this morning?"

"If I had done that, don't you think she would have made noise through the night?"

"Not if she was unconscious."

"You could ask the people from the party next door. One of them knocked on Vicky's door. Maybe they heard something going on in there. Also, some of them saw me arrive. If any of them heard the fighting, maybe they could place me being there after it happened."

"We'll look into it." He leaned forward, setting his chair back on the floor. From thumb to pinky, he dug the dirt out from under the nails of his right hand with the forenail of his left. But he still had enough time to glance up at me and smirk, "You're a smooth talker. Seems like you got an answer for everything." Then he called out a name and Baby Hughie came back in.

I felt tired and disgusted. The guilt game was old already. It was time to stop letting myself be whipped and get down to trying to figure out what had actually happened. I'd definitely had enough of this lengthening list of juicy innuendos. "That's insulting," I told him. "But I guess you're just trying to do your job."

"And you're just trying to help—huh, friend?"

My fuse went out on me. I jumped to my feet and exploded: "Why the hell is every sonofabitch down here my friend? That's what I'd like to know. You can just sit there cool and calm and tell me—"

"Temper, temper."

"You know what you are?" I was whining like a kid now, digging in with some dumb-ass needling.

"No, but tell me."

"A goddamn fucking little sadist. You like to kick people when they're down."

That was enough to make him stand up and smile real big with his eye teeth, just the way a Doberman does before he goes for your leg. He turned his wolfish smile to Baby Hughie. "Hear that? I'm a goddamn fucking little sadist. I'm the kind of guy that kicks ya when you're down."

I should have shut up, but I didn't: "I'm not guilty, but everybody down here seems to want to make me feel that I am."

"He's got a persecution complex," Baby Hughie observed.

The little man agreed: "Which must mean he's got a lot to hide."

I was grinning. "Freud and Jung? You guys should practice in Vienna."

Baby Hughie put his hand on his holster. It was unsnapped already. He was upset as he said, "People only feel guilty because they are guilty."

"Bullshit!"

The little man put one knee over the desk and grabbed me by the front of my workshirt with both hands. I heard a seam rip. Small arms, not the strongest, but still hefty enough to lift my flat feet up into a relèvé.

"Shut the fuck up!" He spit the words into my face. Then he let go of me and let me have a last look at that awful two-way smile. "You're the kind of guy that'd love to have an officer beat the crap outa ya. Then you could really go and make a big stink. That's what jerks like you want. I thought you were an OK guy when you first came in here. Now I've changed my opinion." He looked at Baby Hughie and nodded decidedly as he showed the eye teeth once again. "Unbalanced. This kind of guy here's nuts enough to do anything. Insubordination: all of this goes into my report. He's making it real hard for himself. Talkin' himself right into a murder rap."

He motioned toward me and Baby Hughie approached with the cuffs. "Put your hands out."

I put my hands out. I was looking out the window as I heard the cuffs snap shut over my wrists. The haze had lifted and the sky was getting purple. In about a half hour or so, it would be dark. My escort gave me a rather indelicate shove toward the door.

The little man's voice hit my back, sounding high and shrill as he mimicked a girlish tone; "Sweet dreams."

All the way back to my bunk, I heard those two words strained mockingly through a tough little man's voice. They pierced my back and crawled up my neck like a host of drunken mosquitoes having a party. I couldn't scratch them away. So, in the elevator, I had to just stand there and take it as they sucked the blood out of my head. I knew for sure that I wasn't looking forward to going to bed.

Chapter Eighteen

Round and round, over and over, the same thoughts. Like a broken record of your most hated song. After a while, if it doesn't drive you crazy, it's got to put you to sleep. I must have stayed awake till three or four in the morning, then I conked out for about a half hour or so. I dreamed I was Neil Simon, having lunch with my accountant at the Bistro, and we decided that I had to stop working for at least a year because I was making too much money. I had to take a loss. He recommended that I take the wife and kids and skip around the world a few times just to be safe. I didn't want to be a fool and work to spite myself. It was a good idea. I'd consider it.

Then that beautiful scene dissolved and I got to the bad part. I was in my house, eating breakfast and looking out the window, when Vicky walked up and knocked on the door.

One eye was full of sparkle and laughter; one side of her mouth was grinning. Then her head turned and there was a bloody, unrecognizable pulp. Blood flooded down her neck and drenched her white dress, made a pool of deep red at her feet. She didn't know that she was dying. She asked me if I wanted to go to a movie. I grabbed a towel and pressed it to the gaping wound. The blood gushed out and over my hand. Then she saw it all and started screaming.

I sat up in the dark. My whole body was covered with sweat. I stood up and paced the floor until it was morning.

Chapter Nineteen

Eight-thirty Monday morning, I'd already looked at my Tang, Corn Flakes, and coffee. Someone new came to open my cell. I told him that I wanted to call a lawyer. He said I already had one.

"I haven't even talked to one."

"Well, maybe somebody else did for you."

He put the cuffs on. We were walking out. "Where are we going?"

"Downtown, for your arraignment."

This guy picked up a friend outside. They were both skinny, undeveloped, and the friend had bad acne. My escort's polarized sunglasses were turning dark. It was warm and bright out.

We got into the white squad car, turned right on Santa Monica, cut over to Beverly Boulevard, and headed east. It was only nine o'clock, but there was still a short line of people standing at the outside counter at Tommy's, ordering up some greasy double chili burgers along with soda to help them burp and digest. From Western Avenue onward, the further east you got, the more crude hieroglyphics you saw smeared over the walls, bench stops, and buildings. Most of the stuff looked like it was done by one person. The letters were all capitals, jagged, barely connected straight lines. Scattered ethnic murals, too, on the sides of preschools, liquor stores, and single-story office buildings, done in the style of Diego Rivera.

Inside the courthouse, everyone who was poorly dressed didn't seem to know where they were going. Everyone wearing a three-piece and shiny shoes and carrying a leather attache case walked with authority and led the way.

They stuck me in a holding cell with five other men, and the six of us just sat and contemplated our shoelaces. A couple of old guys dressed in gray county issue had three-day beards and smelled like beached seaweed. One was bald and the other had long scraggly gray hair. Another guy around forty wore Brylcream hair, a cheap baggy blue suit, and a tie with a tic-tac-toe pattern. The two beefy Chicanos were both wearing army dungarees and white T-shirts—one with a yellow-billed woodpecker tattooed on his tricep, the other with a big smile and lots of missing teeth. We were all ushered out into the court at the same time. We sat in a jury box on the side. The two Chicanos and the blue suit were continued until they could get their hands on a lawyer. My name was called and I stood up. The charge was read, and a bearded guy in a beautiful gray on gray pinstripe popped up from nearby and started gabbing about me. I turned my head and caught a glance of Ellen's father sitting in the back row. He was wearing tennis whites. His look was as intense and disinterested as it would be in the middle of surgery. It was cutting right through me like my whole being was one semipermeable membrane.

The lawyer and the D.A. were haggling over my bail, which had been set at a hundred thousand. The lawyer argued my professional status as a writer, my clean record, the fact that I shouldn't have been detained in the first place. The D.A. said that since I was clearly suspect, had no strong ties in the community, and was either self- or unemployed, there shouldn't even be any bail in the first place. My lawyer butted in and said that Doctor Alfred Brockhurst, a personal friend of the defendant, was prepared to vouch for my character and present bail of any reasonable amount. Again, my attorney stressed that the original intent had not been to detain me but to insure that I agreed to submit myself to any inquiries made by the police. I had been emotionally upset at the time and had refused to cooperate. This was why I had been detained, then charged. The judge asked me if I still intended to impede the police's investigation and refuse my cooperation. I said that I'd cooperate fully, then added that I had just as much interest—more, in fact—in determining what had taken place. The judge eyed me disdainfully and told me that my personal sentiments had nothing to do with the matter at hand. I replied that they had everything to do with it. The judge said I was just about in contempt of court. But then he got fatherly, asked if that was what I wanted. I said, "No, excuse me, Your Honor," and he dropped the bail down to fifty thousand.

As I came outside to the main hall, Doctor Brockhurst was standing there waiting for me. I stuck out my hand: "Thank you."

He looked away from me and started walking straight ahead. I had to assume a brisk pace to keep up with him.

"Doctor Brockhurst, excuse me, but if you're pissed with me, why did you bail me out?"

He moved his head to the side and said gruffly, "I do my pissing in the toilet, thank you." Then he stopped abruptly and pointed a finger. "I didn't do this for you. I did it for Ellen."

He winced and dug into his tennis shorts and came up with a cellophane-wrapped antacid tablet, which he tore open and popped into his mouth. He chewed hard and looked away from me as he said something about how hard he had tried to be nice to me and how I'd disappointed him. I asked him if he was referring to my getting arrested. Then he looked at me and said I knew what he was talking about. But I didn't. The doctor was acting like a different person. He had always been more adamant than the Missus in opposing Ellen's "living arrangement." Nevertheless, that hadn't prevented us from having lunch or being occasional doubles partners on guest days at his country club. So when he offered me $10,000 "just to stay away from my daughter," I didn't understand why and I didn't know what to say. I turned away and walked out of the building.

Chapter Twenty

I walked for a long time, up to Beverly and Vermont, where I sat down at a bus stop, then hailed a taxi that had stopped for a red light. I got in, gave the driver my address and some brief instructions, then closed my eyes against the bright early afternoon. I thought about Ellen's father. He had probably had a tête à tête with the attorney and jumped to the conclusion that the reason Ellen and I broke up was because I'd left her for a prostitute. Maybe he thought I was really a pimp. Once that man jumped to a conclusion there was no stopping him. I'd seen it many times in our discussions.

I opened my eyes again and wished I had my sunglasses. By the time we pulled up in front of my house, I realized they were in my car, which was still over in front of Vicky's apartment. I was about to tell the driver to turn around and head back down the hill when I saw somebody standing at my door. Long legs in tight jeans, holding a folded newspaper by her side. She was standing up against my kitchen window trying to see inside. I could hear poor Stanley barking, more out of loneliness than watchdogging. She turned around. It was Vicky's friend, Denise. She shaded her eyes with the newspaper as she bent slightly at the knees and tried to get a view into the car. Then she came down the steps. I leaned across the seat and opened the rear door on her side. She stood to the side, bent her neck, and looked into the car. Her face was pale and drawn. Her bottom lip was quivering, pulling her jaw down into her chin. The eyes were wide and startled; bloodshot and filmy and dilated with no color in the iris.

"Ben!"

"Hi, Denise."

"Ben, is this bullshit or what?" She shook the paper, dropped it into the back seat.

I shook my head.

The driver was a young, slight guy with a much prettier

face than Robert DeNiro and a deep premature suntan that was much too good for late April. He turned around and looked at us without expression, paused, then turned back around. I assumed he was trying to tell us he was an actor, not really a taxi driver, and we were taking up his time. So I asked Denise to get in, then I told him to turn around and head back down the hill.

I turned to Denise. Although she was Vicky's closest friend, I had never gotten along with her. But I was in no mood to harbor hostility toward anyone. I guess I was kind of glad there was somebody to talk to, even if it had to be her. "I got taken in from Vicky's house," I told her.

She didn't hear me. She was squinting at the second page. She looked up.

"They arrested me when I came over to pick her up."

Her voice was soft and shaky: "I've read this a hundred times. Sally called me at eight o'clock and asked me if I'd seen the Sunday paper."

"She must have been pretty upset."

"She was crying so much I couldn't understand what she was saying. So I got it back out of the trash and looked and looked and looked. Then I found it. I went over to her house. After that I hitched up to your house. I was going to call the police, but I was afraid to, I guess, because I guess I knew it was true."

As she cried, she looked away out her window. She didn't make much noise. Her head just bobbed back and forth. I asked the driver if he had a Kleenex. He handed me a couple and I gave them to Denise. She dabbed at her eyes and wiped her face. She made choking sounds as she held herself back, then she stopped and turned around on her seat and faced the front of the car.

The paper was down on the floor. Sunday morning, April 23, 1978. The Sunday paper was supposed to be fun. You allowed yourself to take your time reading it, along with browsing through the funnies and studying next week's TV guide. The news of the moment was that two Palestinians had murdered a confidant of Egyptian President Anwar Sadat, and that the sixth and thirteenth Hillside Strangler victims had lived across the street from each other in Glendale.

I knew where the clip was. Under THE SOUTHLAND, I saw the lead in: *"A 21-year-old prostitute . . ."* I had to look at the others first. I didn't want to find it so fast.

A *35-year-old* Simi Valley man was being held on $50,000 bail in Ventura County Jail on suspicion of beating his six-month-old son . . .

A *retired Los Angeles* businessman paid a $982 filing fee in Orange County in his long-shot attempt to become the Republican nominee for governor in the June 6 primary . . .

Robert Allen Davis, 23, was sentenced to life in prison for the shooting deaths of his father and two El Segundo police officers last July. Davis pleaded guilty to the three deaths, but the charge that he also murdered his mother was dismissed after he rescinded his insanity plea and pleaded guilty . . .

Two guards were seized by prisoners at Terminal Island Federal Correction Institution during a disturbance, prison officials reported . . .

A *pregnant woman* prisoner awaiting trial on robbery charges escaped from the jail ward at Los Angeles County-USC Medical Center after picking the lock on her leg chains, sheriff's deputies reported . . .

I looked back up to the top of the list and my stomach felt like an open wound, but I wanted to read what it said:

A *21-year-old prostitute* was found shot and fatally wounded in her West Hollywood apartment. Police investigators rejected their initial belief that the victim's death may have borne some relationship to the unsolved Hillside Strangler incidents. A television writer, Benjamin Louis Crandel, 32, was arrested and charged with first-degree murder when he refused to submit to questioning. Crandel was seen in front of Victoria Alicia Swall's apartment shortly after the victim's body was discovered.

I heard Denise talking to me. I rolled my window down, threw the paper out onto the street, and hung my arm out into the wind, cupping my fingers together, and letting my hand plane about in the air pocket against the side of the car. Up and down. Dips and dives. The driver had seen me throw the paper out. He was looking at me in the mirror—without expression.

"You should be an actor," I told him. He smiled at me and took his eyes off the mirror.

Denise was saying, "Please tell me what happened." She had probably said it a few times, but all I had heard was the tone of her voice which was sad, tragic, despairing; and all I had done was make sounds with my hand in the wind to compete with the voice. I didn't want any more emotion on my hands. I had enough of my own. But what was I going to do? Tell Vicky's best friend that I couldn't handle any surplus and would she please pick up her emotions and take them somewhere else? I couldn't do that. I brought my hand back inside the car and studied it.

"I don't know what happened."

"Did she suffer?"

I looked at Denise. The skin over her forehead was pulled tight as her brows scrunched down and centered on a large, knobby wrinkle over the bridge of her nose. Her whole being implored me to help her absorb the loss. I was praying for the callous stoicism of a cop.

Gently: "Listen, Denise, I'm trying to get rid of it, not think about it for a few minutes. Is that OK?"

"She was my best friend. How do you think I feel?"

"I know, I know. I'm sorry—it's just that this is pretty hard for both of us."

The cabbie pulled up in front of Vicky's. I paid him and gave him a good tip. He looked at me blankly, said nothing, then burned rubber as he sped away. We got in my car. The gearshift knob had been stolen. Kids always do that. They collect them. I cursed it, and Denise looked at me like she'd done something wrong.

"I can get a ride," she started.

"Some kids stole my gearshift knob. Just get in."

She got in and banged one of her long legs against the dash.

"So, where are you going?" she asked me.

"I have to go home and feed my dog. He's been in the

house alone for almost three days. Would you like me to take you home?"

"Sure."

She sounded awfully bad and I felt like a pig, so I said, "Come on over. We'll talk."

"Thank you. I know we've feuded, but—"

"Fuck it. People are always united in tragedy."

She smirked. "You don't have to be so sarcastic."

"All right."

I was heading up Robertson toward Sunset. After a minute or so, she said, "I'm not accusing you. Can't you just give me some idea of what happened?"

"Denise, you asked me if Vicky suffered. I hope to hell she didn't. But I don't know. I just don't know. If I knew, I'd tell you—I really would. I came over to her place to pick her up for lunch. The cops were there and they wouldn't let me see her. Then they arrested me when I refused to go with them for questioning."

She shook her head in sympathy.

"That's all I know. Before I was with her the last night, somebody who said they were a friend of mine almost strangled her."

"Are you kidding?"

"Nope."

"Where?"

"Her apartment."

"Did she report it?"

"No."

"Well, then didn't you?"

"What the fuck difference would it have made?"

"A lot, maybe."

"Well, we thought we had an idea who it was."

"So you decided you could take care of it yourself."

"Not exactly."

"Who was it then?"

"I don't know."

"What do you mean you don't know?"

She was making me feel terrible. Without planning it, I screamed out, "Don't lay the goddamn blame on me! It's not my fault."

I didn't look at her and she didn't look at me. I wanted to

take her right back down the hill, but I would have had to explain that to her and I didn't want to. So I just kept driving.

Chapter Twenty-One

Stanley looked as pitiful as his namesake, Stan Laurel, used to when he was just about ready to cry. He started wagging his tail, but then didn't. He stared at my ankles and waited for me to fuss over him.

He got to Denise right away. "Poor little doggie. Poor boy." Denise smiled at Stanley and bent down to give him a few pats on his noggin. "He's been all alone."

When she looked up, the smile was almost gone but still there like the after-image on a tv screen. Her eyes were in a foreign country. You'd need a passport to get there, and I didn't have one or want one, for that matter.

"He's a ham. I've gotta walk down to the store and get him something to eat. Why don't you stay here with him."

"OK."

I was in a daze. Somehow I bought the dog food and then found myself back in front of my door. Denise was sitting on the kitchen floor, petting Stanley and bestowing the usual canine endearments. She stopped as I came in. Then she stood up. Stanley started howling. I got the food in his bowl and set it right down on the floor so he wouldn't have to wait another second longer. Denise and I looked down at Stan choking down the whole hunks of burger rounds. Neither of us said anything. Stanley finished in about ten seconds, then sashayed to the screen door, waiting to be let out. I opened the door for him.

"How long did you know Vicky?" I asked her.

"I knew her back home in Phoenix. I was head cheerleader when Vicky tried out when she was a freshman."

"Vicky was a cheerleader?"

"Yeah. Didn't you know that?"

"She didn't like to talk too much about Phoenix, so I didn't ask her about it."

"Her parents."

"Yeah."

"Last year when I moved out here, I looked her up. We got to know each other really for the first time. She looked up to you."

I opened the refrigerator, took out an opened bottle of Chianti, found two clean drinking glasses, and poured them full. I handed one to Denise. She nodded to me over her glass and we both drank the wine down like it was water. I filled both glasses to the brim again, killing off the bottle. I drank mine the same way, although Denise was slower this time, saving hers.

"I'd like to talk to her friends: Sally, maybe Sharon too."

She looked at me questioningly.

"So I can see if they know anything that could help in trying to figure it out."

"I could call Sally. She might be home still."

"Do you have any ideas yourself?"

"Not from what you said."

"Well, what else can *you* think of?"

"I don't know if it has anything to do with it, but she'd just borrowed fifty dollars from me. Maybe she owed somebody money."

"Who would she owe money to—for what?"

"It doesn't make any sense, does it?"

"No."

"Should I call Sally?"

"Yeah, if you would."

Denise looked for the phone and I pointed her toward my desk in the bedroom. I could see her from where I was standing in the kitchen. She dialed the number, then looked toward me. "What should I ask her?"

"If I can come over and talk to her."

Denise spoke into the phone. "Sally, how's it goin'? . . . Yeah, I know . . . Calm down, honey. What do you mean, he won't leave? Tell him to get the hell out of there . . . Listen, I'm over at Ben's house . . . He just got bailed out . . . I don't know. We'll come over, OK? . . . You can handle it. Just tell him to put his pants on and get out . . . See you in a few minutes."

Denise hung up the phone and came back into the kitchen, shaking her head. "She's got a John who won't leave."

"What?"

"He has an arrangement. He's a buyer or something and he comes into town every few months and stays with her. Good money, but he wants it again this morning, and Sally is not in the mood. That's what she said."

"Creeps."

"*Very.*"

Chapter Twenty-Two

Sally lived on Laurel Avenue, around the corner from Greenblatt's take-out deli, in a boxy, two-story, 50's prefab job trimmed with redwood siding. Each apartment had a window facing the aquamarine cement patio and dinky, kidney-shaped swimming pool on the inside court. You walked through one set of double glass doors, then out another before you realized you'd just gone through the lobby. We turned left on the patio and Sally was standing there outside her front door, wearing two articles of clothing: a pair of lacy black panties and a plain white cotton jersey that stopped about two or three inches above her navel. I had never seen Sally when I had not seen her navel and most of the rest of her. There really wasn't that much to hide. She had enough flesh on her to cover her bones and nothing left over, so she marketed that navel for all it was worth. She ran up and tried to put her arms around both of us at the same time. Tears were running down her face, short sobs were catching in her throat, coming out in different notes and key signatures.

After a moment or so: "Hi, you guys."

A tough-looking, sable-haired guy, medium sized and sinewy, with only the slight beginnings of a middle-aged paunch, came out of Sally's door and approached us at a brisk, authoritative pace. His craggy face looked like it probably toughened when he got mad and otherwise stayed roughly genial with a sense of civility that could help him out when he had to stay nice. In other words, he didn't look like the kind of person who had a difficult time getting angry. And if he was mad, as he was now, in order to deal with him, you'd have to get yourself madder than he was. That wouldn't be too easy. There were deep creases on each side of his mouth, engraving a frame around his big-lipped frown.

"I wanna talk to you," he told Sally. He took her roughly by one of her shoulders and pulled her away from us toward the pool. He was buttoning his shirt cuffs, leaning over Sally with his tough-looking face, screaming, "I've had it with you!"

She said, "Look, Harry, I'm sorry. How much do you want?"

He raised his hand as if to slap her, then scratched the back of her neck instead. "What ya want—the whole works—give it to ya, and what do I get? No class."

Denise made a spitting sound. "Talk about class. I don't know how Vicky . . ."

"I know," I agreed with her.

"Listen," Sally was saying, "then just pay me for last night."

"Pretty sharp when it comes to money, aren't ya, kid?"

He didn't wait for an answer. He shook his arms to get the cuffs right, turned away and stormed past us and back into the apartment. A moment later, he came out wearing his suit coat and carrying a white leather suitcase and a large book of carpet samples. He gave me a vicious sneer, flung a couple bills down on the pavement, muttered something like "Goddamn gutter" under his breath, then hoofed it out through the double doors.

We went inside. Sally came up with a joint, so we passed it around. Nothing short of a stick of dynamite could have gotten me more than an inch off the ground. I didn't feel a thing.

"He threw some money on the ground," I told Sally. "Did you pick it up?"

She rushed out the door and found the two bills. They were fifties. She smiled as she came back inside, then looked at us and remembered her mourning. When somebody died, it was a special thing, a rare sort of experience, and if you were privy to it, a reverential attitude was called for. You were receiving the ultimate instruction. About where you were going. Like into the ground. Or into ashes.

Or somewhere. Wherever—it was someplace you hadn't been to. Something to think about. Personally, I was finding the whole process rather disgusting, thinking that every morning, each new ache or pain was only a sign, a harbinger of things to come. Things I sure as hell wasn't looking forward to.

Sally was asking me to tell her what happened. I looked at her and smiled. "I couldn't tell ya, dear. That's why I wanted to talk to you."

"What would I know?"

"Lots of things. Why don't we try to think together if there's anything unusual Vicky might have said or done lately."

"To give us a clue?"

"Right."

"Let me think." She took two long hits and rubbed her chin. "Colombian. Maybe it was dusted." She put the joint out, rubbed her chin, and started thinking again. I could tell she didn't have a thought in her head. She was studying my face and Denise's. Then she went into a stare.

I smiled and Denise shook her head. She put a hand on Sally's knee. Sally blinked her eyes as Denise said, "Vicky borrowed fifty dollars from me. What about you?"

Sally sat up straight. "I knew something was bothering me—'cause she hit me up for fifty . . . no, seventy-five! Really strange."

"Why?" I asked her.

"She said she was goin' somewhere, but she wouldn't say where. She just gave me a mysterious look and sort of smiled. That's strange, for Vicky. Whenever she goes anywhere, she'll talk your head off. You know." She looked at Denise to confirm this, and Denise agreed with her.

I asked if Vicky had still been hustling. Denise objected bitterly, pointing out that Vicky wouldn't have had to borrow money to do that. I asked if maybe Vicky had had any long-standing debts to pimps or other similarly savory characters.

This cut Sally to the quick. "She didn't need them. *They* needed *her*," she trilled indignantly. "Vicky was special."

"You mean she never had a pimp?"

Sally shook her head and started sniffling. Then she was

crying. I got up from the dinette chair by the window and walked over to the couch and sat down next to her. I put my arm around her and she cried into my shoulder.

"Don't cry, Sally."

"Vicky was the best person I ever knew."

I could tell she meant it.

"She knew a lot."

"I know," was all I could say.

Denise got up from the other end of the couch and went into the bathroom and closed the door. I heard her crying in there. I was waiting. My shoulder was getting damp. A lumpy, blue-haired elderly lady came outside wearing a tight, pink, one-piece bathing suit. I could see her varicose veins from across the yard. She stared at Sally's window for a good half-minute. Then she put her rubber nose plugs in place and tugged on her bathing cap. She walked to the deep end, turned around, and let herself fall in backwards like a scuba diver. She started swimming, churning up a little wake with dainty kicks, taking high, rounded, wind-mill strokes that reached up toward the sky before coming down over the surface of the water and slapping it gently with open hands.

Denise came back out of the bathroom and sat on the couch next to Sally. They exchanged a few kind words with each other, clinched for a long hug. Sally told me to take care. I told her to take care and gave her a kiss on the cheek, then Denise and I left. Outside, that old woman was still swimming.

Chapter Twenty-Three

I wanted to go see Vicky's other good friend, Sharon. She was a whore too, but it seemed a little early to be work-ing, so we decided to take a chance. I went down Sunset to La Brea, turned right, and headed down to Melrose past Pink's hot dog stand. I could smell that great combination of mustard, onions, and gluey chili and felt like stopping for a quick one, but I wanted to see if I could catch Sharon first. I drove to Gardner Street and stopped before a cracked and faded one-story duplex that looked like it had been bigger at one time but had shrunk gradually due to over forty years or so of being baked in direct sunlight. The little place had one central wall shared by both apartments and doors on either side that faced each other across a cracked cement stoop. I hadn't been there in probably a couple years, but, the last I'd heard, it was still Sharon's address. I wasn't all that fond of her. I tolerated her. My opinion had always been that she was older and, therefore, should have known better.

I knocked on the door. No answer. There were two thumbtacks stuck right next to the peep window. One of them pinned a folded piece of scratch paper to the old white wood, which looked like a dart board from all the punctures. Printed in bold letters across the paper was TO THE MILKMAN. There was a relief outline of writing coming through the paper. I stuck my nail in underneath the thumbtack and pried it off. The handwriting was scratchy and small:

> Dear Mr. Milkman,
>   Please don't bother to leave any more of my previous order. I hate to sound so very crude. (I hope you're the one getting this note!) But I know I'm way behind on my bill and since I decided against your previous offer, I wish my service to be discontinued. Besides, I am not drinking much milk now anyways.
>   Once again: Sorry!
>   Sincerely,
>   Sharon Bacall

I showed it to Denise, then I stuck it back on the door. As we walked down the steps, I saw a small ball of paper resting in a patch of dried-up geraniums. I bent down, picked it up, and smoothed it out.

> Dear Brian,
>   If you think I'm that dumb you can shove it up

The note was unfinished. Maybe it had been the thought of leaving two missals at the same time. She hadn't wanted to

73

give that milkman any more ideas than he already had. I handed Denise the crumpled piece of paper. She was quiet as we got back in the car. When we were a block or so away, all she said was, "Yick."

"I know what you mean."

She laughed unhappily, the kind of laugh that begins and ends with a shake of the head. "I mean the girl has to give it to the milkman."

"I hear that's how she pays the gas."

"No."

"Vicky told me that the same guy's been reading Sharon's meter for the last three years—quite a savings."

Denise shook her head and laughed again.

"The only thing that bothers me is how she influenced Vicky."

"She let her."

"It still would have been easier if she'd never had anything to do with Sharon."

"But then it would have been somebody else."

I had to agree. And if it had to be anybody, it was probably good that it had been Sharon. She was nutty like Sally, but zestier and more aware. She had sort of been like a big sister. Her theory had always been that everybody was different and everybody had something different to get out of their system. The only problem with it was that Sharon had been spending her whole lifetime getting it out of hers.

We passed by Pink's again and my stomach didn't feel up to the challenge. We opted for the counter at Schwab's. The plan was to eat, then work our way down Hooker's Stroll from La Cienega to around La Brea and see if anybody we might know had seen anything of Sharon that morning. The regulars were there at the counter, tables, and magazine rack. Either before or after they paid their checks, one person after another bought cigarettes and the *Hollywood Reporter* or *Variety* from either the nice old lady or one of the new girls at the cash registers. The magazine rack was really a safety valve so those who didn't want to leave wouldn't have to and could stick around for an extra ten minutes or so looking for someone they knew who might give them a lead on a job. Then, after that, there was always the front part of the parking lot where they could loiter around Elmo's shoeshine stand and pretend as if they were waiting for somebody. The old boys, the guys with long-standing ulcers, cataracts, shrunken limbs, and bulging faces—those guys had all the fun. Schwab's, to them, was just like a cheap country club or bridge club. They had a ball sitting around giving the waitresses a bad time and acting like they still had a foot in the door of show business.

We both had hamburgers. I had to pay twenty cents extra for a slice of onion and a slice of tomato, which gave me another gripe to add to my list. When we got out to the parking lot, I asked Elmo if he'd seen anything of a fairly large girl, chesty, big face and big eyelashes, very blond, almost platinum.

"Wear boots all the time?"

I had never realized that was part of her trademark, but, "Yeah."

"Sharon?"

"That's right."

"Shit, I knows *Sharon*. Everybody 'round here knows Sharon. I don't know if I seen her today though."

I thanked Elmo, then he stopped me as we started walking away. "Wait a sec," he smiled. "There be a lot of action down by the Tropicana last few days."

"You mean by Duke's?"

"Yeah. There's a couple of rock 'n' roll bands in from outa town. You know. I hear the girls been goin' down there."

I gave him a buck for his good ear. He bowed from the waist and slipped the money into the tackle box where he kept his horse tips. We got in the car and I offered to take Denise home, but she said she didn't think she wanted to be alone. So I took her along.

Chapter Twenty-Four

LA.'s Tropicana doesn't exactly match its Vegas counterpart. It was built originally by Dodger fastball artist Sandy Koufax in the early sixties, and at its best probably looked like a very ordinary motor inn. It has since deteriorated and the sheriffs and vice squad detachments do housecleaning there about once a month. The place's main allure is the coffee shop next door, a little hole-in-the-wall called Duke's where people also read the trade papers but are basically less desperate and scheming than your normal Schwab's personality. Chubbier too. These are people who like to eat: great omelettes, French toast, exotic sandwiches like mushroom-onion melts, Brazilian burgers, Swiss burgers, fresh fruit milkshakes, carrot or double layer chocolate cake for dessert.

I didn't know what I was going to do—go up to each little room and knock? Denise and I were standing around the main court of the motel, looking up at the few people we could see moving in and out of open doors along the hacienda-style railing. There wasn't much to see aside from the maids hustling back and forth. I peeked into Duke's on our way back to the car and that's where she was. People were standing in line outside the door to get in and share a table or land a seat at the short counter. She was sitting at the counter, lapping up a fresh strawberry milkshake with a spoon, oblivious to the outside world, staring into space. Sitting next to her was a young, emaciated guy with dark, peroxide-streaked hair that stood straight up in short, wild clumps on top, then tapered out unevenly, getting longer till it hit a straight line just over his shoulders. He was shirtless in a black leather jacket with a zipper in every seam. Even though he wasn't doing much talking, he seemed to be with Sharon who, I noticed, was wearing what appeared to be a rhinestone dog collar around her neck. Slung tightly over her was an artfully torn white T-shirt with a rather large hole placed tantalizingly close to her left nipple. Complementing the dog collar was a chrome-linked leash around the waist of her plain blue Levi's. The Levi's were new, but they were ripped in the knees. Very punk, especially with the dark circles under her eyes thanks to all the smeared mascara. She was concentrating more on her milkshake than her date, so I didn't feel like I was intruding.

I put a hand on her shoulder. "Sharon."

She looked up and a smile lit up her face. "Benjamin, what's happening?"

"Not much."

"This is Lester," she said, introducing me to the punk.

"He's the lead singer in Drivel," she laughed, "That's the name of their group, really."

Lester smiled wide. He had bad teeth and he was proud of it.

"That's great," I nodded to him.

"By yourself?" she asked me.

"I've been looking for you," I told her. "The shoeshine guy at Schwab's told me you might be over here."

"I hope it's not serious," she smiled.

"Can I talk to you outside for a minute?"

"Sure."

Lester was still smiling with his crooked greenish-yellow teeth. He put his arm around Sharon's waist and rested a hand up under one of her hefty, sagging boobs. "Don't be straight, man," he told me. "Sherry and me ain't got no-o-o secrets."

Lester had an English accent. I was willing to bet he was probably a big success. He looked demented, but shrewd and confident. I doubted he was as out of it as he pretended. As far as I was concerned, it was a good pose and he was brilliantly converting all of his drawbacks into assets. Take the teeth, for instance. His face or his mind, for that matter.

"Sorry, Lester. It's nothing personal. I'll bring her right back."

Lester didn't seem to mind that. He scratched his head, then he stuck out a long, gangly paw and offered it. "Pleasure, mate," he beamed. Then he laughed. "If you're straight, what's that make me?" I told him I didn't know. "Crooked," Lester squealed, scrunching face and body into a Hunchback-of-Notre-Dame imitation. "You're so straight, makes me crooked."

People were looking at us. Denise was standing outside as we came out. They didn't know each other so I introduced them. Sharon started telling me that Lester and his band were here in L.A. finishing up a one-month, twenty-five city tour. His first record had already turned platinum. He was taking Sharon and a couple other girls to the Bahamas for a week. She was going to make enough to get a new car. She told me all of this in one breath. After she was finished, I told her what I had to say.

She sat down on the curb in front of the paper stands in front of the restaurant. She said that she had had no idea. I told her that neither did anybody else, and that's why we had wanted to find her. But it was no dice. She hadn't seen Vicky for at least a month or so and had no idea what she'd been up to lately. I thanked her and told her I'd give her a call if I ever found out anything worthwhile. As we drove away, she was still sitting there on the curb. She looked up and waved to us with a limp hand. Then she stood up and walked back into the restaurant.

Chapter Twenty-Five

Before I dropped her off, Denise made me promise to have breakfast with her in the morning. I told her that I wasn't sure what I'd be doing. She got angry and said to forget it. So, then, of course, I had to console her by saying that I would. We both knew that there were arrangements to be made in regard to Vicky; but since she didn't mention anything, neither did I. I'd have to give it some thought when I was ready to. I wondered when that would be. As I was wondering, she was saying goodbye. I thanked her for trying to help, then she thanked me. Her thank-you had a desperate ring to it, something she probably hadn't wanted me to hear—because she turned and walked away quickly after she said it. She had heard herself. And, sometimes, when you hear yourself, you get reminded of the way you are. You hear something that you need to hide, even from yourself. What Denise heard embarrassed her as it embarrassed me. But I wasn't sure what it meant. Maybe embarrassment at having me think she was the sort of person who couldn't make it through an emotional crisis alone. Maybe embarrassment at the admission that I had helped her and she'd been wrong about badmouthing me as much as she had.

I drove away from Denise's apartment, thinking about Denise and what she had represented to Vicky. She had been one of the few friends who hadn't been a whore, per se. Two or three years older, Denise was probably twenty-three or twenty-four. She was the sort of person who had goals for herself. She seemed to know where she wanted to be six months from now, a year from now, and chances were she'd probably be there. Because she worked at what she was and what she wanted. Normally, she was coquettish and bitchy in a heart-throbbing way that seemed to work on lots of men. But she wouldn't let them interfere. I imagined her mind to be like a tight little pocket calculator, right on the beam with the facts and figures, a suggestion of memory, but nothing heavy and long-term to hinder adding up the real vitals and then subtracting or dividing out what got in the way.

She was gutsy, ballsy, sharp, shrewd. She wasn't a sweet, naive pussy like Sally or Sharon who gave it out to squeak by on her monthly utilities. Denise was serious and if she sold herself in any way, she wouldn't tell you about it till much later on if she ever bothered to tell you at all. But she would always know what she was doing. Vicky used to get delirious seeing her strut around Toyotas in those commercials she did for them. If you could see somebody you knew actually getting somewhere, going places, then the impossible seemed more possible. To Vicky, Denise had been all toughness and self-sufficiency. She was making enough money to live in one of those huge old Hollywood Moorish buildings, the kind with gigantic arched windows overlooking a garden courtyard set off the street and barricaded behind high walls. Vicky had said she was furnishing it slowly, tastefully. Denise had probably been a good example for someone as unstable and impulsive as Vicky. That seemed to be the angle, and I wasn't about to argue with it. She had gotten Vicky to join an improvisational theater group about three months ago. I hadn't known any of the people. They had all seemed like morons to me and I had avoided them, although I'd been happy for Vicky.

I dragged myself in the door. Stanley looked at me like he was really sorry, although there was nothing he, personally, could do. I told him that I perfectly understood, and lay down across my bed, took my boots off with the sides of my feet. Then, of course, the phone rang. It was Sharon. She was over Sally's and they were on a crying jag together and wanted to take care of the arrangements. I told her to call the Beverly Hills police and ask for Detective Steifer. He should know where the body was. The body. I couldn't associate it with Vicky. I called it the body. I thanked Sharon. She asked me if there was anything she could do. I told her not now.

I fell asleep for two hours and woke up again at six o'clock feeling more tired. Bits and pieces from the last forty-eight hours had been droning over me in my sleep. I got up, walked down to the Country Store, and bought myself a quart of Jack Daniels. I opened it up and started nursing myself before I got all the way back up the hill to my house.

I gave Stan his dinner and got in my car and drove down Laurel Canyon. Most of the people were navigating either up or down on their way home from work. They looked mean and tight-lipped. It was getting dark out and they wanted to get home as soon as possible. A second's delay was the equivalent of an hour. If you cut somebody off at this time of day, they hated your guts. And all it took was one stalled car to ball up the traffic going either way. On the narrow stretch of curves just above Hollywood Boulevard there was a new Lincoln Continental with the hood up. The first two drivers behind him looked livid, possessed with a self-righteous vengeance. One of them was sitting on his horn. You could only appease these people if you first admitted full negligence, then submitted to a group sacrifice.

I was on my way back over to Vicky's. I didn't doubt that the cops had been through it with a fine tooth comb, but there still might be something there, I could find meaning in that they couldn't—that is, if whatever it was hadn't been taken away. Maybe there was a little bit of self-protection and paranoia operating too. My performance with the Ferret Face hadn't been rich enough for Beverly Hills and I knew it wouldn't hurt if I could find some way to weatherproof my hide. And then there was the guy who'd been such a good friend of mine.

But I'd have to save my sleuthing for some other time. Mrs. McGinty was prowling over the front court. Fortunately, she wasn't covering the street, although that didn't mean she wasn't performing her rightful duties. It was after six and she was still puttering around in the garden. I was parked across the street, a little before the bungalows. From this angle, I could barely see her. She had slacks and gardening gloves on and, after a few minutes, she looked around the yard and out toward the street, then scurried up Vicky's short front stoop, leaned over toward the left, put one gloved hand to her brow, and peered in through the living room window. Then she scurried down again and moved to the other side and out of my view. I'd have to come back later after dark and take my chances then.

Chapter Twenty-Six

The situation was nearly hopeless, so I decided to backtrack and try Herbert. I knew the police would get around to him eventually when they'd exhausted the other more obvious possibilities, i.e., me. But what else could they ask me? A foolish thought. They'd be sure to think of something. All the juvy stuff, my moving violations, my drunk driving, that peace march arrest, whatever. They'd probably be getting around to Vicky's friends, too. My bet was that they'd catch up with Denise and then, from there, pretty much follow the same trail I had.

It was late twilight and the digital clock over the Pacific Federal Building said 6:31. The four corners of Hollywood and Highland were fairly teeming with the typically well assorted array of early evening creatures: half were very businesslike and walked straight ahead, keeping their eyes to themselves and knowing exactly where they were going; the other half were merely pretending—pretending that they'd come from somewhere, pretending that they were going somewhere, pretending that they belonged somewhere. They tried out the bus stops for size, hoping that acting out the real-life drama of following somebody else's bus schedule might give a clue, spark an idea. But people got on and off the buses and the same people stood there watching, undecided, then eventually walked on up the block or crossed the street, gave it some time, then tried again. In the intersection, wearing white gloves, a black cop was directing the traffic with the grace of a mime. The neon up and down the block was starting to pop, and the sky above the rumbling street seemed to know it wasn't being watched. It was just going from blue to black like a bad bruise. The lights were off in most of the buildings, including the fourth floor of the Security Bank building, so I thought I'd go up.

I was alone in the elevator, but I pushed the sixth floor just to be sure, then walked down two flights to where I wanted to be and listened carefully outside Herbert's office. Not a sound, so I took out my key chain and jimmied the door. It had one of those old loose standard locks, so it was a cinch.

I closed the door and moved right toward the desk, went over all the papers strewn over the top, then opened the drawers and went through those. The blinds were open and there was some light coming in off the street so I didn't have much trouble seeing what I was doing. Vicky's batch of eight by tens were in the bottom right hand drawer. I looked long enough to see her face before I closed the envelope back up and put it away. I kept looking back at the envelope, so I opened it again, went through the pictures till I found one with a tranquil pose. I folded it and tore it across from the neck up and put the top half into my pocket. The other part I threw out the open window and watched as it floated down onto the sidewalk along Highland. I put the pictures back away again and went through the rest of the drawer. It was stuffed with cancelled checks, bills, stationery supplies, travel brochures, legal correspondence, everything useless. I went over the stuff on top of the desk again. An envelope with the Bradford Bobby logo. I opened it. It was a short letter straight from Brad on his company's official letterhead:

Dear Harv,
Per our conversation the other day, I received the pictures you promised. I think this Vicky is definitely the item. If she's our ticket, you can count on me for the finance and distribution we already discussed. Talk to you.
                    Sincerely,
                    Brad

I sat down on the edge of the window molding and held the letter up in the light coming in off the street and read it over again. It suddenly made sense that B.B. was the man I wanted. There was a noise outside in the corridor. I just sat quietly and waited for it to go away. I saw shadows flit over the smoky, translucent glass on the door. I was holding my breath as somebody opened the door. It sounded like a man. He cleared his throat and made a hard, gravelly chuckle that ended quickly. There was somebody with him. They were stumbling over each other and breathing hard. They came into the room and moved toward the small couch on the side wall. Then they came out of the dark and into my light. It was Helen, Herbert's wife, and George, the goon. They were so wrapped up in what they were doing, for the moment, they didn't seem to see me. Halfway across the room something dark fell to the floor. Helen's panties. George's shirt was open and his pants and shorts were down below his knees. His arms, legs, and chest were completely shaved and hairless. Each muscle had definition. In this light, his dark body looked greased and primed for posing in a Mister Universe pageant. A squat somber engine of strength riveted to short, bulky froglike legs; a placid pumpkin face—narrow eyes, small flattened nose, long mouth made stupid by its gaping, slack-jawed expression. Helen ended up in front of him and he was pushing her toward the couch, tugging his pants along, hopping like a contestant in a potato race. His erection was wagging around like a divining rod. Helen fell back onto the couch, George collapsed on top of her and they started rolling around as he pulled at her dress.

I stood up from the window sill and started tiptoeing toward the door. The goon made a loud grunt, probably as he entered her, and then he must have seen me. He yelled, "What the hell?" in a low, guttural voice. Helen screamed shrilly and sat up. He started to pull his pants up. "Wait a minute!"

I beat it toward the door, but before I could reach it, one of them threw something toward me that hit the door and shattered it in my face. I put my hand on the door knob, but I must have broken my stride to wipe the glass splinters off

of my face because the goon hit me with a flying tackle that
banged my head forward into the plaster wall by the door
jamb and knocked me down onto the floor. I used my feet
and kicked backwards with all I had. I hit something hard
and the leg grip loosened and I was able to get back onto
my feet. But so was George, squatted down and facing me
with his shoulders jutted up high and both arms extended,
poised and ready just like some stagy wrestler coming out
of his corner in the Friday night matches broadcast live
from the Olympic Auditorium. Only this guy wasn't doing
it for fun. He looked like he was going to pounce on me any
second, and I was afraid to take my eyes off his face and try
another run for it. I had Bradford Bobby's letter scrunched
up in a ball in the palm of my hand. The goon was sober
this time and plenty mad. His lips were turned under and
pulled in and his cheeks puffed out with the pressure of his
held breath. He checked his fly to see if it was up, but
didn't take his eyes off me for a second.

"What ya want here?" He moved a little to the left. I
moved to the right. We were making a circle.

"I just had to check something."

He screamed at me with all he had. "Snoopin'!" Helen
stood up and smoothed her dress out. She looked frightened, which made me all the more scared. This guy looked
like he was definitely going to kill me, had to kill me.
"What you snoopin' around?"

I didn't dare answer him.

"You deaf? Ain't you got no ears?"

We were still circling. He reached out and hacked my
shoulder with the side of his hand. I was numb all the way
down my arm for a second, but then the feeling came back.
Just a love pat and he hadn't even connected. He continued
talking at me, spitting the words out in a jumble I could
hardly understand. "You know what trouble you got me in,
huh? Huh? You comin' over to Herbert's house. Now the
cops wanna talk ta him. What'd ya do that for?"

I shrugged my shoulders.

"Nobody didn't do nothin' to you. What's the chip on
the shoulder? Snoopin' around. I oughta bust your head."

Helen interceded. "George, if you hurt him and he goes
to Irving, you know what's gonna happen."

"You think he's gonna listen to him?"

"How the hell do you know? Remember neither of us is supposed to be here."

George glanced at her, frowning as he strained his patience. "I know that." He looked back at me. "I also gotta do my job."

I tried to put Bobby's letter into my pocket. George jumped me and knocked me back down onto the floor, stuck a forearm down over my throat and dug in as he pulled apart my fist. Then he leaned on the forearm, crushing my wind out and using my neck for leverage as he pushed off against it and stood up, uncrumbling the little ball of paper and squinting as he read. I started to stand up and didn't see his foot coming as he kicked me hard in the stomach. That sent me backward and knocked my wind out for a few seconds. I started to get up again and he let me this time. He was reading the letter over again. He nodded his head as though he'd just thought of something, then he walked over to me and stood about two inches from my face. He had to look up at me in order to place his face in front of mine. His face was worn out. Large crow's feet around the raised scar tissue of the eyes. Bands of wrinkles down his neck. His short hairstyle was too neat. It could have been a good hairpiece.

"Now you're gonna go over and give this poor man trouble, aren't ya? Huh? Ya gotta go bother somebody else 'cause ya got some cockamamie theory. You don't know what the fuck you're even doin'!" He put one hand under my chin, the other over the top of my head, and squeezed it a little, just enough to make my brains feel like a pimple. "All I gotta do is turn it a little left or right—break your fuckin' neck." He turned it just a tad either way. "Bust it," he smiled.

Helen said, "George."

Bless her heart.

"Shut up," he told her. Then he said, "You're hot, though. I can't do that. There could be somebody watchin' your tail." He let go of me and stamped his foot. "I don't know what to do with 'im!"

He turned his back on me and Helen looked at me and motioned toward the door. I ran for it and, this time, he wasn't coming after me. I flew down the stairs and from above, echoing down the stairwell, his voice hit my back, booming, "Run! That's right—run! Little fuck!"

Chapter Twenty-Seven

I didn't feel safe sitting there, so I started the car and drove down to Sunset. I turned onto a side street and pulled over to think. So Bradford Bobby was hooked up with Herbert in the porno business. Stranger things had happened. I remembered Bobby's black eye. Also, the scratches up around his temple could have been from a woman's long fingernails. And Vicky's physical description fit him to a T. The only problem was that nothing else did. The boy king as a smut peddler's errand boy? It just didn't hold water. Could there have been something personal? Maybe this was how Bradford got his jollies—on the S and M express.

I thought of taking my suspicions to the police and telling them about finding Bobby's letter. But I didn't want to do that. My credibility with them was long gone. I couldn't imagine that they'd feel like listening to much of anything I had to say. I didn't know what to do, so the best step for the time being was to put Brad on the back burner and let him stay there for awhile until I could figure things out. I decided to sleep on it, then make up my mind in the morning.

I still wanted to take a look around Vicky's apartment. Like the last time, I drove beyond the center court and parked on the other side of the street. It was a little after eight. There was nobody outside. The old lady had probably fixed her dinner and she was either on the phone or warming up her chair by the tv. I walked around the block and came back around through the alley. The lights were on in the old woman's house as I crept around the path to Vicky's back door. I jimmied the latch on her back window, opened it, then reached in and opened the back door for myself and went in.

It was pitch black. I felt like Vicky was bouncing off of all the walls, flying at me from every angle. She came up to me, just inches away, then stopped. I was afraid to reach out and see if she was there. I shook my head, bent down, and got my hands on a flashlight she kept down in the bottom kitchen drawer. A hoop of soft light lapped the wall above the stove, jerking up and down. No one was there.

I walked into the dining room and sat down. It had been less than three days since I'd last seen her. It seemed like three years. I was consciously trying to remember things: what we had done, funny or endearing things she'd said. I tried to picture her and couldn't. The image was blocked up, her memory was already slipping away from me. And that frightened me, made me feel like a dumb, soulless, callous creature. I took her torn photo out of my pocket and shined the flash on it. I stared at the picture, and still I wasn't satisfied.

After awhile, I went into her bedroom. I pointed the flash toward the bed. The blankets were turned back and there were a couple of large darkened blots across the middle of the bottom sheet. The top sheet and afghan were gone; they had probably been taken into the lab. Scattered spots of dried blood showed on the wall over the headboard. The bright yellow pillow covers were patchy with brown. I looked through her drawers. I turned the whole place inside out down to the bottom of the sugar bowl. Nothing. I put everything back in place, returned to the bedroom, and forced myself to lie down on that bed. In the dark. It was then, with my eyes closed, that I really saw her—alive and hopeful, worried but radiant on the day that we met. So young. And it was then that I wept.

Chapter Twenty-Eight

"Get up, you. Get up!"

Something thick and hard was poking me in the ribs. I opened my eyes and looked up under the brim of a ten-gallon Stetson into a little face that was old, very old, and tanned and shrivelled, with deep, sunken eyes and a big knobbed and veiny nose jutting out over a wide mouth of toothless gums that sucked hard to bring in their breath.

I had fallen asleep on Vicky's bed and a little old man had turned on her bedside lamp. He was leaning over me with the end of a splintered little pine cane and he had choked up on his grip like he was ready to bunt, except he kept hammering away at me like I was one big stubborn nail.

"Get up, you!"

I grabbed the end of the cane and pushed it away, sat up, and stared at this relic. He backed up a few feet, still pointing the cane at me and did the schoolboy's pencil trick as his palsied hand shook hard at the stick, making it look like rubber.

"Put that down," I told him.

I should have known better than to put a dare on an old soldier. He sucked at the air in a rapid succession of angry gasps and came at me like a flurry of Rough Riders stampeding San Juan Hill, throttling and jabbing at me with that damn cane like it was twenty bayonets. Finally, somehow I wrestled it out of his hands, and the next thing I knew I had it right over my knee. I was about to break it in two.

"You wait a goddamn minute there, you," he screamed, waving his hands helplessly.

For some reason I stopped and just looked at him.

"You're gonna break my cane."

"That's the idea."

"What am I gonna do then?"

"Well, then I guess you could throw it at me."

"I'm an old man. I can't walk nowhere without my cane."

"You mean you use it for walking?"

"Don't you go gettin' smart. Now, what are you doin' in my granddaughter's apartment?"

"Granddaughter?"

"That's right, granddaughter." He opened up his wallet, flipped through his plasticene card case, and pointed to an old childhood picture of Vicky I'd never seen before. Then, with that same bony finger, he pointed toward his chest. He repeated this gesture, saying, "Granddaughter, grandfather—get it?"

"I get it. So, what is it that you're doing here—Mister Swall, is it?"

This got him so mad he couldn't talk until he reached into the front pocket of his dirty gray herringbone sportcoat and drew out a half-pint of a cheap bourbon I'd never heard of. He unbuttoned his collar and pulled down the shiny, silver-mounted hunk of turquoise on his Western string tie; then he put his eyes and lips on that bottle and chugged it down like so much water. He smacked his lips, squeezed both his eyes shut, then opened them on me this time. He looked me up and down and screwed the top on the bottle and put it back into the front pocket of his coat. I noticed that the manufacturer's label was still attached to the outside of the lower left sleeve.

"What'd you say your name was?" he asked me.

"I didn't."

He took out the bottle again and gave it another try.

"Can I have a sip of that?" I asked him.

"No, you may not." He squeezed his eyes shut again, sucked it in, then gave me another up and down look frowning and knitting his gray brows as he studied me, trying to make sense out of what I was. He tilted his hat up on his head. What I could see of it was bald and brown and shiny. He rocked on his heels and wiped his hand on his dark baggy slacks. The slacks were held up by a thin belt that had been hand-notched about a half-foot around from where the last hole was supposed to be. The hard leather belt end stuck out from the side of his waist. His pant cuffs were stained with dried dirt and grime and covered most of the shoes except for the rounded tips—they were a dusty dull black material that gave off the slight sheen of imitation leather.

He stowed the juice in the crook of his armpit and slapped his hands together, bringing off a loud popping sound that made him smile as he nodded toward me. "Okeedokee now." He pointed at himself. "This here's Vicky's Grandpa Hal. Now, I don't want no more nonsense outa ya. Where's my Victoria?"

He obviously didn't know, didn't see the telltale spots of blood. He honestly thought that Vicky was around somewhere. I wasn't about to blurt it right out and tell him. "Uh, she's out."

"That little girl." He slapped his knee and wheezed out a round of chuckles. Then he took another long chug on the bottle and set it down on the nightstand. His face got serious. He started hobbling around by the foot of the bed, back and forth, pacing. "I don't like it," he said. "I just don't like it. If I told her once, I told her a thousand times: a young woman's got to watch herself with the men."

"Hold on. This isn't what you think it is."

He looked at me with hope in his eyes. "You mean, you and she, you aren't shacked up together?"

"No."

"I'm relieved," he sighed. Then he went on excitedly, "When she was little, she used to make me so happy!"

"That's nice."

"Well, the presents she used to save up ta buy me—durn but if she weren't the cutest grandchild a man could ever want. Mister, I love that little girl. Where the hell is she? If she forgot I was gonna be *there*. Hell, we got places to be! We do gotta be there sometime tomorra, only she don't think that," he sighed happily, sucking his gums and shaking his head. "I know she don't believe a damn thing I say. I can't blame her. You wouldn't know it to look at me, but I was once worth ten *million* dollars. Ten million—mostly ticker tape. Think she believes it? Better think again. Been a prospector—gold and silver—owned fifty mines. All nothin'. Oil—had that, but I sold it 'fore it hit. Know what I mean?"

I nodded along with him.

"Here." He drew a picture in the air with a shaky hand. "See, here's the shelf a shale. The first load, thousands a gallons—that's up here. Now, down below that we got two million barrels, somethin' like that. But ya gotta dig under the shelf. Under it."

He was beaming at my rapt attention and decided to reward me by handing over the bottle. I took a good pull on it, then he gave a laugh that turned into a hacking cough. He took a stiff handkerchief out of his pants, spit into it, studied the phlegm, then folded it up and stuck it back into his pocket. I handed him back the bottle.

He said, "Thank ye," took a drink, shook his head, and smiled with thin, closed lips. "All's I can tell ya's we're gonna have plenty a money. We're gonna be rich! That's right. Victoria thinks I'm tellin' a big joke." He leaned close. "Tell me confidential—she think I was comin'? No, wait, first, what's your connection with Victoria?"

"Vicky and I were very close friends."

"'Were'—that's a way a puttin' it," he laughed and hacked. "I see what ya mean. But then why *were* ya here?"

"I was just—she told me to wait for her."

"You wouldn't be that tutor she's talkin' about?"

I wasn't sure what Vicky ever told her grandfather about her education or the lack of it, so I just agreed. Since, in a way, it was true I used to work with her on her basic language skills, maybe that gave her an idea when she discussed herself with her grandfather—although I had never heard of any grandfather. I was sure she probably loved this kindly old drunk, at least at one time. She had probably been ashamed of him too. She always felt ashamed when she discussed her family with me. Or at least that's what I thought. She had this distorted notion of my background because a couple of people in my "family" had been horse doctors. To Vicky, that was awesome. Me from a long line of potato farmers and veterinarians.

"How's Victoria doin' in school?"

"Just fine."

"She goin' ta gradiate soon?"

"I suppose."

"Think she should go on any higher after that?"

"I don't know."

"I guess it's up to her. Anyhow, that girl always does what she wants. I believe a person should do what they wants. 'Specially a person that needs to. That's my philosophy. Victoria ever mention me?"

"Sure. It's just that I forgot."

"I didn't know who you was either, but I sure am glad ta meet ya."

We shook hands.

"Mister Swall, so where were you and Vicky supposed to meet?"

"She tell you?"

"No, she didn't exactly say."

"That's my girl," he said proudly. I had put the old man's cane down on the bed. He leaned down and snatched it, then checked it over carefully and sighted it down the middle like a pool shark does choosing a cue. Satisfied, he stuck it on the floor and leaned forward on it with both hands. "If she didn't tell ya, how am I gonna . . ." He fumbled for a name.

"Ben, Ben Crandel."

"See, I didn't even know your name. Just how do I know you're who ya say ya are?"

"Oh, come on, Mister Swall."

"Sonny, lookee here, now if Victoria didn't tell ya, she musta had her reasons, don't ya think? Anyhow, don't let it hurt your feelin's none. I'm the one should be feelin' hurtlike. My very own granddaughter weren't there ta meet me. Can you imagine?" He smiled as he said this. It didn't phase him. He was quite amused by it all. "I can just see her, ya know, sittin' by the phone, thinkin' like: 'Why that old bag a this and that. Tellin' me this an' that 'bout the family fortune. He must be drinkin' enough to swim in. Ha! Don't know night from day. I'm not gonna waste my weekend waitin' for that no good so and so grandpa who's never growed up in all his Lord knows how many years.'"

"Why don't you sit down?"

"Hell no. I been sittin' ten straight hours all the way in from Phoenix. Then I musta sat least two hours in the depot. Then I was sittin' on the buses they told me ta take over here. I'm tired a sittin'."

"Sir, there's something that we have to talk about."

"Now, I jus' told ya I told ya all I can tell ya. Ya don't want me ta tell her she's got a nosy friend—or do ya?"

"Did you know that Vicky's life was in danger?"

"What's that?"

I got up from the bed and took the old man by his shoulders and sat him down on the edge of the bed. "Your granddaughter's not coming home."

He looked at me suspiciously, squinted, and sucked his lips in hard. "What the hell do you want anyway?"

"I liked Victoria a lot, sir. I'm trying to figure out what happened to her."

That got him mad for a change. He stood up and started shaking his cane at me again. "I don't know who ya are, but that's not ta say I don't have no ideas. I got my spies too, ya know."

"Listen, I don't know what you're talking about."

"Why don't you just scoot along then?"

"Sir, please—"

He swung the cane at me and whacked my shoulder. "Sons a bitches. Can't ya mind your own business?!"

He started winding up with the cane again. I grabbed it and flung it out the bedroom door into the hall. Then I took him by his shoulders, only this time I shoved him down on the bed. I reached for his coat pocket, took out the almost empty bottle of bourbon and finished it off. Then I knelt down in front of him and started off slow and easy. "I assure you I don't know what the hell you're talking about."

His nose twitched and he snorted sarcastically.

"You can give me all the looks you want. That's not going to bring Vicky back. Now, to begin with, you seem to know something that nobody else knows about. I don't know what it is, but it's got to be fishy. Otherwise, you wouldn't be so goddamn suspicious of me." I stopped and looked at the old man. He seemed scared. I patted his knee and looked up into his face. "I'm on your side, partner. I loved Vicky as much as you did."

"She don't go for your type."

"What's my type?"

"You know."

Chapter Twenty-Nine

"OK, you win, pops."

I got up off my knee and walked to the front door. I opened it carefully. Papers from the last three days were stacked up on the stoop. I grabbed all three and closed the door again. The old man was standing as I came back into the bedroom. He had retrieved his cane and he was leaning on it, holding on tight. I kept the Sunday paper and dropped the other two on the bed. Then I opened the front section to page two and handed it to him.

He grabbed the paper out of my hand.

"The Southland, far right, first one on the list," I told him.

He read it with his lips. His free hand reacted reflexively and patted his pockets searching for the bottle. Then he stopped as he saw it sitting empty on the nightstand. I went into the kitchen and found half a fifth of Scotch. By the time I got back with it and offered some, he didn't want it anymore. His face had gone slack, the lips had stopped sucking at the air, and his mouth hung open. He was wheezing through his nose and I could barely hear him mutter Vicky's name. "Victoria Swall . . . little Vicky."

"The only thing they got right is that she's been killed."

"Her daddy, ma, cancer—all bad luck."

Big tears were welling up out of the deep-set eyes. It took them what seemed like a long time to gather up enough momentum for the crawl down his face. He tipped his hat up higher. It slid off his head and fell over his back to the floor. Like the unkempt grass on a landing strip, there were two thin, fleecy patches of white hair on either side of his scalp with a thick, long, bald patch of deep tan running down the middle.

"Lies, all lies," he said.

"Yeah."

He laid his cane down on the dresser and drew himself up on the balls of his feet, clenching both his hands into fists. "I'll get 'em." He stopped the tears and rubbed them off his face with the backs of his hands. Then he stared at me long and straight and hard. "That's your name there too, ain't it?"

"Yes."

I slugged at the Scotch bottle as he folded the paper and put it on the bureau. Then he cocked his head to the side and spit on the rug. "If you was guilty, you wouldn't a come back here."

"That's right."

"I can see that." He paused, then looked up at me with one of the saddest faces I've ever seen. "Is it true what they said?"

"You know how they get their facts messed up."

"They should never say anything like that if it's not true. And even if it is, they still shouldn't say it."

"You're right."

He turned toward the bureau and spit on the paper. "Sons a bitches. I'll make 'em take it back. That's what I'll do." He looked at me questioningly. "Can I do that?"

"You can try."

"We gotta say somethin'."

"I know what you mean. But getting them to take it back still isn't going to bring her back."

The real thing hit him then, tore into him, and ripped the vehemence and fierceness out of his face. His shoulders sagged and I could almost feel him crumbling. "I jus' loved her," he said quietly. "You got no idea . . . Victoria, such a pretty name. Jus' like a queen. She was an elegant child." He looked down at the carpet and talked to himself. "Arnold was afraid a trouble, but that never had nothin' ta do with nothin'. He's always afraid a somethin'." The old man shook his head, then he looked up at me. "Bet she was a good student, wasn't she?" I nodded, agreeing. "She used to get rewards." He nodded up and down, remembering.

Then he coughed long and hard, a dry racking cough that didn't bring up phlegm. He took the cane from the bureau and started pacing slowly around the room. "I gotta see that this is cleared up," he told me. "When things get like they gotten, ya jus' gotta step in there. What amazes me is—" He coughed hard and frowned as he patted his chest with a closed fist. "How can they get away with it—that's what I'd like to know. My God, there's the whole goddarn family." He nodded to me and shook his head. "All right. I might as well tell ya. Anyhow, it don't matter now. Ain't no way it can hurt. So here—" He motioned for the bottle, took one long slug, and handed it back to me so I could do the same. We wiped our lips and he smacked his. His eyes brightened as he said, "Let me explain—"

He stopped with a jolt, grabbed his chest with both hands, made a choking sound, then gulped. His face went blank and he fell face forward right over the bed. I turned him over. His eyes stared at me dully. He had stopped breathing. I took the two pillows from the head of the bed, placed them underneath his shoulders, tilted his head back as far as it would go, pinched his nostrils shut, and started in on the artificial respiration. I gave him about fifteen breaths a minute for about five minutes. He started to go into shock. His hands were cold and clammy, so I massaged them. Then he started to breathe by himself—short, faltering, shallow breaths that seemed to be getting stronger. The pulse was slow, then fast, seemed to be starting to regulate. I undid his belt, loosened the laces on his dusty shoes, slid off his string tie, and unbuttoned the first few buttons on his shirt. I got his coat off, pulled up his undershirt and massaged his heart and talked to him gently, telling him he was going to be OK. I had no way of telling how bad the damage was. His forehead was beaded with sweat, but life seemed to have come back into his eyes. He seemed to know I was there.

As long as he remained relatively stable for a few minutes, the thing to do was to call an ambulance and get him to a hospital. I could already imagine the questions if he croaked on me. I took the Scotch bottle back into the kitchen, folded the newspaper back up, put the string around it, and set it back on the front porch with the two others. I came back and stuck the empty half-pint in my back pocket; then I slung his dirty coat over my shoulder, put my arms under him, and picked him up. I lifted up his hat with my foot and put it on my head. Then I laid his cane over him and carried him toward the door.

Chapter Thirty

I had untied his shoes already, and one of them came loose at the heel and dangled back and forth on his foot. I was doing a juggling act trying to balance him and lean down over the bedside lamp to turn it off when I saw something fall out of the shoe. I put him back down on the bed and bent down to pick it up. It was a couple pieces of tattered and yellowed paper folded into a tiny square and wrapped up in a plastic baggy. Without opening it, I put it in my pocket, picked up old man Swall again, turned off the light, and walked through the dining room into the kitchen and out the back door.

I took the pint bottle out of my back pocket and flung it into a trash bin in the alley. Then I came through the court from the back and walked up the steps to Mrs. McGinty's. She was up at the drapes before I'd hit the first step. With her mouth dropped open a mile wide, she stayed right there, staring even as I motioned for her to come to the door. Her cheeks were pinched like the old man's because she'd taken her teeth out for the evening. I took the hat off and, from no more than five feet away, kept waving at her frantically, pointing at the old man and mouthing "heart attack" until she finally moved away from the window and disappeared. After a moment, the door opened four or five inches. Her mouth was still open, but now her big teeth were in there. Her eyebrows were high up on her forehead, the little beady eyes bugged out at me.

"What do you want?"

"This man's had a heart attack. I've gotta call an ambulance."

"Over my dead body."

"He's in shock."

"I'm not lettin' you in here."

"If you won't let me in, would you please call them?"

"What are you doin' here?"

"I got bailed out."

"I know *that*," she sneered.

"I was driving by. He was on the ground in front of the court."

"I don't like it," she frowned.

"If you don't call an ambulance, this man is going to die. Do you hear that?"

"Who is he?"

"He's Vicky's grandfather."

"I suppose he's here for the funeral."

"Right."

She leaned down and stared closely at Mister Swall to make sure he wasn't playing dead, then she made a sour face and closed the door. I heard her talking, then she came back to the window and stared out at us. After another moment or so, she opened the door and said, "Bring him in."

She opened her screen door for me and I carried him in and laid him down across a long, flower-patterned couch protected by thick plastic covers. Grandpa had his eyes closed. He opened them now on the old lady's face. After he saw her, he groaned and closed them again. I had to laugh. The old bag rewarded me with a savage scowl. Then she wiggled her nose and darted her neck out toward me and sniffed me. She pulled away quickly. She wiggled her nose and sniffed me again. Then she turned her back to me and bent down over the old man. After that, she straightened up and turned around.

"This man's had too much to drink," she glowered. "Ya poured him full a liquor ta torture him."

"Why would I want to do that?" I asked her, wishing even as I formed the words that I hadn't opened my mouth.

The map of wrinkles in her face swirled slightly, then deepened at congested points into knots. She twisted her face up toward mine. Her mouth was a grimace that looked like it was setting in cement. Her nose twitched and pulsed with her every word and then some all by itself. "How should I know how your twisted mind works?" She screwed her face up higher, daring me to speak, think, or breathe. "I seen ya around here. I know ya know what I told the police, but I don't care either. I'm old an' helpless an' ya can't hurt me even if ya wanna. I seen ya with that girl that night. Other nights too. Don't think I never heard ya arguin' neither. I heard ya."

"Everybody argues, Mrs. McGinty. You argue, I argue, the president argues. Everybody argues."

"Yeah, but not like you do." She paused, then screwed her face up toward me again. "An' I knew what she was up to too. All along. She tried to butter me up so's I wouldn't make no trouble. I tried ta have her throwed out, ya know. I bet ya didn't know that, did ya? And if ya want my opinion—"

"I don't want your opinion."

She didn't hear me. "—I'd say she got exactly what a girl like that deserves."

"Excuse me, ma'am, but you don't know your ass from your elbow."

"How dare you talk to me like that!" She shook a bony finger in my face. "It's people like you that's causin' a breakdown a society."

"Oh, what the hell do you know about society?" I realized that I wouldn't have even been listening, let alone answering, if the liquor hadn't loosened my tongue and a few screws along with it.

She backed away from me and stared. I felt like a rare type of big insect, the kind that people are reluctant to bash against the wall with a rolled-up paper because they know it will leave too big a smear. She turned around and bent over Grandpa again, turning him over onto his side to get at his wallet. She looked through it and shook it at me. "You coulda made this up and put it there. I can tell you're up ta somethin'. I don't understand what you were doin' outside. Just happened to be passin' by, is that what you said?"

I turned toward the door. The ambulance would be arriving any minute and I didn't see that there was much more I could do. I walked back to the couch, put my head to the old man's chest and felt his pulse, doing my best to ignore the old woman as she stood over me watching. He seemed stable enough. His eyes were open again, so I talked to him quietly and told him that we were going to take him to the hospital just for a few tests, but that he was going to be all right and that we'd sit down and have a talk if he wanted to as soon as he felt well. He nodded at me as I was talking, then he grabbed onto my wrist and held it tight. He told me I was a nice boy, then he turned his face toward the back of the couch and lay there with both of his hands up against his chest. He moaned quietly.

The old woman had backed off long enough to recharge her batteries. She came at me face to face again. "I'm gonna have ta tell the authorities 'bout this." She was pouting and sulking and her small watery eyes regarded me with wary excitement as she waited for me to either say something offensive or, better yet, do something dangerous. I must have disappointed her because all I did was laugh at her and walk out of her house. She slammed her door after me and I could see the blue glow of the tv tube come on, then go off as I walked away. I took a closer look and, sure enough, she was at the drapes, looking out. Her nose was probably twitching, but I wasn't close enough to tell.

I was worried about the ambulance finding her bungalow, so I waited on the street until they drove up. They took an extra minute for tea and finished up a joint before they got out. I pointed them down to the old lady's. One guy was carrying a folded stretcher. They asked me what it was and I told them a heart attack. The empty-handed one sighed and said, "Shit," then he moped back toward the meat wagon to pick up some more equipment. His buddy stood and waited and looked up at the stars. Talk about not straining yourself—when these guys put on their siren, it was probably the Good Humor man's theme song. I told the star gazer it might be a good idea to get a move on it. He took a break to think that over, then he gave me the tired, cocky, put-out look that veterans of every field reserve exclusively for the rank amateur.

"We're goin' as fast as we can," he drawled.

Yeah. Like all get out—if you happened to be a snail. Sometimes it's hard to think of anybody you don't hate. Even jaded thirty-year-old teeny boppers. Hardly anybody really gives a shit anymore, and yet everything costs more. Even a death ride.

Chapter Thirty-One

I felt like seeing Ellen, so I drove west on Wilshire, past the Cadillac, Ferrari, and Mercedes dealers in Beverly Hills and tried to put my mind in neutral. Which was all but impossible. I stopped at a liquor store just a little east of the boxy and hideous Barrington Plaza apartments, bought some J.D. for company, and then drove on to Ellen's, parked in front, and walked up the side path to her little place in the rear.

The drapes were drawn, but lots of lights were on. I walked up to the door and heard laughter—Ellen's and someone else's. Deep, confident-sounding, full and fresh and filled with anticipation. On my part it wasn't pure jealousy or a case of the wounded heart, but they sounded like they were having an awfully good time. Background Billie Holiday sounded soft, languorous, coyly enticing. There was a mood building inside there. It didn't take much just to sense it. And it wasn't any of my business. If I had knocked on the door and broken it, they would have both been nice, she would have introduced me, and then they would have looked disappointed and sat there looking at me and talking to me, not really involved, waiting for me to leave. Ellen would have probably been nervous, over-nice. She would have talked too much, and said something silly or embarrassing that would have made the three of us laugh. I would have said goodbye eventually and wished I'd never knocked on the door. Then the drive home with that guy's face in my mind, hating him for no reason and feeling really shitty. Shitty enough to make me kill the half-pint I'd bought with moderation in mind. With the grand finale on a high chair in the bar at Barney's Beanery, mixing my drinks, getting shit-faced, then letting myself get hustled at pool, busting my pool cue over my knee or crowding a girl and getting thrown out.

I felt lousy enough already, so I didn't knock. I tiptoed back down the path and got back in my car. I hadn't forgotten about that piece of paper I'd found in the old man's shoe, but I hadn't wanted to look at it in front of the landlady either; and when she had started squawking about calling in the pigs, I hadn't wanted to sit there by the curb outside and pass the time while waiting for another night's free boarding. I drove a few blocks up the street, heading for San Vincente Boulevard. I pulled over and turned on my map light, opened up the tucked-in flap of the plastic baggy and took out two pieces of dry, yellowed parchment. They weren't actually tree bark, but they did have a brittle feel. I unfolded them carefully. It looked like an old legal document. It was dated January 1, 1932. There was a heading at the top of the first page: SWALL FAMILY TONTINE. Below that was a short paragraph, then a long list of names and dates.

The type was single-spaced and faded with time. By the little pencil beam of my map light it was almost impossible to read, so I folded up the two pieces of paper, put them back into the plastic baggy, and stuck what was starting to seem like a precious little bundle of information into my glove compartment. I didn't know what the hell this was all about, but, for some reason, instinctively, I found myself locking my glove box.

I started the car, cut down to Santa Monica Boulevard and headed home in one straight line all the way from 17th Street in Santa Monica; through Westwood, Beverly Hills, both dead and lights out except for the all night coffee shops and gas stations; past the Troubador nightclub; past Barney's without stopping, then left by the sleazy teenybop nightclub called Starwood and left onto Crescent Heights. Just before Sunset, I stopped at Harry's Open Pit Barbecue. It was eleven-thirty and they were just about to close. I got a half slab of ribs and a whole chicken, a plate of salad with their standard French dressing, the side of fries, dill pickle, and a Bud. All to go. Then I continued straight up the canyon and turned right by the Country Store. Stanley heard me park in front of the house and took up a terrible plaintive howling. I unlocked the glove box and took out the legal paper.

After checking the mail, I took a couple of last weary swigs out of my bottle and flung it up toward the hill, blowing out a "Bombs away!" sound as the bottle came down and struck target. It didn't break. I was disappointed and I was drunk. I got my key in the door, flicked on the kitchen light, then sat down on the kitchen floor and let Stanley slop his tongue all over my face. He started sniffing at the bag, so I took out the plate of chicken, peeled a hunk of breast off the bone, and set it out on the paper plate for him. Then I dug into some ribs. Stanley was finished in about ten seconds, so I pulled off some more chicken for him. He ended up eating just about all of the chicken except for the drumsticks. I saved the ribs for myself because I knew he'd get carried away and gag on the bones.

I took a cereal bowl out of the sink, rinsed it out and filled it up about a quarter of the way with beer, and set it down on the floor. I washed my hands, finished the beer, took Stan's empty bowl and filled it up with water. He drank a little of that too. I went into my bedroom and sat down at my desk, pushed my typewriter to one side, and set out the two sheets of legal paper. The terms of it seemed to be fairly succinct. My main problem was focusing. If I gave it my all, I could see the letters clearly, but then I didn't seem to have enough wherewithal left over to read them and make sense out of it. That last little bit of beer seemed to have sent me over the edge. I read over the list of names. Grandpa's was there at the top. He was one of the original trustors and his children's children appeared to be the beneficiaries. That much I was able to figure out.

I looked up the word *tontine* in my dictionary. Tontine, it said, can be pronounced two ways: *ton*-ten or ton-*ten*. Aside from that, it was a noun with French and Italian roots coming from the Italian Tontina and related to a gentleman named Lorenzo Tonti, a Neopolitan banker who introduced the system into France in the seventeenth century. It was defined as: "(1) an annuity shared among a group of people, or a loan based on a group of annuities, with the provision that as each beneficiary dies, his share is divided among the survivors until the entire amount accrues to the last or last two or three survivors."

I reread that part. Seemed quite interesting. I wasn't really sure how it applied to Vicky, but I still felt that somehow it did. It just seemed to be a matter of figuring out what applied and what didn't, which pieces were relevant and which were not. I walked into the bathroom and threw cold water on my face. It helped.

"We declare that there are ten (10) children currently . . . that there are ten (10) children currently . . ." As with a child or pet straying too far from home, things got hazy and unfamiliar just a few blocks or sentences away. I kept mulling over the beginning; it seemed to be the only thing I could keep in focus. I nodded out over the page, for just a few minutes or so, but when I woke up I realized that the little piece of paper probably deserved more than a cursory perusal from a half-wit. So I folded it up and shoved it into one of the cluttered cubbyholes in my rolltop, hoping that I'd be spared a hangover and wake up clear-headed in the morning. Then I could give this thing the full and undivided attention it deserved.

When I tried to stand up, I felt as though I had weights on my feet. I pulled them out from under the desk and got addressed by a mild grumble that was actually the beginning of a snarl. Stan. He'd been sleeping on my toes. Somehow I found my way to the bathroom. I stood over the toilet and aimed carefully. Stanley stood next to the toilet bowl and watched my steady stream arch downward. I flushed, then moved over to the sink and washed my face. I even brushed my teeth. That made me proud of myself, so I went one step further and took two aspirins to prepare myself for the morning. I let Stanley out for his nightly airing, then I turned out the rest of the lights and got into bed. Stanley jumped up and curled himself up at the foot. He was snorting. I took that to be an invitation to talk.

"OK, the fact of the matter is that I am now a suspect in a murder case. I thought I should tell you. I've had my name in the paper; I've spent two nights in jail; I almost got rubbed out by a thug tonight—can you believe that?"

I shut myself up. A man raving to his dog. I was thinking of what people might say. You have to do that sometimes—think of what people will think. You can either object or concur, but whatever you decide, at least you've given yourself a reference point. And that's better than raving.

I put my arms outside the covers and let the cool night fortify me with its dizzying stillness. The dizzying stillness of the cool night. A good phrase, especially if you could say "dizzying" without sounding like a Chinese buzz saw. Two years back if I thought of a good phrase, sentence, or interesting idea for a story before I fell asleep, I used to get up and go over to my desk, scribble it down, and then go to sleep feeling fulfilled. Lately, I had fallen out of that good habit. I wondered why. I didn't feel like thinking about it, though I knew the answer right off. There was no need to beat around the bush. I wasn't pleasing myself anymore. What would people think? What would people think? A year or two ago, I had been able to keep my marbles all in one place without worrying foolishly over stupid things. I had done what I wanted and I had loved writing, even the handful of crappy jobs I'd done for tv. I had had momentum. But now I had let myself lose it. I had let myself slip.

Chapter Thirty-Two

Howling, desperate agonized howling out of the pits of hell. Three-headed Cerberus couldn't keep them out. So strangers came in and plundered the forbidden place, shook penitent souls loose from their precarious moorings, and the souls fanned out on a thin and stifling wind, drifting into a void of space, lost forever, cut off from the Elysian destiny. I was with them. The awful wind got hotter, overripe, putrescent, sent us barreling upward, then dropped us headlong down at the ground. Tons of bodies piled in a dark ditch. Smothering. They were dumping the dirt in. I was gasping. I could feel myself slipping away into a nothingness, but not a nothingness completely, more an oblivion brought on by the constant pressure of pain. At my throat. Terrible pain choking me.

I opened my eyes and saw a shadow looming over my face. A tall and narrow human shadow that was breathing hard as it bobbed over me, jerking up and back as I floundered battling against it. Moist fingers squeezed at my neck, wringing it as if it were a wet rag. I reached up and battled the fingers. Something dark smashed down toward my face, grazed the side of my head.

I tried to scream. My larynx was cut off. I heard myself grunt and gurgle, make loud animal sounds. I tried to lift my knees and kick at the sonofabitch's back, but my blankets were stretched out over me like a strait jacket and he was straddled over my legs. I bit into one of his wrists and he yelped at a high pitch. He dropped something that hit the floor like a rock. I got a hand in his face and then he went a little off balance. I heard the dog snarling and barking at the side of the bed. I reached for my lamp and got hold of it, then I crashed it down toward the silhouetted face. An arm slashed at my arm, knocked into the lamp as the other hand hammered my nose. The punch wasn't hard enough. I let go of the lamp and grabbed at the hand. The wrist was narrow and bony, the fingers long and delicate. He made the yelping sound again. Stanley had gotten hold of something. He was off balance. I took a pillow from behind my head and heaved it into his face and pushed him off the side of the bed onto the floor. Then I rolled off the bed and fell on top of him. He clipped me hard on the chin, harder than I'd been thinking he could hit.

It dazed me a little. He got back on his feet. The bedroom was almost pitch black, but I could still see most of his face. It was angular and young. His voice sounded young. He was laughing, wanted me to think he had my number. It wouldn't have taken much to make me believe it—because he wanted to kill me and I didn't know why. That was enough for me. His hair looked smooth and slick in the dark.

"One more step, I will shoot your face off." The words were carefully enunciated, stiff and formal. The r's were slightly rounded, just the vaguest touch too long. They sounded French.

"Why didn't you do that before?"

"That is what I'm asking myself."

"Where you from?"

He ignored that. "I had thought you and the girl were partners. You were a fool to take so long on her."

"What?"

"If you had acted more quickly, you could have had both of us."

I asked him what he was talking about. He laughed his mocking laugh and backed toward the door with his hand behind his back. Stanley howled at him.

"Stay there," he said.

"If you're gonna shoot me, why don't you do it? How do you know I'm gonna be here next time?"

"If you're not, I'm sure you'll find me, won't you?"

He turned on his heels. I saw he didn't have a gun. He ripped out the kitchen door, slammed it after him. I hauled out on his tail, but the guy was as fleet as a goddamn deer. He seemed to take two or three strides to my every one. And I had nothing on but my briefs. I stubbed my toe before I was halfway down the hill. I saw him turn left on the residential street adjacent to the canyon boulevard. From that point, he could dip in and out of back yards, cut up and down side streets. I kept running after him, but before I even entered the long block, I'd lost sight of him completely.

Chapter Thirty-Three

I came back inside and looked at the wall clock above my stove. It was four o'clock in the morning and I had been asleep close to four hours. My nerves were shot. My hands were shaking; my head felt heavy and hollow. Suddenly I got seized with panic that something had happened to Stanley. Then he came waddling out of the bedroom. That relieved me somewhat. I sat down at my kitchen table, dropped my head into my hands, and started to think.

What had happened so far? Vicky had been beaten up, almost strangled to death by somebody who said they knew me. Vicky and I had surmised that it had something to do with Herbert. Then, after Vicky had been murdered and I had talked myself into getting arrested, I had gone back to Herbert's office, found George and Herbert's wife, Helen, and a recent memo to Herbert from Bradford Bobby. I had gone back to Vicky's and met her grandfather, who had started out from Phoenix and had come here after Vicky had failed to meet him somewhere else—where, he wouldn't say. A legal paper dated 1932 had fallen out of the old man's shoe. It mentioned something called a tontine, which was an annuity shared among a group of persons, or a loan based on a group of annuities, with the provision that as each beneficiary died, his share was divided among the survivors until the entire amount accrued to the last or last two or three survivors. This Swall Family Tontine dated back to 1932 and mentioned the Bank of America in San Francisco, which was probably where Vicky was supposed to have met her grandpa. Finally, after giving Harold Swall a heart attack, I had come home, then been manhandled in my sleep.

Then I remembered my little outing to the Dodger game and how I had been pushed over the railing during the seventh-inning stretch. One guy had bumped into another guy buying peanuts, that guy had bumped into the peanut vendor and knocked him off balance, and he had bumped into me. I'd felt kind of sorry for the kid. He had a harried, thankless little job that took the fun out of watching baseball, and he had lost his whole box of peanuts.

The Frenchman's silhouette: it was the same face. I just knew it. The guy who had just tried to snuff me was the same guy from the ballgame last Friday! No accident. But the really amazing thing, what topped it all off, was that this had taken place a few hours *before* Vicky had first been attacked. He had tried to get me before he went for Vicky. It didn't make sense. Was it because he thought Vicky had told me something? But if she had said anything to me, she could have easily said at least a word or two to a dozen other people just as well. None of her other friends that I'd seen had found their lives in jeopardy.

Yes, it was definitely the same face, so definitely that maybe it just wasn't. But for some reason, whatever it was, someone was trying to do away with me. They were doing a pretty sloppy job of it, but they were trying. Whether it had all started before or after Vicky's death, whether it was the same guy who had been at the ballgame, these were important points, but the main thing was that I had become a marked man—a dubious distinction. I didn't like it one bit.

I got myself a good, tall glass of water. My throat was all bunched up and lumpy. It hurt when I swallowed. I thought of Vicky and put down the glass. I turned on the shower in my bath, leaving it a little on the cool side, and got in, hoping it would settle me down. Instead, with my translucent shower curtain pulled across the bath, all I could really think about was the shower scene in "Psycho." It had never once occurred to me before that my bathroom, in its starkness, bore at least some faint resemblance to Hitchcock's hallowed stomping ground. I let the water keep running and opened the shower curtain, but that still wasn't enough. I turned it off and got out, dried myself off, and put on a clean pair of cords and a fresh shirt. Then I boiled some water in a soup pan, put three tablespoons of Instant Maxwell House in a big cup, and poured the hot water over it. I put in just a touch of milk and drank it as hot as I could. It loosened up my throat, numbed it a little, which felt good.

I got on the phone and called the UCLA Medical Center. They transferred me to a half-dozen stations until I finally located the right one where a woman said that old man Swall was in intensive care. I asked her if he was out of shock, and she said that was all she could tell me. She hung up before I could ask anything more.

It was past four-thirty now. I made some more instant coffee and took it with me back into the bedroom. The blankets were all over the floor. I picked them up and heaped them on the bed. Then I got down on my hands and knees and went over the carpet carefully to see if I could find anything that might have been left behind in the scuffle. I found a dark, handsized rock underneath my desk. I put it on top of the desk and found the paper in the cubbyhole right where I'd left it. I sat down and spread the two pages out in front of me:

SWALL FAMILY TONTINE

On this first day of January, 1932, we, *HAROLD DAVID SWALL* (a married man), *RICHARD LIONEL SWALL* (a married man), *STEPHEN SETH SWALL* (a married man), and *AUGUSTA BEATRICE SMITH* (a married woman), of San Francisco County, State of California, hereinafter referred to collectively as "Trustor," hereby transfer and deliver to the Bank of America, San Francisco, hereinafter called "Trustee," the sum of Two Hundred Thousand Dollars ($200,000.00), representing the Tontine Estate of an express trust and to be held, administered, and distributed by the Trustee as provided in this Agreement.

ARTICLE 1

We declare that there are ten (10) children currently alive representing the offspring of our respective marriages, whose names and dates of birth are as follows:

Name	Date of Birth
Harold David Swall, Junior	January 14, 1918
Selma Janice Swall	March 3, 1920
Robert Ernest Swall	September 5, 1928
Oliver James Swall	February 9, 1910
Marian Robyn Beck	April 4, 1912
John Bruce Swall	May 5, 1920
Raymond David Swall	June 14, 1921
Elizabeth Ann Smith	August 12, 1926
Deborah Frances Smith	July 8, 1922
Cecilia Allyson Smith	January 27, 1920

The first-born of each child above-mentioned are

hereinafter referred to as the "Income Beneficiary," and the Trustee shall pay to or apply for the benefit of the Income Beneficiary the net income from the Tontine Estate as hereinafter expressly provided.

Sifting through the rest of the legalese, I established that three generations were involved. The four trustors, including Vicky's grandfather, were the first generation. Vicky was probably the first offspring of one of the ten names following, of which at least one was either son or daughter to Harold Swall, making her an income beneficiary. The initial amount had been put into trust where it would remain accruing interest until the beneficiaries came of age. At this time, they would receive an initial lump sum of interest that had accumulated since 1932, and thereafter would receive an annual stipend.

Important to note was that if any of the ten individuals failed to bear an offspring, their share of the trust went to the other members remaining who were able to meet the trust's requirements. Furthermore, if any beneficiary died before his or her twenty-first birthday, the full sum of their accrued interest went to the surviving members of the trust. This applied as well to those who attained their legal age and received their interest payments from the trust. The annual payments representing their proportionate share of the earned annual income would be accumulated and added to the corpus of the tontine, then distributed in equal shares among the tontine's remaining survivors.

One could not transfer, give, or will interest to anyone else. You were rewarded for living; punished for dying. This appeared to be the essence of the tontine. It was the very inverse of the normal sort of insurance policy where you were rewarded for dropping dead. It seemed Darwinian in nature, celebrating the survival of the fittest as financial wager or doctrine. You were recompensed for being strong and proving yourself a long-distance runner when the others from your same brood fell victim to natural selection. In other words, the survivor benefitted directly and substantially at the expense of the dead.

The initial sum of $200,000 was nothing earth-shattering; but forty-six years of sharing compounded interest on the original principal, in conjunction with the inevitable streamlining effect as the list of qualified participants dwindled gradually over time, was something to make you stop and think a minute when you considered the eventual prospect of just two or three people sharing a big lump of interest payments. The end result, too, was that the final survivor received the full trust, meaning the original capital sum, interest payments and all. At this point, the tontine would be completed.

It was a strange thing to make up a raffle for your own family. But in the continuity of a closely knit family, it could be one method that elders, possessing a natural gaming sort of instinct, might employ for providing for the family's future. It could be assumed that any money benefiting the lucky beneficiaries would also benefit their respective families and be a help to the overall family. It would be a way, too, for the old ones to make sure that a good chunk of dough would be around for their dotage in case they ever found themselves in a real spot. And, considering the times, 1932 had been the right time for anybody, whether they had money or not, to be a little worried about the future.

It seemed that Vicky had come from fairly good stock. As I remembered looking at old man Swall, it was pretty hard to believe. I could see Vicky patiently persevering through the old man's endless tall tales. That nice old silly grin, the excited gestures, and overall zestiness must have been trying to live with. It had probably become so that the most simple and obvious thing the old man said sounded more like a fib than anything else. To be sure, he was quite a talker, quite a schemer. If he had told me about this thing, I probably wouldn't have believed him. And it was now only because of all the chaos, the killing atmosphere, that I gave it any credence. Also, the fact that it was one day before Vicky's twenty-first birthday. She would have been eligible for her income as beneficiary and that was why somebody had wanted to do away with her. Somebody had been so greedy they hadn't wanted her to see a penny of what was due her by her natural birthright.

I figured that if all ten folks had had a first-born child that had survived and was still alive—compounding an average five percent interest derived from $200,000, the original

111

capital sum would have hovered up around at least $1,800,000 and Vicky's share would have had to have been worth a minimum of $180,000. If a few of the ten folks had died, or hadn't had children, or if a few of the children had passed away for one reason or another—let's say that only five nominees were currently participating in the tontine. Well, then Vicky's share would have been twice as big: $360,000. That was a good hunk of money.

I picked up all of the scratch paper I'd been scribbling on and carried it into my living room and piled it up on the small grate of my fireplace. Then I put a match to the pile and watched it curl up and burn. It was seven-thirty already and suddenly almost bright out. I washed my hands, spread the curtains in the kitchen, sat down at the table and wrote a note to Ellen. I thanked her for getting me bailed out and asked her to hold onto the tontine document for me for the time being. I let her know that many odd things had been popping up in regard to Vicky's death and that I was trying to filter them out. Then I signed off feeling like we had already become strangers.

Chapter Thirty-Four

The phone rang. It was eight o'clock.
"Hello?"
"Crandel?"
"Yes."
"You fuck-up, Crandel."
"Who is this?"
"You fuckin' sonofabitch. I oughta bust your ass. If you think you can go runnin' around stickin' your nose into everybody else's business, you're in big trouble, buddy."

I recognized the voice. It was Bradford Bobby. He sounded great on the phone. Like George C. Scott playing Patton. Very commanding.
"You hear me?"
"I don't know what you're so upset about."
"What I'm so upset about," he mimicked me. "I talked to Herbert. He told me what you've got up your sleeve. If

you're so cunt-crazy and stupid that you're going to blame the murder of some whore girl friend of yours on anybody in sight, I feel sorry for you, buddy."

"Hey, wait a minute. Let's get this straight. I'm not cunt-crazy. I'm not stupid—you got that? And my girl friend was not a whore."

"You can call her anything you like. But if you think you're gonna hook up what happened to her with anything I might be responsible for, you're outa your mind."

"Who said I was going to?"

Then he really started screaming. "I can put one and one together. I get two. What do you get?"

"If you can't get a hold on yourself, what you're going to get is a nice long dial tone because I'm going to hang up."

He lowered his voice, although it still threatened to blow up at any second. "OK, so you stumbled upon a little bit of info. Just because Harv Herbert comes to me with a set-up on a movie doesn't mean I'm involved when the girl gets killed. I don't even know why I'm even bothering to tell you this."

"I guess you must be worried."

"You make me sick—know that?"

"The only thing that confuses me is how you used to poke fun at me for writing porno when you were shooting it. That's kind of funny, isn't it?"

"Crandel, I don't shoot porno movies. I finance them only very occasionally when I need revenue."

"Oh."

"I had nothing to do with that girl. I never even met her, and if you think you're going to try to rub my nose in some bad PR, I—"

"I don't suspect you or Herbert."

"Then why have you been hassling him? He's goin' nuts."

"I had a hunch that I was wrong about him. And now I've changed my mind."

"Well, then, I think you owe the man an apology."

"Thanks, Brad. Now that you've got me straight on my etiquette, maybe life will be better."

"The only way it's gonna be any better is with you out of it."

"Is that a threat?"

"You can take that any way you want to," he said, banging his end of the conversation down at my ear.

Boy, there's nothing a pseudo big man gets more upset about than his PR. I knew that B.B. was out of the picture. His involvement with Herbert and Vicky's theory had both been red herrings. That whole avenue had fit together too well, too easily. I thought it would be fun, though, to fuck up Bobby's PR just for the hell of it. The bastard deserved it.

I made myself some more instant coffee. My throat was still lumpy, but the heat was working on it. I went into the bathroom and shaved, ran a brush through my hair, picked up my letter to Ellen off my desk, then moved quickly through the bathroom into the kitchen, failing to beat Stanley to the door. I caught him peeing by the lemon tree around the side of the house. The window screen was on the ground. I hadn't seen that from inside. The foreigner had taken the screen off, came in through the side window in the living room, then closed it after him. I started wondering whether he'd been amateur enough to have left any traceable prints when the telephone rang again. I got Stan by the neck, pointed him back toward the house, and he waddled slowly back inside. I got to the phone by the third or fourth ring and picked it up. There was no one there. I started walking back to the door, telling Stanley to stay, when it rang again. I cussed it and picked it up before the second ring.

A loud and twanging, self-amused voice spoke before I could say hello. "Mister Crandel?"

"Yes?"

"Mister Benjamin Crandel?"

"Yeah, this is Ben Crandel."

"Mister Crandel, you don't know me, but I been thinkin' that maybe we could help each other."

"How's that?"

"Well, I'm not sure now, but I said that I was thinkin'. I'm playin' my hunch on the come line, if ya take my meanin'."

I didn't know what this cowboy was talking about. It sounded like he was about to segue into a smooth and fancy phone sales pitch for putting a pool into my nonexistent back yard. When he asked me if I were a homeowner, I was going to hang up. So I wasn't sure I heard him when he added his name.

"What?"

"I said my name's Arnold Swall. That mean anything to ya?"

"Of course it means something to me. Are you related to Vicky?"

"I'm her first cousin—one of 'em."

"I see."

"I was eatin' in the coffee shop when I seen it in the papers, so I called ya up."

"Did you try to call Vicky's grandfather?"

"Why I sure did. But I couldn't catch him."

"Because he was on his way out from Phoenix to meet her in San Francisco."

"How'd you know that?"

"I ran into him last night."

"He have any idear 'bout what happened?"

"He didn't know that Vicky had been killed—no."

"Did you tell him?"

"Yeah."

"Well, what'd he say?"

"He didn't say much. He had a heart attack."

"You're shittin' me."

"I shit you not."

"Ben . . ."

"Yes?"

"I know ya don't know me too well, but I gotta talk to you."

"I'd like to talk to you too."

"If you gotta say somethin', don't say nothin' now. *Nada.*"

"Where do you want to talk then?"

"Ya see, my line may be bugged. Can't take *no* chances. Understand?"

"Sure. So where should we meet?"

"We can talk at my place."

"Where's that?"

"The Dunes."

"In Las Vegas?"

"I'm sorry. Yes, that's where I'm callin' ya from. I'm stayin' here for awhile. I'd come to see you, 'cept I think ya better come to see me."

"All right."

"Is the old man OK?"

"I don't think they know yet."

"S.O.B. Ain't seen him for years. I send him some plush when I don't piss it away."

"Did you know Vicky at all?"

"Never did meet her. Was she really a cottontail?"

"No."

"That's good for her granddad. He thought she was a princess—"

"She was."

He got my meaning. "Gee, I'm sorry, fella."

"Forget it. So, if you were out of touch with Mister Swall, how'd you know he was coming out here?"

"He called me and asked me for some money 'cause he was gonna go see Vicky for her birthday. I thought she was twenty. I shoulda known this was the whole hog. He wouldn't tell me. That old goat hates my guts."

"Why's that?"

"'Cause I'm just like him. I don't have money, but money has me by the balls. I never have nothin' I can help him out with. He hates my fuckin' guts." He had a good belly laugh at this.

"What do you do with it?"

"My money?"

"Yeah."

"Mister, I don't know. If I knew, I'd probably have it." His voice was mellifluous and self-satisfied. I could tell he was proud of hanging loose with his dough. Then he said, "I told that old goat right when he called me—I told him I smelled skunk and I told him why."

"How's that?"

"I can't tell ya that over the phone."

"You mean your life's been threatened before too?"

"That's right. I guess you do realize somethin's involved here."

"Like a family trust fund?"

"My cousin tell you that?"

116

"In so many words."

"She oughtn't to have said that."

"She didn't mean to."

"She tell anybody else?"

"No."

"Are you sure, Ben?"

"Pretty sure."

"She probably thought the whole thing was a joke. I did . . ."

He paused, so I finished the thought. "—until the checks started coming in."

"You got it." He sounded like he'd taken it well, but then he started getting jumpy again. "Listen, Ben, it's been nice talkin' to ya, but I gotta go now."

I was afraid he was going to hang up, so I said quickly, "Aren't we still going to meet?"

"You got anything else ta tell me?"

"I might."

"You might," he laughed. "You're startin' ta sound like a real sharpy, Ben."

"I wouldn't say that. But there's no reason why I should trust you either."

"True enough, but you ain't said nothin' 'bout gettin' a glance at whoever that did it."

"Is that what you're interested in?"

"Well, yeah, and a couple other things I can't say over the phone."

"Well, I saw him, if that's what you want."

"You mean you were there when it happened?"

"No."

"He thought you'd been a witness then, and he came after ya?"

"That's part true."

"What do you mean?"

"I mean that I think he came after me before it even happened."

"Before Victoria was done in?"

"Yeah."

"No shit?"

"No shit."

His voice got full and resonant. "Ben, we gotta talk."

"That's what you've been saying."

"Can you make it up here?"

"Sure."

"You fly up and I'll pay ya back for all your expenses."

"Thanks."

"There's a side room where they got a couple poker tables—right beyond the lobby. The dealer there's one a my friends. I'll either be there or you ask him for me. Got it?"

"What's his name?"

"Roger. You just ask him. He'll know."

"OK. I suppose I'll be up there by late afternoon."

"Good. Now, you take care a yourself, ya hear?"

"Sure."

"All right then. I'll see ya later."

Chapter Thirty-Five

"What?"

"I said how's your omelette?"

"Oh. Fine."

"Really?"

"Yeah. How's yours?"

"Fine. It's amazing."

"What?"

"How you can eat something without tasting it."

I had a glass of water in my hand and I'd been drinking that and nibbling on the ice cubes and hadn't noticed my food arriving. I looked at the omelette. I wasn't hungry. Denise was studying my face and, by the look of her expression, I could tell it wasn't getting her anywhere. "I'm not much of a breakfast eater," I told her.

"So I see."

"It's not that, really."

She put her fork down and folded her hands together over the edge of the table. "I know," she said.

"I've just got a lot of things on my mind."

"Tell me about it." She picked up her fork and jabbed at her food mechanically, eating with all the gusto of a tractor making a land fill.

118

I watched her and felt bad because I was making her feel worse than she felt already. An old man in the adjoining booth right behind Denise was hard of hearing and yelling to his friend sitting across from him. He was reading from the paper—an article about the twenty-three-year-old Saudi Arabian sheik who had paid three million in straight cash for a big mansion along Sunset Boulevard in Beverly Hills—and it sounded like he was screaming right in my ear even though I was sitting on the far end of the conversation:

"'They are now painting the once white plaster maidens fronting the grounds in flesh tones with pubic hair.'"

It was all over town. Large crowds had been stopping by the front of the place and staring in wonder. It was an ultimate fantasy, a luscious exercise in bad taste. The mansion's chimney had been covered with rainbow-colored tiles. A copper roof was going up on top. Brown and black rock pebbles had been glued over the walls surrounding the estate. All of this had been stopping cars, causing traffic jams and accidents.

Denise made a sour face and shifted herself in the booth, trying to move away from the voice. The old guy stood up then and left and Denise leaned back against the divider, sipped her coffee, and stared into the cup. "I'm supposed to tell you that the funeral service is this afternoon at one o'clock." She didn't look up. "Sharon called me this morning," she added tonelessly. "She and Sally took care of all the arrangements." I didn't say anything, and when she spoke again feeling came into her voice. "It really hurts that they didn't at least ask if I wanted to help. They could have asked, at least, don't you think?"

I nodded that I agreed. I realized that if I wanted to go to Vegas, I wouldn't be able to make it to the funeral. I didn't want to go to the funeral anyway. The very thought of it made me sick. Some pastor who would mumble words that would depress me more than his looks. The girls crying, leaning on me for comfort. The closed casket, the cloying smell of too many flowers. Suddenly, the smell of my food nauseated me. I pushed the plate away. Besides, it seemed that somebody was trying to kill me. I thought that Vicky would understand.

"Well?"

119

I looked at Denise. I didn't know what she meant.

"I guess I have to ask you if you mind taking me."

"To the funeral?"

"To Disneyland." Hurt and malice: Her eyes and mouth spelled out the words.

She was jabbing at the eggs, tearing them apart with her fork. I took her wrist, then pried the fork out of her hand. "I'd take you. Only I'm not going."

She pulled her hand away. Both of her hands disappeared beneath the table. "I hate Schwab's," she said. "All the stupid dreams, stupid conversations, stupid memories." She opened her handbag and started digging through it. Things emerged and were placed upon the table: a red plastic hairbrush, imitation tortoise shell comb, wallet, checkbook, ticket stubs, torn half-page from the casting calls section of the *Hollywood Reporter*, a paperback biography of Vivien Leigh, a page of dialogue torn from a script with lines underlined, annotations in the margins, till she finally found what she wanted, her lipstick. It was just a faint shade of red. She dabbed her forefinger into the little fingerbox and rubbed it on. Then she gently smacked her lips and studied them briefly in the tiny mirror on the inside of the case. She rounded her cheeks, pushing up a quick perfunctory smile, then frowned, smacked her lips again, and closed the case. She took her arm and swept the things off the table back into her purse. Then she looked at me and stood up. "Shall we go?"

"The check's not here yet."

She sat down again and drummed her nails on the table and looked around the restaurant. A young couple, conspicuously handsome, came into the dining area and sat down at a nearby table. Both their faces were pale and sad and airbrushed to an unblemished perfection. They leaned back against the wall and stared out at the room, waiting for something to happen to them. The waitress turned around from the pickup counter and Denise waved toward her and caught her eye, then mouthed, "Check, please."

"I'm only partly not going because I don't want to," I said.

"That's fine." She shrugged her shoulders and seemed not to care.

"There's another reason."

The waitress came over and tore the check out of her book. Denise thanked her, then rechecked the figures after the woman walked away. "What's that?" she asked me as she was adding.

"You know how you said you'd like to go over Vicky's and check the place over yourself?"

She stopped adding and looked at me with a quizzical expression. "Yeah?"

"Well, I had the same idea myself. I went over there later after I dropped you off yesterday. Only the landlady was out front, so I came back after it was past her bedtime. Three guesses for who I ran into."

Denise squinted and put her finger to her lips. "Let's see. Paul Newman? Robert Redford?" She dropped the silly look and addressed me with hard, determined eyes that demanded facts and wanted them right away, straight and fast and to the point.

"Her grandfather."

She started looking very angry. "Why didn't you call me and tell me this?"

"I didn't have a chance to."

"What do you mean? I want to talk to him. Did you mention me to him?"

"I didn't have a chance to."

She took a big breath and swallowed and sat up straight and poised. With strong apparent effort at restraint, she said slowly, in a poor imitation of equanimity, "Didn't you realize that I would want to—"

"If you could just let me finish what I was going to say. I didn't get to mention you to him because he had a heart attack before I finished talking to him."

"What?"

"The man had a heart attack. He must have been very upset."

"I think that goes without saying."

"OK, let's not get bitter about it."

"Who's getting bitter?"

"You are. You seem to have this notion that the whole world's excluding you from sharing grief that's rightly yours."

"I'll thank you to keep your asinine comments to yourself."

"Denise, what do you want me to do? Call you in the middle of the night and tell you that Vicky's grandpa's just had a heart attack? I thought you had enough already."

She calmed down a little and her voice got softer. "It's just that I would have liked to have seen him."

"I went over to the hospital this morning before I came to meet you."

"Can I see him?"

"He's dead. He died this morning."

"That poor little man."

"That's not the whole story. Get a grip on your seat."

I leaned over close to her so the other people in the restaurant wouldn't hear me. "Somebody tried to kill me last night."

She shook her head. "What?"

"I had Mrs. McGinty call the hospital, then I went home and went to bed and fell asleep. When I woke up, this guy had his hands around my throat. Then he said hello by trying to club my brains out."

"It doesn't make any sense."

"I know it doesn't, but what's even stranger is that this guy tried to kill me before—in fact, before he got Vicky—and I didn't even know it. I thought it was an accident."

"Somebody tried to kill you before they killed Vicky? How can you be sure?"

"Either him or his clone quote unquote bumped into me at the Dodger game last Friday. Almost sent me flying over a guard rail."

"You're positive it was the same person."

"Yes and no. The first time there were crowds, the second I didn't have any light."

Denise paused and thought for a moment, then she said, "If you're right, I don't know what the answer is. But if you're wrong, it could be that whoever this person is, they think you know who they are."

"So therefore they have to rub me out before I can tell anybody—is that right?"

"I don't know."

"But if I knew and I was going to tell anybody, I could have told them already, couldn't I?"

"I suppose so."

"So what point would there be in coming after me?" Denise shook her head and I joined her. "I know. It's totally crazy. The final straw is this morning a distant cousin of hers calls me and says he wants to talk to me. He saw the story in the paper."

"Well, what did he say?"

"He said he couldn't say because he thinks his phone's bugged."

"What do you think?"

"Maybe he's nuts, but he claims his life's been threatened before too."

"This is the strangest thing I ever heard."

"Tell me about it," I smiled, getting one back C.O.D.

I asked Denise if Vicky had ever said anything to her about coming into some money. I told her about finding the tontine document on Vicky's grandpa and about what it said.

Denise asked if I had said anything to Vicky's cousin. I told her I had just mentioned something about a trust fund and that he hadn't disagreed with me. He had wanted to know who told me, so my guess was that there had to be something to it.

Denise said she recalled Vicky's grandfather babbling about some amount of money Vicky was going to come into—but Grandpa Swall had babbled about a lot of things, and if you asked him what he meant, demanded that he back up a claim, why then all he used to do was smile or mutter under his breath and walk away. Sure sounded a lot like old man Swall.

And it was almost like I could still see the old man's empty toothless mouth sucking in the air, his eyes small and rheumy, gray, distant, yet scowling at me smugly, demanding either my attention or a piece of my leg. I could hear the stubborn, hoarsely strident voice barking at me, commanding me with little gruff and whining growls while reciting fantasies for the sheer pleasure of hearing himself inject new life into dying thoughts that sounded less real when kept to oneself. I could see and hear him. His life was still there—talking at me, following me around.

Chapter Thirty-Six

"What time is he expecting you?"

"I just told him some time this afternoon. I'm supposed to ask a dealer named Roger in the poker room."

"Don't you think you better go ask him?"

I patted Denise's hand, let it go, then came back to it and did what I wanted with it: I held onto it tight, like a lifeline. It was three o'clock in the afternoon and there were three bottled blondes in full-length sequined evening gowns, one black with silver spangles, one pearly with silver, one midnight blue. One seat down and three in a row, they crossed and recrossed their legs quite casually but with expertise, operating the slits that ran halfway up their thighs with the adroitness and dexterity of cool and perfect fighter pilots opening and closing their wing panels while veering through the sky. I could feel my eyes going up and down according to what they wanted to do with me. They didn't have to look around, strut the stuff, or pretend to be interested in anything around them. As long as they kept those wing panels going, all they had to do was sit there on the bar stools sipping tonic water over ice and chatting with their friends. People were passing in and out dressed for carrying luggage or going to the pool. Most men who walked alone carried a glass. It was lonely here: Vague-ass. Timeless, dayless, nightless. After a while, meaningless chance games dulled even the sharpest senses, then soured the stomach. A middle-aged Lothario sporting an inner tube about his middle was sitting two seats down from Denise drinking a glass of milk, which seemed to fit well. Sour stomach. He'd had enough of Scotch and now he was back to milk and cookies. One flight on the tail of ice-cold wings fleeced in fool's gold, and he'd be ready to trundle on home and snuggle back up to what he had once called life and love and what he now probably looked upon as responsibility in drag.

Denise looked at me. I thought she was a little surprised, possibly embarrassed. She just looked at me with a questioning sort of smile. I let go of her hand, feeling like Alice in Wonderland. One second small as an ant, the next ready to take on a bevy of street gangs. I'd gotten this far, to Vegas by plane, by taxi to the Dunes; you'd think the rest would be easy. But it wasn't.

"How do I know this guy is really Vicky's cousin?"

"He says he is."

"That's the problem, and that's why I'm sitting here at the bar instead of blowing a bugle to announce my arrival. And that's why I'm going to have another double and think it over a little longer."

The bartender glided down my way. "Could I have another double Jack Daniels?"

"You betcha." He stood there in front of me and poured a liberal slug into a fresh glass, then set it out before me. I picked it up and sipped from it slowly but steadily like a sick man taking down his chicken soup. Somebody called out a drink and the bartender glided down toward the other end of the long bar. I looked back at Denise.

"I mean, I am getting paranoid. I'll be the first to admit it, but how do I know that this guy isn't connected to the first guy or wants to do me in for some reason I don't understand?"

"That's why we should call the police," she told me.

"We will," I said. I patted her hand again. "I just appreciate that you came along, that's all. I just wanted to tell you that."

Almost too quickly to see, her eyelids fluttered. Then she was relatively calm. "I feel like this is doing more good than standing at Vicky's funeral. I also appreciate you were nice to me the other day. Besides, I figured you wouldn't have bothered to tell me all about this unless you felt you could use help."

The man drinking milk finished his glass and ordered some hard stuff. Then he stood up and walked around Denise and me and planted himself in front of the commando air squadron. I heard him ask the girls how they were. A couple of them returned the favor asking him the same. I figured if he could handle this town, so could I, especially if I might be able to help myself in the process. He was helping himself, and I was going to help myself. He was helping me and the girls were helping him. And he was also, of course, helping the girls. We were all helping each other. Life was really wonderful. I felt ready to come out of the desert reciting the parable of the burning bush. I stood up, told Denise to wait for me there and buy some yarn and knit booties if she didn't want to be picked up.

I found the little poker room at the side end of the main casino. The Dunes isn't a poker hotel, none of them really are. They make their money at baccarat, craps, and black-jack. Still, it was amazing they only had a couple of poker tables—three to be exact. Two were covered and there was a low-stakes, five-man game going slowly at the third. The dealer had his white shirtsleeves rolled to the elbow and a green plastic visor high on his forehead, only he looked too nice to be a dealer. Black-rimmed glasses, an honest trace of rough stubble, and a thick-lipped, cautious, O-shaped mouth made him look more like somebody's nice uncle in the furniture business, the kind of guy who was generous and ready to give you a deal if you knew somebody he knew. Big hands on small arms and a stooped, lumpy little body. Nobody looked up like they'd been expecting me, so I waited till somebody won a few cents pushing a pair of jakes, then I asked the man if his name was Roger. He nod-ded, so I told him that Arnold Swall had asked me to drop by when I came to Vegas. He smiled, told everybody to ante up, then invited me to sit down. I asked the guy if he'd talked to Arnold. The guy told me that we'd have to reserve the social chit-chat for a little later on in the day. If I wanted to sit down and play, that was wonderful, but he'd have to talk to me and Arnold a little later on. Well, so much for nice guys who gave away furniture. The only thing this guy would give away was his indigestion. I thanked the man, excused myself, and went back out into the lobby and up to the girl at the registration desk. Before she could hesitate or ask me anything, I told her I was a friend and that Arnold had told me he'd meet me in the lobby. I'd been waiting for some time and Arnold had yet to show up.

The girl smiled, shook her head. "You know how he is."

I shook mine back and chuckled with her and told her

that I sure did. She gave me the room number, I thanked her and—knowing it could leave at any moment—I strolled off quickly to find the elevator, riding my short burst of courage for all it was worth. I could see the cocktail lounge across the way as I passed back through the lobby. Denise was still at the bar. I waved to her but she didn't see me. She was reading her Vivien Leigh book.

Chapter Thirty-Seven

I got off on the fourth floor, saw the room numbers and arrows on the aisle walls opposite the elevator, turned left on the aisle on the right, and walked halfway down the hall. A maid's cart was out in the middle. As I went by the doors, it seemed like most of the rooms were empty. People were either gambling or sitting by the pool. I heard a bunch of little kids laughing wildly behind one of the doors. They were screaming, making thudding noises. It sounded like a knockdown, drag-out pillow fight. I came to the end, hit a right angle, turned with it and ended up on one of the short ends of the rectangle. There was another cart down this way. A wide-hipped, big-bottomed girl in a white miniskirted maid's uniform bustled quickly out of a room, grabbed a can of Ajax and an oval, bristled toilet brush from her cart, looked down the hall at me, swept the hair off her face, then turned and walked back into the room. I came down the hall, reading the numbers on the doors. The number I wanted was the one where the maid was. I stood outside the open door and tapped on it gently, then peeked in.

"Hello?"

The girl was already on her way back out. "You want somethin'?" She moved by me and grabbed a handful of clean rags off the bottom tray of her hand truck.

"No, I guess not. You wouldn't happen to know the man whose room this is?"

"Mister Swall."

"Yeah. I was supposed to meet him. Have you seen him around today?"

"Sure have."

The girl went back into the room. I was standing by the short entryway next to the bathroom, and from there I could see the foot of the rumpled bed, the side of the long, mirrored dresser. Clothes and personal effects were strewn messily over its top. I was thinking about how I'd like to get rid of the girl and have a look at them.

"You remember where?"

The girl turned toward me, smiling and showing me a wide but pretty face. Her eyes glinted with a mischievous look. "He's right there in his bed if you can wake him up."

I stepped further into the room and looked up at the head of the bed. I couldn't see anything, mostly forearm and elbow, then a bit of hair sticking up out of the covers. The man was lying on his side, his head was cradled inside the crook of his arm.

"I didn't see him."

"An' you musta thought I wouldn't be cleanin' his room if the guest was in here."

"You might say that."

The girl laughed. "It would be hard to do it without him here considerin' the guy's usually in here all day long."

"A night owl, huh?"

"Oh, you better believe it. Sleeps all afternoon, makes whoopee all night. And I mean whoopee."

"Is he asleep?"

"Out like a light."

"He was wide awake when he called me this morning. I may be wrong, but I thought he was sober too."

The girl was going over the carpet by the window. There were two cushioned sitting chairs by a small, round side table in front of drawn drapes. Underwear, expensive snakeskin boots, high-legged riding boots, silver-studded belts, elaborately embroidered Western shirts, empty shirt-backs from the laundry, were all over the floor. The girl picked it all up and piled it on the table.

"You can never really tell. 'Course I don't usually see him in full glory. Mostly it's the morning after." She thought for a moment, then added, "Maybe he found somethin' to get his nose into after he talked to you. This man is incredible, I'm tellin' you. As soon he's awake, he's lookin' for some excuse to waste his money. I never seen anything like it in my whole, entire life."

I was standing by the dresser. There were two framed eight by tens lying on the counter. One pictured a cowboy in spurs and chaps bareback on a huge, randy-looking bull kicking high off the back. One hand was waving wildly in the air, the other held onto the horn. You could see half of a contestant's number card standing out from the checked shirt on his back. The other picture was of the same man in the same shirt down on his knees and roping up a calf in what looked like the same arena with the same patch of crowd in the background. The girl saw me looking.

"That's from when he won some rodeo."

"How do you know so much about him?"

"The guy's lived here for almost a year. I clean his room every day. He won't let no one else close to it."

"Why's that?"

"Mister, he leaves so much money and valuables around here, it ain't funny."

"Don't you think our conversation's going to wake him up?"

She started back toward the entryway and began hanging up some of the clothes. She laughed through her nose. "Nope. Not till he's good and ready. Sleeps like a stone. I'm not kidding."

I went back to what she'd been saying. "Why is it that he trusts you so much when he doesn't trust anyone else?"

"How should I know?"

"I'm sorry, I don't mean to pry. I'm just curious. I've never even seen the man, so what you're telling me's interesting."

"You guys were supposed to get together this afternoon?"

"Yeah."

"I see. Family?"

"Yeah. Why?"

"Nothin'. He said somethin' yesterday 'bout family, that's all."

"How'd you happen to talk to him yesterday if he's always sound asleep when you're here?"

She wheeled on me. "Listen, what is this?"

I put my hands up in a stopping gesture. "That didn't come out right."

"It sure didn't. What are you—a cop?"

"Nope."

"You don't look like one."

"What does one look like?"

"You know."

"Well, I could be one," I smiled.

She finished hanging up the clothes, walked past, ignoring me, and started to straighten up what was on the dresser. She picked up the two framed pictures and stood them up and leaned them against the base of the tall mirror above the bureau just the way Arnold liked it and told her to do it, probably. She picked up the discarded laundry packages, then went past me again back out into the hall where she threw them into the ten-gallon plastic bag tied to the side of the truck.

When she came back in, she looked at me firmly. "You can leave him a note if you wanna."

"I know he needs his beauty sleep, but I'm going to have to wake him up."

She smiled sardonically, her wide face dimpled, and shook her head. "Oh, if I were you, I wouldn't do that. He'll make you wish you hadn't."

"He will?"

The acid went out of her face, the smile got sweet. "How I met him was I came in here and asked him when he wanted me to clean up. That was when I'd been tryin' to come in and clean for over a week. He was asleep and I woke him up. Know what he did?"

"I could guess."

"Sat up and socked me on the jaw."

"You're kidding?"

"They told me I was unconscious for over two hours. Had ta wire it. The hotel insurance would have paid for it, but—" she pointed at the bed—"he felt so bad, he made them let him go for the whole shebang. Another time I thought he was up, so I asked him somethin'. He pulled me down an'. . ." Her smile faded, the soft blue eyes moistened slightly, shifting into gray. She looked down at the bed.

I lowered my voice a little. "Why would you do his room then?"

"Guess."

"He pays you because you put up with him and do it the right way. Plus, because he's generous with you, he doesn't have to worry that you'll rip him off."

Her face flushed, her lips tightened. "Hey, man, I'm not a prostitute."

"I didn't say you were."

"The fucker raped me, man. I didn't enjoy it, I assure you."

"I didn't mean that."

She screwed her face up at me, started to say something else, then turned on her heels and walked away. "Wake him up if you want to. What the fuck do I care?" She went into the bathroom and started cleaning in there.

Maybe what she'd said should have been advice well taken, but I was there in Vegas because this guy had said he wanted to talk to me. A hangover should be nothing new to either of us. If he was going to have one, he'd have it whether I was there or not. I decided to stand at arm's length, pat him gently on the shoulder, then ease him into it gradually. I went to the window to open the drapes, but then rejected that tactic. Too harsh. I came back to the bed, leaned over Arnold Swall, and tapped him on the shoulder. No movement. Like stone. I tapped him again—harder— then bounded away ready for the claws of tigers. It wasn't until I started to shake him by the shoulders that I noticed a large stain darkening the rust colored bedspread pulled up around his head.

I pulled the covers back far enough to see that the man in this bed wasn't asleep. He was dead. There was a remote possibility it was someone else, not the man who had called me and told me to come here. Maybe Arnold Swall was really sitting poolside downstairs soaking up the rays. Or maybe it hadn't even been Arnold Swall who had called me in the first place.

I walked into the bathroom, told the girl not to be shocked but that the man in the bed wasn't sleeping. She came back out into the bedroom and, before I could ask her whether the dead man was Swall, she looked down at him and screamed. What she screamed was "Arnie!" which answered my question quite well and added another dimension to the reserved and rather hurt and hostile things she had just said. Not that it mattered much now.

The girl was sobbing loudly. I closed the hall door, then came back and asked her what her name was. Her hands were over her mouth and she whimpered "Betty" through them.

"OK, Betty." I put my arm around her shoulder. She grabbed me and held on for dear life, sobbing into my chest, "It's not your fault," I told her. "You didn't have anything to do with it."

In a few moments, she stopped the sobbing as suddenly as she had begun and started wiping her eyes with the sides of her hands. I went into the bathroom and got her some Kleenex.

"What are we gonna do?" She stared at me waiting for me to tell her.

"All right. Let's get a few things clear. One, I didn't have anything to do with this—do you believe that?"

"I don't know."

"What do you think?"

"I don't know." Her voice was shrill and panicky, lost.

"Accept that I didn't. My second point is that I think I have a chance of finding out who did. I don't know what you really thought of Arnold Swall—maybe you don't yourself—but other people's lives are involved."

"So what do you want outa me?"

I walked to the closet, grabbed a handful of clothes off the hangers, tossed them back onto the carpet by the window, then I ran my hand over the dresser, messed that up too. "When the coast is clear, I want you to give me a couple minutes, go back to the room before this one, clean it up good, then come in here and scream your lungs out, call downstairs to the front desk, report it, then wait for them to come upstairs. Tell the story with one very very big exception—me." She opened her mouth to say something, but I continued on before she could get a word in edgewise. "Unless you do, I'm not going to have a chance to get to the bottom of this thing. I'll probably get blamed for it—which isn't fair because I didn't do it."

"I don't know."

"You wouldn't be lying completely. You don't know my name anyway. All you could do is describe me."

"I don't know."

"We'll make a deal. If I don't call you in two weeks and give you a good explanation for why this all happened, then you can call the police and tell them what you know. That's all the time it should take me."

"If I hold back information, they're gonna think I'm an accomplice."

"True. But tell them I threatened your life and you were afraid to say anything."

After a long, long moment: "OK."

I took her hands. "You're a very good person." I didn't know what else to say. Now, if the bartender in the lounge, Roger the dealer, and the girl at the front desk all got temporary amnesia, I'd be home free.

Betty went back into the bathroom, picked up her rags and bottles, dipped quickly into the hall, and dumped them into her cart. She shoved the cart back toward the room she had just finished. A door opened halfway down and across the hall. She leaped back inside Swall's door and closed it. Then she walked around the room looking for anything she might have left behind.

I had one more chance to ask her something. "I still don't know how well you knew him," I said carefully, "and we couldn't really get into that now. But I'd like to ask you if he ever said anything to you about where his money came from, where he earned it, how he earned it—anything?"

Her face was blank. No, she didn't know. She had never had any idea. Swall had joked about it once or twice when he was carrying an especially heavy roll. Said it fell from heaven. I believed her. On her part, the vague relationship had probably existed out of necessity; on his side, the mindless perverse pleasure of physical domination, guilt, and also trust. She was like a pet that wouldn't bite the hand that fed it. Aside from some of his crass and obvious aspects, she hadn't really known a damn thing about the man.

She peeked out into the hall, opened the door a little wider, then rushed out. I heard the door next door open and close. I went back to the bed and looked through

133

Swall's wallet. There were a couple of pictures of young women, really girls, a couple of pictures of horses. I was on the verge of finding this amusing, then my eye caught the man's face. There was a horrible grimace set over the mouth. It made him suddenly seem very much alive. I felt my own mouth molding itself into the same shape. I closed my eyes to shake it off, opened them again, and looked at the whole face. At one time, it had been ruggedly hand-some, a beefy version of Monty Cliff in *The Misfits*. His eyes were almost closed, but I couldn't imagine they would have looked quite as tortured as the actor's—probably more on the happy-go-lucky side. Good solid features: a full head of dark fine hair flecked with gray—matted, sticky in the back where the skull had been smashed in; bushy eyebrows; a sculptured nose—a little red and just a touch bulbous like Grandpa Swall's; handsome squared-off chin with a tiny dimple in the middle. In contrast over his blood-streaked neck, his complexion had a distinctly whitish pallor, but I imagined that in life it had been fairly ruddy, jacked up with the excess of living this man had practiced with such diligence. There were bulges in both pockets, so I went through them. Twenty hundred dollar bills on one side, eighteen on the other. Thirty-eight hundred cash on him. I folded the money back up, put it back, tried to think of any-thing in the room that I'd touched, couldn't think of any-thing, so then I quietly opened the door, peeked into the hall, saw nothing. I let myself out, closed the door behind me, and walked toward the exit door at the end of the hall.

I went down the four flights to the first floor and found Denise sitting where I'd left her. The bartender was talking to a couple in matching leisure suits down toward the other end of the bar.

"What did he say?"

As I started to speak, I couldn't stop picturing Arnold Swall. The action from the slots and tables in the main room swarmed up and surrounded me bodily. My ears were ringing. It felt like all the people down there were talking about me.

"Ben?"

I swallowed, then all I could say was, "Let's get out of here."

As we walked by the main desk, I looked out onto the gambling floor. The chatter was still echoing around me, assaulting me from every direction, but no one looked my way. They looked down at their chips, their wallets, the green sward. But that still didn't mean that one of them might not know. Know what? That murder happened every minute of every day. They knew, of course they did, everybody did. The only difference was that when you were in Vegas, you didn't have to care. They covered that for you. It came with the room. At least it was supposed to.

Chapter Thirty-Eight

"Flush—ace high."

"Goddamn it! I had a king. What's that you got, an ace?"

"Yep."

"That eight's a diamond."

"Excuse me, sir, but that's not a flush. King high takes the pot."

"What d'ya mean?! Five hearts—count 'em—ace high. Look at the cards, would ya?"

"Ben, your eight's a diamond."

The dealer swept the cards out from under my nose, picked them up, and shuffled the deck.

"What kind of hotel is this? That's what I'd like to know."

"This is the MGM Grand, sir, and if you don't like it, perhaps you better play someplace else."

"You're just givin' it away, buddy." A voice from somewhere around the table.

"The ante is one dollar, sir."

"I put it in already, for god's sake."

"How could you have put it in when you have no chips in front of you?"

"Huh?"

"Do you want to buy some more chips?"

"I put in the goddamn ante!"

"Ben, please, I think you've had enough."

"Oh, what do you know?"

A couple pairs of arms reached up under my arms and pulled me from my chair. A pleasant sensation, really. I was hoping they'd swing me back and forth. I waited for a deep voice to croon, Whoopsa daisy!, but instead I was being pushed, dragged, and manhandled from the casino floor.

"Are you and your husband staying at the hotel?"

"He's not my husband."

"Sorry."

"He's in seven twenty-nine."

"We'll help ya take him up there."

"Thanks."

Chapter Thirty-Nine

"I'm gonna be all right now. Don't you worry."

"Ouch! What do you think I am, a fullback?"

I thought I had just patted her on the back. "Don't get mad now."

"I'm not mad."

"When you're mad, you don't look pretty. Some women do, but you don't—definitely."

"That's very interesting."

"I can tell you're fascinated."

"If you won't be needing me, I'll be going down to my room."

"Where's that?"

"Seven-fifteen."

"How did we end up getting separate rooms?"

"You might ask how we ended up getting rooms at all."

"How did we?"

"At the rate you were going, I figured if you get nauseous when you're sober, you certainly wouldn't appreciate flying when you're this drunk."

"What? I'm relaxed. I could fly anywhere."

"Sure."

"What do you think I am, an invalid?"

"I won't answer that."

"I'm just a little drunk. I know what I'm doing. Think I didn't know whether I had that hand? Ya gotta bluff sometime—name of the game. Keeps everybody on their toes."

"They wouldn't have let you on the plane."

"OK, so let's make the best of it."

"Would you look at yourself? Just look. Look at both of us."

She turned me around toward the mirror over the dresser. I laughed and slapped my knee like a real yokel. I had a great shit-eating grin on, so my reaction was completely in character. Denise looked a little flea-bitten and weather-worn herself. Her black hair was wind-blown and tousled. Her cheeks and forehead were redder than rouge. Her eyes looked a little like they were trying to read road signs while the rest of her was caught in the middle of a pirouette that wouldn't stop. And her mouth was just a touch on the silly side too. Not like mine, but still not altogether sewed up and careful either.

"You're drunk," I told her.

"Not like you."

"How did you get drunk?"

"I don't know. How did you?"

"Really, I'm curious. I didn't see you drinking."

"That's because you were too busy doing your own."

"You're cute. Before, I never noticed you."

She was pleased, but, nevertheless, still turned toward the door. "I think that means it's time for us to get some rest—separately."

I got in front of her, leaned my back up against the door. "Tall girls aren't usually my type."

"Writers aren't usually mine."

"Who's a writer? I couldn't write if you paid me!"

"I think you better get some rest." She motioned for me to step aside.

"Hey, how often do we get a chance to be together like this?"

"We didn't come here for a vacation—or don't you want to remember?"

"No."

"Hey, I'm sorry."

I wouldn't have been able to do it if I had thought about it too much or if I hadn't moved in quick before she knew what was happening to her—because what I did next was simple: I reached out and yanked at her shoulder straps hard, as hard as I could, in fact. They were thin, but not spaghetti strings either, and needed a good strong pull if I expected to get them both at the same time.

I did. She lifted both her arms up to stop mine as they came toward her. After the straps tore, her arms were still up in the air for that brief second, just long enough to pull the whole dress down. Like a sack, the thing dropped down over her feet.

She stood there with her mouth open, gaping at me. It looked lost out in the cold, so I covered it to make it warm and let it know I was there. She pulled her face away, took a few steps backwards, then stood there, turned her body to the side and froze. She was as naked as the day she'd been born. Small breasts and the pale pink areolae were hardly even noticeable, though the nipples themselves protruded like the tips on a baby's formula bottle. I couldn't have seen them underneath the sun dress. They'd been tucked under its tight straight line. These were nipples I'd waxed salacious over at two dollars a page, the kind of nipples you didn't see too often, the kind that lonely truckers, soldiers, and shy, deprived men loved to read about, see, and drool over.

I reached for one of the small breasts, took it in my hand. Tiny and firm, it was just like one of those small lemons from the tree in my front yard. I covered it with my hand, closed it up between my fingers and palm. I squeezed it with care, found it fresh, then held the nipple between thumb and forefinger and rubbed it gently to and fro.

She turned away again so that her back was to me. Then she pulled the bed cover off the bed and covered herself. I patted her buttocks and smoothed them out. They were long and narrow and cool to the touch and fit so easily into my hands that it felt like I was molding and creating, putting the last finishing touches on the clay.

"Stop it, Ben."

"It's exciting you weren't wearing underwear."

She turned around. She was holding onto the bedspread with her left hand. She held up the right, pulled it back far enough to send me a telegram, and came down on my face. I let her do it. The hand was open so it didn't hurt much, although it sure sounded like it. So loud it seemed to have shocked her and she stood there and let the blanket drop to the floor as she watched and waited.

I smiled and leaned down toward her. I took both of the little lemon breasts in my hands, cupped them and turned them toward each other. The long nipples came together, side by side, and I took the spouts into my mouth and licked them tenderly, nibbled ever so gently.

I looked up. The nipples were still in my mouth. Her mouth was gaping wide open, wider than before. Her eyes were popped wide with hysteria. Her hands were raised above her head in small fists ready to come down upon my head and back. I waited for the screams: Police! Rape! Murder! What was a little murder? After a while, you got used to it. That was how squeamish boys became good doctors. They got used to the sight of blood. And if they couldn't get used to it, then they kept trying. I hadn't had to go looking for mine. It had come to me. And maybe I was getting used to it. So if Denise wanted to scream bloody murder, I was willing to let her. I thought I could handle it now. I kept up my sucking and nibbling, alternating between the two with tenderness and care.

Fists, small and round, came down on my back. Harder and slightly smaller than the little lemon breasts. They hurt, they stung. Then I thought she was probably ready to scream, so I leaned forward with all my weight and we fell onto the bed.

I pumped her from on top. I still wasn't inside her. I wanted her to want me.

"Fuck me. Now, now—put it in and fuck me!"

For some perverse reason, I don't think I've ever enjoyed it more.

Chapter Forty

Hangover took care of breakfast, made it something very quiet and devotional—a low mass, I suppose, in liturgical terms. On the plane homeward, the single high-ball didn't do a bit of good. We compared headaches and

139

neurasthenic symptoms, and I dozed. Then we were north-bound on the San Diego Freeway, making time toward the west end of town. Aside from that, I didn't know where I was going, her place, mine, wherever—alone or together. It was too quiet and I had the uneasy feeling that it was time to say something.

Finally, "I feel like I deflowered a virgin." A stupid thing to say and I had no idea how she was going to take it.

She decided to take it as a compliment because she said, "Thanks."

Then she laid her hand across my thigh and gave me a there-there pat. After a pause, she added, "The quickest way is to take the Santa Monica East."

It was the quickest way to my house too, but I assumed she'd been giving me directions to hers. We didn't talk again until I was a few blocks from her apartment. She looked at me a couple of times like she wanted to talk, so I asked her what was on her mind.

She shook her head. "I don't know what to say."

"Neither do I."

"I'm glad we got to know each other."

"Me too."

"We shouldn't have done it, but we did. Now a lot of the pressure's gone."

"Snap, crackle, pop, poof, gone."

"I know it's shitty, but let's not make it any worse than it already is." She suddenly sounded bitter.

"My apologies."

"You feel bad, don't you?"

"Just hung over." She didn't like that, so I revised it. "I guess I'll feel kinda lousy until all this is settled. It's like Vicky's dying, I know she's going to die, only she isn't dead yet."

Denise seemed to know what I was talking about. "Strange."

"Yeah."

"Listen, don't blame yourself. You think you did every-thing, but I let you. I wanted you."

"Really?"

"How many times do I have to say it?"

"Were you attracted to me before?" I pulled up in front of her apartment building and turned off the car.

Her forehead wrinkled. She frowned and shook her head "No, don't be soap opera. It's being thrown together under odd conditions—you understand?"

"Sure."

"I'm not trying to put you down."

"I realize that," I smiled. Then, just for the hell of it, I asked her, "You think we should see each other—like once in a while?"

She lifted her head up and smiled back, looking embarrassed, coy, and yet a trifle confused. I leaned over and kissed her hard. In a second, we were licking each other's teeth and tonsils and she was sucking my tongue down into her throat. I put my hand up her repaired dress and she pulled away and swung open the passenger door and jumped out. I thought I'd offer to buy her a new sundress, but first I asked her if I could come in.

"No."

"Why?"

The top was up so she had to crouch down as she leaned back into the car. She held her dress daintily to her neck so I wouldn't be able to look down it. "Ben, I've gotta have some time. Please try to understand, won't you?"

I nodded.

"I think we can both use it."

I had to agree with her. Then I told her that I was going to go to San Francisco the next day or the day after. Denise shook her head and said she thought I should go see the police and tell them what was going on. Maybe they'd be able to help. I laughed and said the police could go fuck themselves, even though I'd have to give them some song and dance to explain how I had happened to come across old Grandpa Swall in the throes of a fatal heart attack. They were certainly going to insist upon being privy to a good little tale in that case, and I'd have to give it to them before I split for San Francisco. Otherwise, they'd probably be able to stop me before I was able to get there.

Denise told me that she thought I was just trying to defeat myself, make things harder. She offered to come along for moral support, but I told her I didn't think that was a good idea. Besides, she'd been saying that we both needed time to think and the only way that could be done was alone and in separate places.

She said she'd be worried about me. I said I'd be worried about me too and that I'd call her as soon as I took care of what I could and got back. She leaned closer and I kissed her again, lightly.

I started the car and drove home. On the way, I thought about Denise's fabulous nipples. I could picture myself sucking on them. I could see my hard, hot, and hungry cock sawing back and forth, playing those taut tips just like a cellist tightening his strings, then plucking with finger and bow to test for trueness of tone. I hadn't gotten around to that one and I was regretting it. Seemed to figure that I had forgotten to perform a simple erotic fantasy that I now found I was craving over and beyond anything the two of us had actually done. I was primed up. If I went straight home, I was sure I could sit down and whip out a quick thirty to forty thousand smutty words by mid-morning the next day. But I was finished with that chapter. From now on, Herbert and his kind could have their fun with another turkey. This one'd had all his feathers plucked, but he was trying to stay away from everybody's chopping block. Gobble, gobble . . . Gobble, gobble . . .

Chapter Forty-One

"Glad you could make it."

The Ferret Face with that peculiar smile-frown of his, drumming his fingers over the desk top. I was in a spot. I knew it. He knew it. It was all a matter of what he intended to do about it. As for myself, I'd already decided I was going to be on my very best behavior. There were things I had to do, and I couldn't do them sitting in a cell.

So I smiled and said, "Sorry I'm late."

He thought that was very funny, so he tilted his head back and gave out a good guffaw, then cut it short, dropped his chin and bored through me with the leechy eyes. They sucked out what little composure I possessed, poured back in a will-weakening venom that left me perplexed.

Baby Hughie was back in again on this one. He stood to the side, waiting for Ferret Face to tell him what to do. Steifer left his eyeballs in my bloodstream and turned toward the other man: "I'm not taking one fucking chance. Put the cuffs on him."

Baby Hughie put cuffs on me. I kept a pleasant expression on my face. Didn't say a thing, sigh, complain, or suggest that I might. I held out my hands and let Baby Hughie do his business.

Steifer told Baby Hughie to go get a candy bar, then he told me to take a chair and sit down across from him at his desk. Except the chair he indicated was across the room and my hands were tied. I walked toward the chair and started dragging it by the inside of one of its legs with the side of my foot. Then, before I knew it, Ferret Face had popped up standing next to me. He grabbed the chair away, swung it through the air with an arcing motion of his right arm, and crashed it down before the desk. I followed him and before I could sit down, he helped or rather pushed me down onto the seat. Instead of grumbling, I thanked the man. He sneered in return. But by the time he had perched himself back behind the empty desk, he seemed genuinely amused.

"Changed your tune, haven't you?"

"What do you mean?"

"You know what I mean. You haven't called me a mean, sadistic fucker yet."

"Give me time," I smiled.

"Crandel, know what I think about people when they suddenly become very cooperative?"

"What's that?"

"They're definitely hiding something." He made a church out of his hands and leaned toward me across the desk. "If you don't tell us now, you're gonna tell us later, or we'll find out anyway. Why make it harder for yourself?"

"I don't know what you're talking about."

"You stupid asshole, don't you know I'm aware you're holding back on me?"

"You must be clairvoyant." I was trying to lighten it up a little, but he wasn't going for it. The tips of his fingers squeezed together, turned the church roof of his hands all white and red. I blabbered on, saying, "If I did know anything, don't you think I'd want to tell you? I don't want some maniac running around killing people. I'm not that big of a jerk."

He ignored what I was saying, sat back in the chair and drummed his fingers along the desk edge again. "The landlady called yesterday morning," he said tonelessly. "She said she called the night before, but she fell asleep after we put her on hold. Told us all about the girl's grandfather *and* how you carried him over to her apartment."

"That old lady—"

"Without *her*, we wouldn't know a goddamn thing about this case. Were you going to call us, phone in any information you came across?"

"I didn't consider the fact that Vicky's grandfather had come into town to be a vital piece of information. I'm sorry, but it seems to me that you're letting Mrs. McGinty's—"

"Forget the old lady and the grandfather. The real issue here's that you're on bail. That means you're supposed to be available."

"I was available."

"We had men at your house from one o'clock yesterday to one o'clock today. Twenty-four hours."

"What was the big deal?"

"The big deal is that we wanted to talk to you and we couldn't find you. Something like that's bound to make us start thinking things. Which is what you seem to want."

"If I had realized this was going to cause such a stink, I would have come in yesterday. I just didn't realize." Steifer smiled with clenched teeth. "I was over at a friend's house."

"We'll have to check that out."

"I didn't know I was supposed to be on call."

"Don't get cute."

"I'm serious."

He rubbed the back of his ear, came up with something on his forefinger and flicked it on the floor. "That's the problem."

I wasn't sure what he meant, but I was starting to wonder whether I'd given this guy all the credit he deserved. He was good with his hunches. My only hope was that he didn't have anything concrete to trip me up on. If he could link me up with the killing in Vegas, I'd really be in trouble. I gave him Ellen's name and address. He didn't write it down, so I told him it might be a good idea if he did.

"You know that's a lie and you know I think it's a lie, so why are you insisting on it?" he asked me.

"Because it's the truth."

"Level with me."

"OK."

"You don't really think cops are crooks or something, do you?"

"No. Just generally incompetent."

"Don't you realize you're contributing to and abetting that incompetence by not giving us your full cooperation?"

"Yeah, I guess so," I tried to say sincerely.

He took it or at least pretended to: "Then why don't you try to help us?"

"OK, I will, but you didn't have to come and arrest me in my own house. I was going to come in today anyway."

"Of course."

"What can I say if you don't want to believe anything I'm telling you?"

"So how did you happen to run across the girl's grandfather?"

"To be honest with you, I was doing some snooping around the apartment."

"What for?"

"To see if I could find anything else out—on my own."

"Were you inside the apartment?"

"Yeah."

He winced, then he asked, "What about the old man?"

"He just showed up, that's all."

"So then what happened?"

"We talked for a little while. He was drinking heavily, and then he had a heart attack. I'm sure Mrs. McGinty can tell you the rest."

"And you're still not going to say where you disappeared to."

"How can I say anything if I didn't disappear?"

"We checked out a few locales on you. You're in for some very big problems."

"I drove around. Then I went over Ellen's."

Ferret Face asked me Ellen's last name again. He picked up the phone and made a few calls. When he had somebody on the line, he asked me for the address, mumbled a bunch of yeah, yeah, yeahs. When he had hung up, he said, "They're going to call the girl."

"Good, that's fine with me," I said calmly while the inside of my guts churned away like a garbage disposal.

"Let's get back to the old man."

"Sure."

"Did you have any thoughts about anything the two of you talked about?"

"Nothing in particular."

"What did you talk about?"

"Vicky's childhood, what she did out here. He was very upset about what he'd read in the paper."

"Hooker?"

"Yeah."

"So then he just had himself a heart attack and you carried him over to Mrs. McGinty's and that's all that happened."

"Right."

"If you knew that the old lady was going to get all hysterical, it would seem logical to me that you would want to call us first before she did."

"I just didn't think it was relevant; plus, I've given up caring about anything that old bag wants to say about me."

"You're walking on thin ice."

I leaned forward. I wanted to make what I next had to say sound as rational and even-tempered as I possibly could. "Mister Steifer, if I hadn't been so hot-tempered, overwhelmed by my emotions, we wouldn't even be sitting here having this conversation. I wouldn't have been jailed, then put on bail, and you wouldn't have the wise-ass image of me that you do."

"Is that so?"

"All I mean to say is that, in my opinion, I think you're reading too much into me."

That affected him. He didn't show it, but, somehow, after that, his eyes didn't feel quite as leechy. The smile, too, wasn't quite so ambiguous. There was a pause, then he said, "Well, for your sake, I hope you're right."

I thought it might be good to repeat what I'd already said, so again I told him that if I had thought there had been anything important about what had happened at Vicky's, I would have called or come in right away.

Baby Hughie came ambling back into the room. Steifer told him to take my cuffs off. I rubbed my wrists, twiddled my fingers as I closed and opened my hands, and said thanks. Steifer looked at me and didn't say anything, so I stood up.

"Would a return-trip ticket to San Francisco mean anything to you?"

"No, why?"

"She had an airline reservation for the twenty-first."

"I'd have no idea."

For a split second there, I almost wanted to tell him everything I knew. The sequence of events had fallen into a definite pattern, but I wasn't sure I could crack it all by myself. And it wasn't that I didn't trust Steifer. I guess it was a primitive, superstitious inkling that Vicky wanted it this way. And as a friend I felt I owed it to her to do everything I could. As for myself alone, this death-wielding puzzle had become my responsibility. In an abstract sense, it could have been anything. It was just something that I had started and now had to finish. I hadn't followed through on anything for a long time. I wanted to reacquire that old touch. I wanted to remember that Iowa farm boy in his senior year at the U of I— the one who had believed in possibilities. Somehow, it seemed necessary to go back in order to go forward.

Steifer's eyes got leechy, the smile ironical again. He didn't believe me, but, now, at this point, I didn't have to care. I had been cooperative and he didn't have a thing to hold me on. What he didn't know now, he'd find out soon enough—that is, if I was still around to tell him.

Chapter Forty-Two

Frenchie, *mon cher,*
    Bonjour! Bon nuit! Comment ça va? Bien ou non? I'd like to talk to you and discuss terms. If you wish to contact me, please go to the corner of Crescent Heights

and Sunset. See Elmo, the shoeshine man, in Schwab's parking lot. He will give you a number where you can reach me. Don't waste your time trying to weasel information out of him. He won't know anything.

So long or *à bientôt, mon ami.*

That Vicky had made a reservation to San Francisco, of course, came as absolutely no surprise to me. Whether by air, land, sea, or carrier pigeon made no difference. San Francisco was my inevitable destination. There was just one other thing it was imperative that I do first. I had to die first, then I could go to San Francisco; and, perhaps, after taking care of what I anticipated to be rather rough and complex business, I might even enjoy myself, relax and have a little vacation if I had any money left. But first things first. I had to die and die fast, and I wasn't exactly sure how I was going to go about doing it.

I picked my blankets up off the floor and draped them neatly over the bed, patted the pillows, smoothed them out, and pinned my note to Frenchie to one of the pillows. I stood back and admired my work. Perfect. Your eye caught it as soon as you stepped into the room. Because my desk was messy and there were clothes strewn all over the floor, and the broken lamp still lay on its side in the middle of the floor, it was incongruous to find the bed made. Your eye picked it up as a contrast and from there moved to the note.

I walked down to the Country Store and picked out two cans of Kal Kan with scrumptious-looking labels and hurried back to make a peace offering of two pounds of solid horsemeat to pacify my sad-eyed pooch for his long confinement.

Doing penance to Stanley made me think over what else I might have forgotten and neglected over the last few days or weeks. Who was there—anybody? I was just about ready to drop it, when it slammed right into my guts: Petey! Oh, God, Petey. The Auto Show on Sunday. Over a year of building, cementing a relationship with a sensitive, volatile, highly explosive kid, and then when I'd almost gotten him into the palm of my hand, swish, like the wave of a wand, I had gone and blown it. I'd never stood the kid up before. You couldn't even consider standing up a kid who considered his whole life to be a stand-up.

As I called, I was hoping that he'd transferred a little bit of his budding prepubescent maturity from his sex glands into the gray matter. I was praying that he'd be able to summon up enough good-natured optimism and sound judgment to read a good reason into my absence.

"Father O'Connor?"

"Speaking."

"Hi, this is Ben Crandel."

"Hello, Ben. How are you?"

"Fine. I—"

"I was just going to call *you* this evening."

"About my not showing up last Sunday."

"Yes, Ben. I'm sure you had a good reason, but you know how these kids are."

If he hadn't read the paper to find out where I'd been I wasn't about to tell him. "What did he do now?"

"It's nothing serious, except he's been truant on both Monday and Tuesday. And he picked a fight with one of the older boys here at the home, I'm afraid."

"That's all?"

"Aside from a bloody nose, that's about it. You want to speak with him?"

"Yes, please. Thanks a lot, Father."

Not being a Catholic myself, and having mainly resided in either foster homes or nonsectarian places, I'm always unsure about the little rituals. I'm never sure whether you're supposed to address a priest all the time as "Father," or whether it's all right to slip in a "sir" once in awhile. I was thinking about this while I was waiting for Petey to pick up the phone. It was some wait too. I started to wonder if whether, under special circumstances, it was ever all right to call an older priest by his first name if you knew him well enough to know what it was. I doubted it.

"Ben?"

"Yes, Father."

"I'm sorry but I'm afraid Peter won't come to the phone."

"Oh, boy."

"I told him he was being immature. But he says he doesn't care. Do you have any suggestions?"

He asked it nicely. I liked this guy. He was pretty human for a guy that lived the way he did. I doubted that I'd be able to handle his sort of life. And he probably felt the same way about mine. My mind was drifting. What could I do to get the kid on the phone? "Would it help if I asked you to explain to him that I had to cancel due to unforeseen circumstances?"

There was a pause, then he said, "I hate to sound like an adversary, but I'm sure he'll be thinking, if not saying, that you still could have called."

Well, he was getting his digs in, after all, wasn't he? What the hell. It was warranted. By being forgetful, irresponsible, I'd gummed up part of the works around the padre's place. It was more work for him, made life harder than it was already. He had a right to gripe. "Listen, Father. What time is lights out over there?"

"Nine o'clock."

"Well, it's eight-forty-five right now. It'll take me about fifteen minutes or so to get over there."

"I'll make sure he's waiting for you in the lobby."

"Thanks a lot, Father."

"My pleasure," said the padre.

Chapter Forty-Three

The drab, Spanish-style building looked considerably better covered over in darkness and shadows. I much preferred not seeing the gray, rotted potholes in the thick, decaying plaster, which had once probably been a dead ringer for adobe brick until the clay red had faded over time into a very foolish pink. You wouldn't have thought of it as being a home, but that didn't change the fact that it had once been one, still was, in principle. And it wasn't that the padre and his crew couldn't do anything about improving the conditions. They weren't rolling in dough, but being a good old Catholic charity, they weren't exactly begging for handouts either. They had the plans and just needed a few more thousand before they could raze the old heap to the ground and construct a whole new, specially designed facility in its place. In the meantime, they didn't want to waste money on restoring something they were soon going to do away with. A few months or so after Petey and I had started cruising around, he took up calling the place the old Pink Pussy. If he was having a good time, the joke was that he didn't want to go back in there. If I sent him back into the old Pink Pussy, he might never again come out. Such was life. We must be brave—or some crap like that—I'd say with a smile as I dropped him off.

I was thinking about just that, the old Pink Pussy, as I knocked on the big old dark door. Unintentionally, of course, there was something of the old tired-out womb about this place. Inside, a slew of rowdy, parentless boys thrown together without choice, bristled, pounded on the walls through all the minutes of the day, waiting, wanting to bust out and go somewhere, do something real, be somebody for somebody. Mean something. Be wanted.

Father O'Connor greeted me at the door, rushed me into the main recreation area, and left me with not much more than a howdy-do. He did make time to say that the only way he'd gotten Petey down there was by locking him out of his room. I knew enough not to volunteer for an automatic putdown, so I didn't bother to try and say hi when I walked into the room and saw him standing with his back to me. I just walked over to him.

So there we were, me and him standing in between the ping pong and pool tables, him with a paddle and ping pong ball, his eyes locked on the ball, his lips counting silently, seeing how many times he could bounce it without dropping it. In the Guinness Book, the record for this must be something like three days. The kid himself looked like tonight might just be the night. He knew I was there, but didn't lift an eyelid. His pace was steady. He didn't have to move his feet at all, and flicked his wrist ever so slightly every time the ball hit the paddle, just enough to pop it back up and keep it going. I went over to the candy machine along the side wall and bought a couple of Baby Ruths, picked up a couple of Cokes from the machine next door. Then I walked back over and stood next to Petey again.

I opened up one of the candy bars and started eating it, chewing loudly, making an ostentatious display of smacking my lips as I tried to make it sound indescribably delicious. I stomached the whole candy bar, finished half a Coke, then I said, "How's it goin'?"

No answer, of course.

"What number are ya on?"

His lips worked emphatically, mouthing what seemed like long numbers, making every effort to keep the count and blot out the sound of my voice.

"Care to tell me?" I continued. "I betcha if I keep talking like this, asking you what number you're on, how long you've been doing this, what you're goin' for, you're gonna have to start counting outloud, aren't you, Petey?"

I kept it up. After a while, a small hard voice spit out numbers like rounds of ammunition: "Four hundred-five, four hundred-six, four hundred-seven, four hundred-eight, four hundred-nine—"

"Four-o-nine. That's nothin'. You've only been at it a couple minutes then. If you were further along or something, I'd beg off and leave ya to it. But since I'm already over here and you've kinda just got started, would you mind if we shot the breeze for a few minutes?"

"Four hundred-fourteen, four hundred-fifteen, four hundred-sixteen, four hundred-seventeen, four hundred-eighteen, four hundred-nineteen."

"Pete, I can't talk to you if you're just going to count your ping pong balls."

"Four hundred-twenty-four, four hundred-twenty-five, four hundred-twenty-six."

"All I've gotta do is knock the ball away. Of course, then that would give you a good excuse for getting real mad at me, wouldn't it?"

More numbers.

"You can start up again after we're finished—from the point where you left off."

"Four hundred-thirty, four hundred-thirty-one, four hundred—"

I slapped the ping pong ball with the flat of my hand. It went bouncing out across the floor, rolling toward an old, beat-up right piano in the far corner. Petey held onto his paddle, turned away from me and started scurrying after the ball. I hurried after the kid and grabbed him by both his

152

arms before he could bend down and pick up the ball.

"Jesus Christ, Petey, I'm sorry. I really am—I'm sorry."

"Sure."

"There's no excuse. I forgot, that's all. Something came up. I know it sounds bad."

I let go of him. The kid sat down on the piano bench. Barely. Fell there might be a better way of putting it. Just like a sack of bones. "Somethin' came up. Hey, man, I can get behind that. Somethin' came up. No shit. Stuff comes up with me too. I guess when I fuck up, it's different."

He wasn't needling. The tone wasn't lancing, piercing with the normal repartee. It didn't really care. The small voice was listless, indifferent. It brought out the father in me, made me realize I loved this kid more than anything. If I had a good home for him, I'd . . . That was a tangent, the wrong tangent, especially for this moment.

"It's no different," I told him. "But when you screw up, I don't throw the towel in, do I? I don't pretend like it's the end of the world and we're not friends any more."

"You can afford to be like that. You can do whatever you want. I gotta stay here."

"In the old Pink Pussy."

It didn't make him smile like usual. I had to do better, so: "Say, did I ever tell you I used to live in places just like this? Must have had four—no, five—sets a foster parents, plus I lived in more of these types of places than you could count. I didn't get along with people very well."

I could tell he was listening. His neck jerked a little in surprise, I think; and though he kept his eyes on the floor, he was poised delicately, tensed up like an animal picking up a scent.

"My dad was a drunk. He beat up my mom so she left us. Then he beat up on me." I rolled up my shirt and stuck my forearm down under his nose. "See those little scars—he used to put his butts out on me. Some neighbor reported it. He killed himself when they took me away from him. He must have loved me, 'cept he didn't know how to show it—huh?"

He didn't say anything, so I went on: "So, I gotta confess I don't just mess around with you to get a break on my income tax. Somebody like me knows where you're coming from. I thought I had something to offer. That's why I do it. So now you got the truth."

My history lesson didn't seem to have any bearing upon the current situation. After that first jolt, the kid hadn't budged an inch. I swallowed my pride and knelt down by the piano bench in front of him. It was the only way I could really get his attention. I put my hands up on his shoulders. "Petey, you don't realize it, but I'd never do anything in the world to hurt you. You're a very important person in my life—as a matter of fact, pretty close to first place."

"Sure."

I shook his shoulders. "I mean it. You're the tops, god-damn it."

He looked at me then. His eyes were damned up, watery, dark with hurt still, as he said, "How come you forgot about me then?"

"My life's in danger, that's why." There it was. Before I knew it, I'd said it.

His eyes widened and he lifted up his head. He looked at me like he believed me.

"Really?"

"Really."

"What'd ya do?"

"I don't have time to go into it. I just came over here to make sure you were still on my side."

He wasn't listening. His mind was too busy rolling out fantasies of incredible espionage and intrigue. "Are the cops after ya?"

"Not yet," I said, almost thinking aloud. Which was a real mistake.

"What do you mean?"

"Nothing. Forget it."

"Come on, Ben. Maybe I can help, huh?"

"You can help me mainly just by giving me your moral support."

He broke away from me and stood up. "That's the same as saying, 'I don't trust you,' man."

"OK, man, fine" I mocked him. "But I feel like you're playing chicken with me—just to see how far I'm willing to go."

He shook his head and started walking toward the double doors leading to the hall. I talked to his back, saying, "All I'm trying to do is keep you out of it so you won't be involved."

He whipped around, yelling, "I am involved 'cause I know you. I suppose that don't matter to you, does it?"

"OK, OK. You wanna deliver a message?"

Chapter Forty-Four

Well, from there on out, I could say or do no wrong. It was all a bed of roses and more entertaining, besides, than the "Six Million Dollar Man," "Charlie's Angels," "Starsky and Hutch," "Wonder Woman," and the "Hardy Boys" all rolled up into one superduper sexy car chase mystery. My life had suddenly become a prime time tv show with me as star, Petey as my sidekick. I asked him if he had gotten a look at the peanut vendor from the Dodger game. He hadn't seen anybody, and all he remembered was me hanging from the railing like a monkey; but as soon as he made the connection linking seeming accident with rampant murder far afoot, there was no stopping him. Somebody was trying to get me. Geeze. No shit. Really. Were we both secret spies or something? To the best of my ability, I tried to convince the kid otherwise, but I could easily see he didn't quite believe me. He nodded, agreed as I said that I wasn't sure why, but that maybe we'd both find out if we could catch the guy. Petey was cool. It was OK if I couldn't tell him. After all, I probably had my secret orders. And after he proved himself in this clandestine operation, maybe he, too, would attain select and privileged access to the secret files.

Well, at least the kid didn't hate me any more, and the way I was setting it up, I'd be making him feel important while still essentially keeping him out of trouble.

Mon cher Frenchie,
 If you want to talk to me, call this number at exactly 5 P.M.: 451-0789. Today is the 25th. I'll wait three days for your call. After the 28th, I'll assume that you've

rejected the deal and would rather not discuss anything.

Ben Crandel

I clipped a ten spot around the note, gave it to the kid and told him to deliver it to Elmo at the shoeshine booth the next day after school. I gave him five bucks to buy an old pair of clodhoppers from a hock shop. Inspired by Grandpa Swall's subterfuge, I told Petey to slip the note down into one of the shoes, approach Elmo when the stand was empty, show him the shoes, let him see the note inside and tell him to shine them for Frenchie and make sure he got the note. Then ask him if the ten spot would cover the shine as a favor for Ben Crandel.

"What if he says no?"

"All he's going to do is smile at you and say, 'Thank you, young man.'"

Petey was terribly excited, but his brow was deeply furrowed. He wanted to make sure he had it right. "OK," he said. "I buy the shoes. What kind?"

"Any kind. Just don't get any that stand out too much or look too clunky. Ordinary shoes—you know."

"I don't have any dough. What if five bucks ain't enough."

Like a genuine moneybags, I peeled off another five. "Here." I started hoping I'd have enough left to fly back from San Francisco.

"So I buy the shoes. I take them to the shoe guy named Elmo. Crescent Heights and Sunset. I guess I can take the bus."

"Right. Petey, don't worry. All you have to do is hand him the shoes and show him the note inside."

"Then I say, 'Shine 'em for Frenchie.' Will the ten bucks cover the shine?"

"Righto." I bear-hugged him with one arm. He looked happier than a fat kid eating cotton candy.

"But I can't say anything if there's anybody else standing there."

"That's what you shouldn't worry about. If you can't say anything, Elmo will probably get the message anyway. OK?"

"Ben," he began slowly, "I'm glad I'm doin' this for ya."

I laughed.

But the kid was serious. "I mean it. You're putting your life into my hands kinda."

"That's because I trust you, kiddo."

"Thanks."

He didn't pull away from me. Let me hug him. Which was odd. It felt good.

When he walked me out to my car, he wanted to know what was going to happen after I talked to this Frenchie guy. I told him that I didn't know. I also told him that he shouldn't worry if he called the house and I wasn't there. I was going to be staying in a motel for the time being. Petey said he understood. I could tell he was very impressed. He asked me who was going to take care of Stanley. Stanley, I said, was going to be in the kennel at the vet's for the time being.

Even though I hadn't deliberately intended to, I'd said things that had planted images in a boy's mind, things that had sugar-coated and painted over the real core of the danger, made it phony and fun, packed with adventure. It was a pretty bogus way of winning back a kid's affection. But it had worked. And the thing to remember was that he'd surely be safe. My hunch was that the Frenchman had never really gotten a good look at Petey, plus I was almost positive that the first message wouldn't be picked up until the next night. Which left Petey completely in the clear—unless I'd been tailed.

I started to Indian-give on the proposition. I didn't want to take any chances. Petey, of course, immediately started getting mad as hell. So I gave up after he promised he'd get a haircut, comb his hair differently, really do it up. The kid has a great imagination. He could talk me into jumping over Niagara Falls in an inner tube. In a second, he had himself transformed from a corn-haired, pig-pen street urchin into little Lord Fauntleroy, every teacher's pet. When I told him not to overdo it, he rolled his eyes like Jack Benny.

So I gave up. I reached into the car and came up with a record album. "Ever heard of Drivel?"

"They're a new group."

"Well, here's their latest album with their lead singer Lester's autograph."

"You got his autograph?"

"I thought they were just some new group."

"How do you know this guy?"

"I know a girl that goes out with him." That was a nice way of putting it. I'd rushed by Tower Records, grabbed the album, ripped by the Tropicana on the way over to Petey's, hoping to find Sharon and her punk boy. I had found them, taught the guy how to spell his name. When he saw his picture on the album jacket, the Quaaludes laid back easy for a second and he opened his eyelids. He had been so pleased, he'd scribbled something on an eight-by-ten glossy.

"I heard it's a good album."

"I heard it's loud."

Petey found the picture inside the record sleeve. Lester, shirtless in dirty blue jeans and red shoes, was squatted over a six-pack of Heineken on an empty white floor. The pants were unzipped and pulled halfway down the knees; both arms were crossed over the crotch. Lester's face was scrunched up, strained. He looked like he was trying to take a crap. I hadn't read the inscription before, so I looked over Petey's shoulder: "Pete, Punks Rule the Night!!!"

"Far fuckin' out. If these guys get famous, this might be worth somethin'."

"Better put it in a safe place."

I got in my car.

"Thanks, Ben." It was hard to say, but still he had said it.

"Any time."

"Are you sure you're gonna be OK?"

I told him that I was. I also told him that if he hadn't heard from me in a week, he should call Ellen. That would give him a good excuse to call her.

"You better get back inside."

"Yep. Better get back into the old Pink Pussy." He smiled ear to ear.

"It's not that bad," I reminded him.

"That's what you think." He held his nose. I laughed because he was happy. "Someday, I'll be leavin' here and never comin' back." He said this proudly, with confidence. His words seemed to linger ever so slightly, hover over the night air a little like a question. I couldn't really see them, but I could distinctly feel his eyes on me, his ears perked and waiting for what I'd say.

"Damn right."

"Night, Ben."

He turned around and sprinted back into the house.

Chapter Forty-Five

It was five to five on the second day and I was standing in the phone booth on Pico and Ocean Avenue, staring at the black dial face and waiting for it to do something miraculous. By now, I'd become so paranoid about being followed, I was looking behind me wherever I went. I got galvanized with a short surge of adrenalin as I blanked out for a second on where the hell I'd ditched my car. You feel naked in this city without one; crazed, like you've suddenly become paralyzed. Twelfth and Broadway. I loosened up a little. Barely.

A blur of seagulls, gray sky, steel sea lit bleakly on its landward edge—a knife blade—as the miniscule waves picked up sand and silt, lifted up, then slashed straight down, pulled out, started the same little massacre over and over again. The dreary, dilapidated, hulking, red brick Synanon junk house looked like it wanted a wrecking ball for dinner.

I was really worried about Petey. How many nights ago was that? Two. The Frenchman could have been following me then. Easily. For some reason, I had been assuming I had a day's grace because I'd just returned from out of town. That was bullshit. Total stupidity. I felt like calling him, but I stopped myself. I had to cut off contact until this was over. I got this image of Petey being strangled in some back alley in broad daylight. No one was there and it was playing in my head and I couldn't help him. It was completely my fault. Made me shudder. Goddamn fucking sonofabitch. Ring, you cocksucker! Ring! I slapped at the dial with an open hand, hit the heel of my hand into the cluster of metal touchstones. Pain felt really good. I wanted to hurt myself because of what I was thinking about Petey.

He had Petey and he was going to use him on me for bait. That was exactly what I was thinking. So that meant we were both as good as dead. Sitting ducks. Good man, Ben! Way to go. Five o'clock on the nose. If he didn't call today, he probably wasn't going to. All because of a crummy hunch, a theory. My compulsion to make *my* world conform to *my* ideas. Well, at its worst, the end result would hopefully either be nothing or no more than *my* life.

5:01. A squad car cruised by. I felt like they were checking me out. Right. Elmo got thrown off track, gave my little love note to the cops who thought a big score was coming down right in my phone booth. I waited for them to pull a U-ie or come back around the block, but no black and white.

I opened the door, took two steps, then sleigh bells jingled at my back. I stood still and listened, then something exploded inside me. I made one lunge and the phone was against my ear.

"Yeah?"

"I received your messages."

"Well, I'm glad you did."

"What have we to talk about?"

"I think we can come to an agreement."

"Oh yes?"

"Yes."

"That's very good. I'm happy you say that."

"Well, I'm glad we both agree that we can agree."

"Clever!"

"Carl's Market—the corner of Melrose and Doheny. You know where that is?"

"I suppose I could find it. Why?"

"I want you to meet me there at one o'clock—tonight."

"Why should we meet in a market so late?"

"Number one, it's a public place. Number two, at that hour the area is well policed. I'll feel safe there. After we check each other out, then we can go somewhere else."

"Let me think." There was a solid minute of silence.

I was afraid he'd dropped the line. "Frenchie?"

"Yes," he said. "I'll meet you there."

"I'm telling you now, my attitude is that there's enough for both of us."

"Yes." That was all he said.

"I'm going to have somebody outside. He'll check you out before you come in the market. I think it's reasonable that I be suspicious. Come in the entrance from the parking lot. As you approach the door, take out a Kleenex and sneeze. When my guy says 'Gesundheit,' you go over to him and he'll frisk you."

The Frenchman laughed.

"*Comme le* Mickey Mouse Club, *les* Masons, *le Légion Américain*, FBI, CIA."

There was a delayed reaction. I didn't hear anything, then he laughed louder than before. "Is there a special secret handshake?"

"Not yet."

"We should have one."

"Nah. Secrets are like food. If you keep them, they get spoiled."

"Maybe so," he said cheerfully.

"Well, *mon cousin—*"

He laughed.

"We can continue this nice talk later this evening."

"Perhaps we can design a coat of arms."

"*Pour nous et pour touts les autres* cousins, aunts, uncles."

We both laughed. He hung up before I could get the phone off my chin. I realized that Petey was safe and stood there smiling, listening to the buzz, thinking of nothing.

Chapter Forty-Six

I went back to my motel, tried to call my schmucky friend Alex, the guy who hadn't even bothered to thank me for setting him up for the break of his life. I called him at his apartment, let the phone ring for about five solid minutes because I knew the guy had to sleep during the day. I called him at Carl's. He wasn't due in till eleven P.M. At least he was still there. Then, on a complete lark, I called Paramount. They buzzed me right through to Alex Freeman's office, and I got a holier-than-thou mentholated voice. "Yes, Alex is in. *Whom* shall I say is calling?" I felt like doing some heavy breathing, then telling her where I'd like to put it. Instead, I just gave her my name. When I got him on the line, he hemmed and hawed, had at least a million and one excuses for why he hadn't connected with me. I congratulated him, told him it was all fine and dandy and asked him if he was going to be around awhile longer. He told me that, as a matter of fact, this was his first day in his office. He was just moving in and he figured he'd be going in and out of there until at least eight. I told him I had something I had to talk to him about. He said fine, didn't ask me what, and said he'd put my name in at the gate. Great. He wanted to take me to Lucy's for Mexican and Margaritas. Whoopee do and gee whiz. Weren't that nice?

I shaved and showered, put on my suit and had to hold my breath to latch in the pants. I walked over to this restaurant by the Santa Monica pier that did early dinner and happy hour with the beachside tourist and local business trade. Thirteen or fourteen Cadillacs and Mercedes parked in the front of the lot. A couple banged up Pintos and VWs in the rear. Three parking lot attendants—dumb-looking surfer boys. I crossed the street and walked in through the bar entrance so the surfer boys wouldn't see me. I went to the Olde English pub, parked my carcass on a stool and ordered up a double shot of old Irish just to keep in tune with my surroundings. I drank it slowly, then ordered another and put it down the hatch, stood up, paid the barman, and walked out the main door to the parking lot. I took a crisp one spot out of my wallet as I came out the door.

Two of the boys were moving Caddies in and out. A third one, with hair in his eyes, looked like a blond sheep dog. He hustled toward me on light and springy feet.

"That gold Mercedes, second from the far left." I pointed toward the car.

"Yes, sir."

He fetched the car. Good boy. Good, good. Stanley would have been proud of this one. He brought it straight out and up alongside me, swung open the door, and popped up like a Jack-in-the-box. I handed him the dollar and traded places.

"Thanks."

"Thank you."

Chapter Forty-Seven

"Benny, you're making me feel so guilty—I can't tell you."

"Good, Alex, good. That's what I want. I want you to really feel like you owe me something, 'cause I want ya to do something for me."

We were walking through the parking lot by the gate on our way to Lucy's El Adobe across the street. I slapped Alex on the back and left my hand there, rubbed my fingers into the nape of his neck. People, mostly parents with carpools of neighborhood kiddies, were lined up outside to see the filming of "Laverne and Shirley."

"You make me feel terrible."

"Wonderful."

"So I'm a heel, a jerk, Mister Despicable. Do you know how many times I've tried to call you?"

"Sure, Alex, sure."

"Benny!"

We stopped at the light and waited for it to turn green. I put my hands in my pockets, slouched, scratched my head, and stared down at the tips of my boots. I was thinking of saying something like, Do you ever get the feeling that life is passing you by? That was a little too much, though. I didn't think he'd go for that. But I really wanted to play up this forsaken Sad Sack routine for all it was worth.

"Hey, you've been busy. I can understand that—really."

"I drove by your house. I called you. You should get an answering service."

"I should have a valet too."

"They aren't expensive, Ben. Buy yourself an answer-phone at least."

We crossed the street. "You mean you want to have to call back every damn person who calls you?"

"Of course not. Who wants to talk to anybody? I'd rather

be night manager of Carl's market for the rest of my life. Wouldn't you?"

"Don't get sensitive, Alex."

"I'm not. I just don't understand you, that's all."

We got to the front door of Lucy's and had to wait while a large party filed out. There was a Jerry Brown for Governor poster on the window and three or four Linda Ronstadt albums lined up on the inside ledge underneath, which meant to say that this was one of their favorite places when Linda and Jerry went casual. Who cared? The food was still mediocre as hell, but the Margaritas were good so they could get away with it. People will rave over anything when they're drunk and hungry.

Alex put his hands up on my shoulders and turned me around to face him. He looked kind of like a muscular twelve-year-old with a Teddy Roosevelt moustache, except for his serious eyes. Twelve-year-olds don't usually capture your attention via their eyeballs. "If I could, I'd do the same for you." He looked like he wanted to cry, and I was hoping he would.

"That goes without saying," I smiled. Then I pinched his cheeks and told him, "But you won't deny the fact you owe me one, will ya?"

"If they ever make this piece of crapola, I'm gonna owe you one every day for the rest of my life."

"That's exactly what I was thinking."

They seated us. We looked around at the has been star pictures and chit-chatted about B.B. and his eccentricities until the pitcher of margaritas came. I waited until he started sipping. "Alex, since you do owe me so much of your recent found success, I'm going to ask you to collaborate on something really creative with me."

"You got a concept for a script or somethin'?"

"I'm in trouble."

"Good. Tell me about it. And don't leave out any of the gruesome details."

"Listen, *I'm in trouble!*"

"You're kidding! Is it serious?" He was still smiling, wasn't thoroughly sure whether he should believe me.

"Somebody's going to try to kill me tonight."

"Jesus." His smile looked like it was receding.

"Is that serious?"

"Are you kidding?"

I lowered my voice. "Calm down. No, I'm not."

"What do you want me to do?"

"I want you to help me."

"What? How?"

"I've got to make him think he's killed me, but I've got to do it so I don't actually get killed. Does that make sense?"

"What in the world are you talking about?"

I felt like an absolute ass talking about this stuff right in public, so I stood up and asked for the check, then walked Alex back over to his office. It was a large, shabby cubicle in the old writer's building, with half-opened venetian blinds and a view out over the flood-lit asphalt on the inside parking lot. There was a big beige metal desk, a tattered couch against the side wall. Alex assured me how it was only temporary. I sat down at the desk and he paced, studying my face with a quizzical, rather frightened expression. I could tell he knew already that he wasn't going to like whatever I told him.

"I've got to fake a scene so this guy thinks he's killed me when he hasn't. It's a plot as old as the hills, but if you do it right it's gotta work."

"Why does this person want you dead?"

"If I started to tell you that, we'd be here all night and I'd probably end up dead besides."

"Try to tell me," he said.

"I can't."

"I think you're being obstinate, Ben."

"I'm not."

"You should tell me as much as you can, and then we'll go to the police."

"The police can't help."

"Why's that?" He sounded peeved.

"Because I know more about it than they do." I asked him if he had seen the thing on me in the paper. He didn't know what I was talking about. I traced back my memory and tried to recall whether Vicky and Alex had ever crossed paths. I couldn't remember the two of them ever being together or even meeting. Alex was never interested in having anything to do with "lady friends," as he called them.

And he wasn't the type of queer who enjoyed chit-chatting with women. It had always been very apparent to me that he didn't find them too amusing or palatable in any shape, form, or permutation; so I didn't feel any compulsion to re-hash the crazy chain of events for him. Originally, when we had somehow gotten put together on a "Policewoman" episode, this weird little guy, who had said his name was Alex, had treated me suspiciously and said flat out that the only way to write a good one was to see Angie Dickenson as a dyke, then everything would fall into place.

Alex: He was a half-foot shorter than I am, wore tight pants and a half-sleeved, skin-tight T-shirt to show off his taut and veiny arms and ripply washerboard tummy. He worked out at the Hollywood Y no less than four days a week and looked like he was fit enough for any form of hand to hand combat; but you never would have known it from his loose, slightly moist handshake or the skittish, frightened way his eyes danced around when they looked at you under tension. Tonight, though, they were somewhat placid—for Alex, that is. I wondered whether he'd been flirting with me and up until now I'd been missing it. That's the only problem with having a gay friend. You worry about things like that; especially when, in Alex's case, as I'd heard lately, there was an element of self-righteousness attached to the consideration of sexual preference. I personally didn't see any reason why he had felt it so necessary to wave around his gay flag before Bradford Bobby's nose. It didn't seem to have anything to do with his script. But that was Alex. If he was insecure about anything, he liked to air his thoughts. He never held onto his fears. He liked to fling them in your face in a way that made you feel culpable. Alex was really good at that. I admired him for it.

"How can you say that if you haven't checked with them?" he was whining.

"Alex, I have checked with them. Take my word for it."

Alex started rubbing both his temples with the tips of his fingers. "I think I'm getting a migraine," he said.

"A big schtarker like you. Come on, boychik. Taka, tatala."

"Ben, no Yiddish expressions, OK?" His jaw was bulging, his lips were set with tension.

"You're the one who's Jewish."

"I know all about that. We've been through this before, haven't we?" He shut his eyes and massaged his scalp with the whitened knuckles of his closed hand. "Oh, my head."

"Oh, stop being a faggela—I mean a fag—for a second, would you?"

He glowered at me, clenched both his fists and held them down by his sides. "Benjamin, I like you, but—"

"I just want you to help me. I don't want to watch you put on a whole show of your vast range of histrionics."

"You have a very funny way of asking for it."

"I'm sorry."

"Don't call me a fag."

"OK."

He started pacing again, paused rubbing his chin, trying to make up his mind whether or not he should say what was on his mind. And I knew, of course, that he'd say it. "You know, it really did blow my mind that you'd help me out at all."

"Why's that, Alex?"

"You know. You're so fascist, macho-hetero."

"That's not true and you know it."

"I've always been just a fag to you."

I stood up and started toward the door. It was the most theatrical thing I could do and I felt like it was going to work.

"Benny, what do you want?"

I turned around silently, imitating one of Stanley's saddest looks.

"Come sit down."

I got back to the desk, sat down and laid the whole thing out. The Frenchman was coming to the market. I had to have someone there to check him out. I knew that if my young man had any marbles at all, it was more than possible that he might leave a plant somewhere in the store. If he did, I had to get my hands on the gun, put some blanks in it, then stick it back into its hiding place. If he didn't, the situation was more complicated. I'd have to plant my own and somehow manage to get it into the Frenchman's hands. I had a nearly new .32 Smith and Wesson stuffed with blanks and sleeping in the cozy glovebox of my stolen

Mercedes—I'd picked it up for ten bucks off a gnome—pawnbroker—in Culver City.

Finally, I came to the part that had made me think of Alex in the first place. One of Alex's old boyfriends was somewhat of a special effects wizard of the kind that specialized in blood and gore. Alex had told me that he had been responsible for some of the grisly authenticity in a few of Peckinpah's recent films. Alex, by this point, had out the Valium and was stretched out over the shabby couch on the side wall.

"I cannot call Michael," he said.

"Alex, let bygones be bygones."

"Would you just up and call an old girl friend right out of the blue?"

"All the time."

"Well, I don't," he said, adding confidentially. "It's very involved."

"I know I'm asking for a lot, but don't you realize—"

"Stop!"

"A moment's embarrassment on your part might save my life."

The phone rang. It was Alex's new boyfriend, David. David wanted to know why Alex wasn't home yet. Alex started to explain the situation and David hung up. Domestic difficulties. We all have them. I asked Alex for his home phone number, got on the line and tried talking to David. He asked to speak to Alex. Alex's voice cracked as he pleaded with David. Eventually, I was seized with the brilliant notion that, perhaps, if David could be brought in on the circus, then we might be able to clear the way and proceed on with the show. I interrupted Alex and made my suggestion, and we made plans for the three of us to visit Michael if he was home, then for Alex to go to work and for David to rendezvous with us at the market to search the Frenchman for me at one o'clock.

Chapter Forty-Eight

INT. CARL'S MARKET—NIGHT
BEN CRANDEL, a six-foot, overfed, underexercised 32-year-old crazy man, strolls slowly by the produce bins wondering why he's here and trying to keep away from the planted gun—the one the killer left. It's all too perfect and Ben finds he's feeling very, very nervous. Nothing unusual about that. CAMERA PANS grocery shelves from Ben's POV, taking in condiments, juices, Uncle Ben's fried rice.
TIGHT SHOT—BEN
standing there, obviously not knowing what he's doing. CAMERA then PULLS BACK and TRACKS Ben down frozen foods aisle to main aisle by check stands. Ben's good buddy, ALEX FREEMAN, a nervous, flaming faggot, ENTERS SHOT dragging his feet, his eyes big and fishy, and slumps down and falls over Ben's feet. Alex has just O.D.'ed on his prescribed Valium, Quaaludes, reds, and other medications reflecting his zany eclectic tastes.
Ben calls out and Alex's boyfriend, big macho DAVE HOLMES, rushes up and slaps his beloved who then opens his eyes with a slightly perverse smile. Coffee is sent for from the restaurant next door, and Alex is soon on his delicate feet again, his eyes alive with their normal dose of apprehension and impending hysteria.
There is waiting to be done. Macho Dave returns to his post by the door. CAMERA resumes TRACKING Ben down the grocery aisles as he studies cans and boxes, removing some from their shelves, reading labels. Finally, the CULPRIT appears and rather than rummaging through the avocados for his hidden Smith & Wesson, he pulls another just like it from his pocket, takes aim and FIRES at Ben who is walking toward him from the back of the produce department. It's a direct hit with real bullets. Ben's jar charge goes off. He flies backwards into cans of beans, then slides down to the hard floor. He is now DEAD.
And what's more, he really looks DEAD, double-DEAD

with the help of the ingenious blood gusher props he's wearing underneath his dress shirt. That doesn't stop the old bullet from going right in there. There's a good quart of real and fake blood spreading out from his side, sending numerous tributaries out across the floor. The bad dark desperado FIRES stray SHOTS about the market and everybody else remaining flees into the streets. CAMERA FOLLOWS ACTION!!!

TIGHT SHOT—BEN'S MUG AGAIN

His face looks dumb but peaceful in its final repose.

FINAL CREDITS

FADE OUT

THE END

Oscar! Oscar! I was walking around the damn market. My brain was bouncing so hard and fast my skull felt like it should be split open to let the damn thing shoot up into orbit. Everything looked like it was jumping all around me, and all I could do was read boxtops on Cheerio packages and walk by the produce bins and think about Frenchie's gun keeping nice and warm buried down under a blanket of avocados. Alex had started going bananas from the moment macho Dave found the precious little handgun. Dave had supposedly been doing an inventory. At least that was what Alex had told the other checkers. But, by the time he passed out cold, they started looking a little grumpy, curious, like they would have appreciated being told what was going on. I felt like I should have told them, but I was too busy looking forward to all the live action, pondering the important shots. It was important where you placed your camera. This market was really too small, though, to accommodate all the cinematic razzmatazz that should be done. I was thinking that it would have been better in a Ralph's or an Alpha Beta.

I knew perfectly well that the damn thing wasn't going to work out as planned and just as I'd almost made up my mind to get my ass out of there and back to the drawing board, the asshole wheeled in. Dave walked by the front of the store from the outside and gave the handsign as planned. I saw it from the end of the soup aisle and walked up toward the checkstands.

Catching a stroke of luck, Frenchie walked right up to my aisle, looked down, and saw me coming front before I could get all the way there. And then it all started happening just the way it had in my head. Only there was no more waiting and now it was a lot scarier. He smiled wide, baring his little pearly fangs, bent down quickly and took a small gun out of his boot. The asshole had the gall to say *"Bon nuit,"* then he laughed loudly, insanely, so that I was sure there was no way of stopping him. I was down in the middle of the goddamn aisle. Couldn't go forward, cut to the side, or inch back. The cans on both sides were as high as my head. I swiped both my arms across the shelves as I heard shots go off. Something punched me in the shoulder and I felt the shock charge go off inside my coat. Without thinking, I clamped my teeth down on both of the plastic blood packets inside my jaws. Fake blood spurted from my mouth, gushed down my shirt. I fell over a big pile of cans. Felt like I'd split my head open. Frenchie was moving down toward me. He was saying something, flashing a victory smile as wide as a goal post. No more than ten feet away. I heard another shot go off, but I didn't feel anything. I heard people screaming . . .

Chapter Forty-Nine

"Where are you taking him?" demanded a shrill, familiar voice.

"Cedars." A voice I didn't know.

"For God's sake, David. They don't take outpatients."

"What do you mean they don't take outpatients?"

"You have to be referred by your doctor."

"They are not going to turn away somebody that's seriously hurt."

"But I just told you that—"

"Alex, shut up—please."

David, Alex, somebody that was seriously hurt. That had to be me, I guessed. It was time to sit up, time to prove a point, as much for my benefit as for theirs. I opened my eyes, rubbed them, then I started to sit up. Somewhere in the middle, though, thousands of invisible sledge hammers shattered my left shoulder, then proceeded down my chest. I screamed out, then pushed myself up the rest of the way. I was in the back seat of a late-model Ford or Chevy. Alex's boyfriend was driving. We were moving fast, making time down Doheny, going south toward Wilshire.

"You passed Beverly!" cried Alex. He leaned over the seat and gently patted me on the head. It felt like a massage because his hand was shaking. "Don't move, Benny. You're gonna be OK. I never should have let you talk me into this. So stupid, stupid. Why? Why did I let you do this?"

"Does he think he killed me?"

"Don't talk."

"I wanna know, goddamn it!"

"What are you talking about?"

"He wants to know if his plan worked," said Dave.

"I know what he means. Who gives a shit about your plan? You're hurt, Ben."

I was ready to get hysterical myself, so I said, "Alex, would you mind calming down?"

"OK, OK. You just relax. That's what's important." He patted my head again. "Lie back down."

"Since I did get hurt, it'd be nice to know whether my efforts were worthwhile."

"Ben, I don't know. I have no way of knowing. Right now, we're on our way to the hospital. I don't think you should talk. You've lost a lot of blood."

"You can't take me to any hospital."

"What?"

"Don't take me to the hospital."

"I think I'm losing my mind," Alex mumbled, holding his head between his hands, turning it slowly from side to side.

"Don't forget to breathe," Dave reminded him.

"If I go to the hospital, they're gonna call the police or something. I'll be brought in for more questioning."

"Don't overestimate your importance," said macho.

"What do you mean?"

"Nobody's gonna hassle you, man. They'll just patch you up, that's all. You're delirious."

"I am not delirious."

We went on like that for a while longer. By the time Dave approached Cedars-Sinai Medical Center; I'd convinced the two of them that I wasn't bleeding to death, that I'd live at least another half-hour or so, long enough for us to get over to Ellen's parents' home.

We plowed out Wilshire to Beverly Glen, then headed up to Sunset and drove through the west gate into Bel-Air. We turned into the hedge-lined circular drive and stopped up by the front door. On the outside chance, I was guessing that it had to be at least two-thirty, probably closer to three. A dim twenty-watt yellow bulb on the porch was the only light, although lights went on in the bedroom upstairs before Dave rang the doorbell. The house was secluded on a cul-de-sac; therefore, the approach of any vehicle resonated like the call of wheezing trumpets. When a car came in their drive, it was meant for them and they knew it.

"Yes," was said sternly from behind the closed door.

Dave spoke to it, saying, "I'm a friend of Ben Crandel's. He's in the car, hurt. He insisted that we bring him to you."

The voice grumbled inaudibly, then the door swung open and Dr. Brockhurst came flapping out, his leather bedroom slippers clicking like castanets between his heels and the surface of the drive. He looked surprisingly vulnerable, smaller and more delicate, out of his usual impeccable attire. His gray hair was piled up on his head and stuck out at odd angles, giving his face a pinched and narrow look. As he approached, he was frowning, but with a slack jaw. He was still half asleep.

"What's wrong, son?"

Before I could get my mouth open Alex piped in, "He's been shot, doctor. He's lost so much blood."

Mrs. Brockhurst came shuffling out from inside the house. From a distance, as she drew up, I almost thought she was Ellen. She was wearing a sheer white house coat over pajamas, holding it closely to her. Her neck and chin were high, aristocratic without meaning it. She was a beautiful woman and carried herself, I thought, like a huge dove. Her back was straight and her large breasts sloped out like the chest of a bird.

"Where?" asked Brockhurst.

"What is it, Alfred?" Then she saw me. "Ben, what's wrong, honey?"

"Nothing, Mrs. Brockhurst. I just need a little help."

Dave came around and helped me out of the car. Dr. Brockhurst was there on my other side and the two of them helped me up the steps and inside the house with Alex and Mrs. Brockhurst right behind. I went out again for a few seconds. When I came to, they were lugging me into the maid's room off of the kitchen. The lights went on and the maid sat up in bed, yelling something in Spanish. Mrs. Brockhurst talked to her in Spanish and the girl got up, put on a robe, and went out to the kitchen. I could hear her banging some pots and pans around.

They put me down on the maid's bed. The doctor took my shirt off carefully. He saw the emptied blood packet stuck to my skin, made a questioning face, but didn't say anything. When he saw my shoulder, he whistled softly. "Madeline, call Emergency. Tell them we're bringing somebody in." He turned to Alex, saying, "Why didn't you take him right to a hospital?"

"He wouldn't let us. We wanted to, but he kept saying they'd arrest him. He tried to jump out of the car while it was moving."

I went out again. When I woke up, it was light out. Mrs. Brockhurst was sitting in a chair next to the bed. She was wide awake. She took my hand between both of hers and held it.

"Where am I?"

"You're in our house, dear. The doctor didn't want to take a chance on moving you again. Why don't you close your eyes and try to go back to sleep?"

"This was very nice of you, Mrs. Brockhurst."

"Shush."

"I know how imposing I am."

"You're a very nice young man." She paused, then added, "Maybe a little confused," as an afterthought.

"Is Alex here?"

"No. We sent Alex and his friend home. We had to convince them first that you were going to be all right." She smiled broadly.

"I'm not trying to do the wounded soldier routine to win back my sweetheart," I told her.

"I know, darling. Don't you worry. Ellen doesn't even know about this."

That was a little too assuring, but anyway, I still said, "Good. I just didn't know where else to go and I was afraid because I—"

"Try to hush, Benjamin. You'll feel better."

"I just want you to understand."

Mrs. Brockhurst said she understood. We didn't say anything for a few minutes, then, almost to herself, she said that she hoped that Ellen and I would be able to work things out for ourselves. We were "such a nice couple."

I kept trying to say something, but each time I started to open my mouth she told me I should lie still and not talk. She went on to tell me that, although he hadn't said much, the doctor had appreciated my apology. I had made a big start toward breaking the ice between us. I guess I'd been delirious because I had absolutely no recollection of what I'd said. But, from piecing together Mrs. Brockhurst's remarks, I gathered that my oath of contrition had covered two main areas. Number one, that I deeply regretted the rift between the doctor and myself as evidenced a few days back in the Hall of Justice and fervently wished that I had stayed to explain myself and dispel the misunderstanding that existed between us. Number two referred to the Brockhursts' twenty-fifth anniversary party at which I had imbibed to excess and made a spectacle out of myself by climbing the highest palm tree on their grounds and getting stuck up in the fronds until a handful of firemen had lugged a ladder out to get me down. This little scene had been over a year and a half ago, but my contention had been that this was when my rapport with the doctor had first started turning sour. The fact that this faux pas still bothered me had touched the Missus and the doctor. I had apologized at the time, but I suppose they thought I had been prodded by Ellen or had just felt compelled to be polite.

I looked up at Mrs. B and felt glad for what I'd said. It relieved me that my abiding guilt had made the doctor a little more convinced I was capable of sincerity.

I fell asleep again. When I woke up, I cleared my throat.

The house sounded completely dead. Then I heard footsteps from the kitchen. The maid put her head in the door.

"You like soup?"

"Where's Mrs. Brockhurst?"

"No one here."

"Yes, I'd like some soup."

The girl brought me a bowl of beef broth. It tasted better than everything on the menu at Scandia, and after I finished a few bowls I felt like I was ready to climb Mount Everest. So I stood up and walked to the bathroom. After that, I came back and lay down again to celebrate my adventure. I started worrying about whether the doctor had called the cops and reported anything. It probably was his duty. You couldn't just go around yanking bullets out of people without telling somebody about it.

I knew that this was really the right time to vamoose before anybody came home to stop me. So I got up and put on my pants. They were caked with dried blood and ripped in one of the knees. My shirt was nowhere to be seen. I sat back down on the bed and listened to the maid as she moved around the house. After about ten minutes, I couldn't hear her anymore and concluded that she'd stepped outside for a minute. I hobbled upstairs as fast as I could and went into the doctor's drawers, picked out underwear, then opened the closet and chose what looked like one of his old suits. The lapels were narrow and one sleeve looked like it was on the verge of fraying. The pants fit surprisingly well and, wearing boots, I could get away with them being a little short. I went into the bathroom, shaved with the electric razor, washed everywhere that wasn't covered by the bandage over my shoulder, then spent about fifteen minutes trying to put on one of the doctor's freshly laundered shirts. When I was all finished, I called a cab. Then I draped the coat over my shoulders Italian style and walked outside and leaned against the mail box on the curb. The cabbie defied reality and got there in about ten minutes. As we pulled away, I heard a car approaching behind us and looked up into the rearview mirror. It was Mrs. Brockhurst in her Coupe de Ville. I waved goodbye, but she didn't see me—which was just as well.

Chapter Fifty

"How many times are you gonna take my picture?"
"How many do you want me to?"
"None would be fine."
"I gotta have something to remember you by, don't I?"
"Listen, I don't know where you're comin' from, but you been here every day—seems for a week. All you do is walk around the plaza, take a cable, then come back and walk around the plaza some more."
"I happen to like it here. Is there anything wrong with that?"
"What's your trip, man?"
"I don't know. What's yours?"
"My trip is sittin' here in the flower stand all day."
"Well my trip is walkin' around the flower stand all day."
"I get paid for it. What do you get?"
"Enjoyment."
"You are *really* weird."

I walked back up toward the top part of the plaza by the bank. Yes, it was certainly nice to be in San Francisco. There was nothing typical about this girl and, at heart, I knew she didn't represent the hospitality of the city, but still, nonetheless, for three days running, she had been the only person I'd spoken to outside of the night shift clerk in my quaint hotel.

I looked like shit. I felt like shit. My thoughts were like shit. It was no wonder the girl wasn't exactly crazy about me. I looked back over toward the flower stand on the corner and saw her. She was standing outside the glass enclosure, staring after me with equal parts of incredulity and disgust crinkling up her button nose and pulling up the corners of her mouth into a smiling sort of wince.

I kept walking away and sat on a short brick side wall facing out toward Montgomery Street. I tried to step outside of myself and see the part of the picture she was looking at. Here was a guy who was standing there somewhere around the corner of Montgomery and California Street every morning by the time she got to work. He was wearing a pair of unpressed wool slacks over scuffed-up pointed boots; a baggy T-shirt with captioned illustrations of Fisherman's Wharf, Coit Tower, Golden Gate Bridge, Harbor Tours, Chinatown, and Cable Cars in bleary color across the front; the T-shirt bulged over the chest because his left arm was hanging from a sling which could be seen tied behind his neck; and it was all topped off by an unshaven face and a pair of aviator shades with the right lens shattered (I had sat on them on the plane). This guy was standing there on her turf every single day as she arrived. It was obvious he didn't belong here. He wasn't an executive in the 52-story tower or the bank next door. He wasn't maintenance apparently. He didn't seem to be a wino either. With those possibilities eliminated, what else could he be? A lame, pathetic vagrant with a crummy little instamatic who walked around all day taking pictures. At five o'clock when she was ready to leave, the guy was still there. Just when you thought he was gone for good, there he was again with his crummy little camera, hopping off the cable car and walking briskly across the street. As if he were going somewhere. But where did he go? Up the plaza steps around the tower, then back again to those same steps and down. Then he walked around the block, came back to the same place, and started all over again.

Crazy, some kind of rare nut. That's what she was thinking. Suddenly, it became important to me to prove myself otherwise. I walked back to the flower stand and told the girl that I wasn't really as strange as I seemed. She was actually quite pretty. Dark, long, frizzy hair held down the sides of her face with a colorful Indian headband. It was amusing to me, in some ways almost consoling. People still lived like they were in the 60's up here. I felt sure that most of them didn't even know what a Nielsen rating was or how the stock at Fox and Paramount was climbing like all get out.

She told me to get away from her or she'd call for the police. I told her that I had just given up a career in the Coast Guard. I was wandering around because I hadn't been able to decide what I wanted to do. She didn't go for it. She looked over my head at nothing, then returned to the Robert Heinlein novel she was reading.

I felt like shit. I was going buggers. I crossed the street and walked down a block or so until I found the first bar. One, two, three doubles of dark fire water and the flames were still rising up my back. The only thing I felt was more sober. It smelled and looked stale in there. An Olympia waterfall ("It's The Water") in perpetual motion over a well-seasoned cash register and a black, Naugahyde-cushioned bar with matching high seats down the line. The seat at the far end was turned over on its side. The bartender looked like he belonged here. Like a piece of furniture, he was just there, didn't give a damn about what he had to look at or listen to. It didn't matter. I watched him washing the glasses. His eyes looked interested. Like an alchemist polishing his stone, he took a certain pride in things inanimate. Fuck the rest of it and why worry. It'll give ya trouble. Right. I put my head down over my free arm along the cushioned edge. The bartender told me there was no sleeping allowed. My nose was down in the crook of my arm and I smelled myself under the armpits. It was a rotten smell, a stink of inactivity, shiftlessness, not the healthy stink you give off after you've been working out, letting off some good steam. I lifted up my head and took another whiff around the watering hole. Smelled just like me. We were twinsies.

I got back on the street. It was 4:45 and I didn't give one holy shit about the fact that the buildings would start emptying out in about fifteen minutes. I passed a drugstore and saw a pair of aviator shades in the window and thought about buying them with the halfhearted notion of improving my image. Then I reached down into my pocket. I had twenty-eight dollars. I knew I wouldn't be able to fly back to L.A. I had confronted that little inconvenience from the start. So, at eight bucks a night, I had three more nights in the Stanford Arms, which was fine with me. Even though the black and white tv in the lobby and all the young and old derelicts and flies that came with them were compliments of the house, a man still got that hankering feeling for his very own slum.

At the rate things had been going, with three days down

the tubes and another three to go, I was thinking that I'd better get back over to the plaza and put in some more time, regardless of how it all looked in the flower girl's eyes. I passed up the sunglasses and walked back over there.

The girl didn't look up, although I knew she saw me. I walked around the bottom of the tower and mulled everything over again just for the pure entertainment of it. I wanted to stop the last leg of a murderous scam, a monetary affair that had taken the life of someone close to me, the lives of others not so close, and almost—but not quite—mine. I had a sore arm and shoulder to prove it. I had put my money on the hope that the Frenchman believed that he'd killed me. He'd therefore be coming to Frisco at some time soon to make the final arrangements for transferring the full trust estate into his control. My hunch was that this young foreigner had to be the last remaining survivor. Therefore, the tontine would be terminated. Frenchie would inherit the original principal sum and the interest that had accrued. It was his dough and I believed that there was enough of it—and probably enough papers to sign and be notarized—so that he'd have to be right there in the flesh.

All of this made sense. What didn't was the strong possibility that I'd been framed for a tontine member myself. This frame could have been honest, unintentional. But important things just don't happen that way. There was somebody else involved. Somebody else had been coaching Frenchie, giving him pointers, telling him where it was he had to go. The bank obviously had a list of all the official players. But what was going on here was lost and buried far beneath the paper work. Identities can be borrowed, traded, or created at the drop of a hat. The Bank of America wouldn't be the one to know. The only thing I had in my head was that I had to follow Frenchie to the truth. He'd lead me to somebody or something that would wrap it up completely.

Chapter Fifty-One

I was so wrong.

I was coming down the short stairs by the tower, angling in toward the corner of the plaza so I could pass in front of the flower booth just for spite before I headed back over to the other entrance on Kearny Street. A sharp cold gust, and a billowy dress filled up like a sail and caught the corner of my eye. A flash of leg, long and thin, dark, perfect, fluting upward into a narrow thigh, slight like the tip of an arrow. Hands came up, then down over the pleated navy front. Long hands. Red, red glycerin lips that struck the late sunlight and shattered it. Dark, glossy hair brushed back off a fair face. Like a highdiver making her approach on the board, her head was thrown back, and her shoulders jutted back further with every step. She knew where she was. She knew where she was going. Her hands stayed along the sides of her pleated skirt, holding it down against the wind. The closer she got, the better she looked—the kind of woman who, although good in clothes, is always better without them. I felt pretty sure about that. In fact, I was certain. Because it was Denise.

We were ten feet apart and she hadn't seen me. I crawled to the side of the flower girl's glass booth, looked over toward the curb. Her car was still there. It was a four-door Volvo with an elderly driver in livery, double-parked, drumming his fingers over the steering wheel. I looked back toward the tower. She was going in the entrance.

I was feeling something, but I wasn't sure what. Shock, alarm, confusion, depression? No, none of these. Peace, calm, tranquility, surcease of pain and sorrow. That was more like it. Also, not surprised. It was so simple, so obvious, and the simple reason for not having overtly suspected was because it had been that way. I thought that I must have known without knowing all along and that was why I had this sense of equanimity. It was almost religious, the feeling. I looked up at the sky. The wind was blowing the clouds, keeping the air clear and blue. The bank and the 52-story tower, the scene on the street, all of it looked beautiful because life once again made sense. The particular timing and the claimed shared experience were what had held me back from confronting it, from transposing feelings into thoughts. My reluctance, my doubt—I traced back all of my more subtle inklings to the obvious knowledge that we had had a history of not liking each other. And that had been so logical, too. If I had gotten to know her better while Vicky was living, then, well, of course, I would have wanted to know more about her. Not big things necessarily, but little things that could be pieced together artfully into all kinds of tales once Vicky was gone. And even if for some irrational reason they just hadn't seemed right, who could have proved them otherwise? Who would have denied that Denise and Vicky had been neighbors and high school chums? It had taken her and whomever she was working with a minimum of a year to set the stage. That was a lot of time and work. It had to be because this was all worth something, something in dollar signs that would probably be more than the wildest calculations I'd had in mind.

The flower girl was closing up, pulling in her pots of white and yellow chrysanthemums. She was either pretending that I wasn't there or she'd forgotten about me. Fine. I was standing in the middle of the plaza trying to keep an eye on everybody coming out. The Volvo was waiting, so she'd most likely be coming out the same door again. I wanted to shield myself from view but still keep a good angle on her when she came out of the building, so I walked up California toward the bank building and leaned up against a parked car. My arm and shoulder hurt again and it felt good to lean back. I took another look up at the sky and then I started daydreaming about her nipples, how long and taut they were. I could see myself bent over them, taking the two of them together, kneading the little breasts to bring the points together so I could suck on them both at the same time. I could see myself fucking her. Almost, but not quite, I could hear her moaning at me, "Put it in and fuck me;" then, "Harder!" I laughed aloud remembering all the naughtiness. Down below I was as hard as steel. I still felt like fucking her. Which amazed me. At that moment I felt I'd rather fuck Denise than anybody else alive. I wanted to slap her face and paddle her little butt. I could hear her shrieking in my ear and all it made me want to do was slap and spank her harder. What I really wanted to do was kill her. I realized that, and I could feel the excitement so bodily it made me shiver.

I glanced back toward the Volvo, then ambled over and took in the license. The driver didn't even see me. As I was walking back over toward my waiting place, she came out. She had her arm around somebody a head taller than she was. Smug-looking, gray wings around his temples, a ruddy, bony face with a square, pronounced chin. Looked and dressed just like a magazine model. Their hips rolled in stride; they were fused together like incestuous Siamese twins. He leaned over her lips and she came up on him hard and swift. I watched him open the back door of the car, let her in, then follow after her.

They drove away and I just stood there. The flower girl's glass cage was all shut up. She'd left without my noticing. The excitement had drained out of me. I felt spent. I was thinking about my shack in Laurel Canyon and the place seemed like a palace to me. I wanted to take a nap, but I couldn't face walking back through that lobby full of sour-looking strangers in the clean light of day.

I walked down to Bush Street, went on up and plopped myself down in a small booth in a large Chinese-style coffeeshop a little off the main drag on Grant. It was fairly busy, so I ordered up some won ton soup, a steak sandwich with fries, chocolate milkshake, tea, and coffee, wolfed it all down, bided my time; and, when the moment arrived, I put the check in my pocket and cruised out the door. I felt guilty but promised myself I'd send them something at a later date.

Then I covered every square inch of Chinatown, trying to relax. I pretended I had money and window-shopped for a pair of silk pajamas. Finally, well after dark, with swollen feet and a throbbing shoulder I could no longer ignore, I went back to the hotel.

Chapter Fifty-Two

"*B*on soir. Stick 'em up."
  "*Merde.*"

"*Merde* is right, my friend. Let's go inside."

"How have you been?" he asked me nonchalantly. "I thought you were no longer with us."

I had Frenchie's own gun to Frenchie's own back and I pushed the barrel into his vertebrae and urged him forward. "Ring the bell."

He did so without another word. A snowflake of refracted light glinted out toward us from behind the bevelled glass door. Somebody had flipped a switch in the entry. This was a slum for Russian Hill. The bell was manual, the door knob only brass, and I could just tell by the looks of it the place probably didn't even have a bowling alley in the basement or more than one library on each floor. Denise's dashing gentleman swung open the heavy door unassisted and we were standing face to face.

"Good evening. May we come in?" I shoved the heel of my hand into the back of Frenchie's neck just to throw him off guard in case he'd been thinking about doing anything, then I held up the gun and waved it in the air a little for effect. The only problem was that my sonofabitch hand was shaking.

The guy looked genuinely surprised. "What do you want?"

"I've got so much to talk to you about, I don't know where to start," I told him chattily. "You're not going to be rude, are you?"

"Who the hell is this?" he demanded of Frenchie.

Frenchie answered him, sounding just as put out as he was. "You know who this is. Move, for God's sake."

Frenchie stormed in brushing past the larger man. I came in behind him and shut the door. I switched the gun from my right to left hand, which worried me a little although I hoped it made me appear relaxed. The sling seemed to be holding me steady, at least.

"Ben Crandel." I offered my hand and all he did was look at it, then glance over toward Frenchie with a supremely reproachful expression.

I patted the fellow's face with my palm. "Boy, you are really rude. Especially after all the trouble you put me through."

He backed away from me, still staring at Frenchie. "What did you do?" droned his hollow voice. "What did you do?"

"I thought I had succeeded when I hadn't. What can I say?" Frenchie said. "I'm much more surprised than even you."

"Listen, fellas, I'm sorry I'm not dead," I told them both. Then I put the gun back into my right hand and nudged Frenchie over toward the dapper fellow before he moved too far astray on the periphery. I moved up close on the dapper guy. The face was pale and waxy, the thin-lipped mouth slack and slightly open, but the eyes were hard, stony, predatory. He was wearing a double-breasted gray worsted blazer over a collarless red-green checked flannel shirt, tailored blue chinos, neutral suede loafers. Fashionable wasn't the word for it. He was a goddamn paper cutout of every latest trend, from his diamond deco stickpin to his tapered pant cuffs. I was standing nose to nose with him. He smelled like a walking beauty shop, but he was big enough to get away with it. "So, let's see," I said. "Are you a Swall, a Smith, or what else could you be?"

He looked at me like he didn't know what the hell I was talking about. Of course. And of course the whole thing was going to demand an awful lot of explaining. I knew he was going to deny it all, but I realized I was almost doing it more for myself than him. He'd just have to bear with me.

"Why don't you just do the honors and get it over with," he told me.

"Oh, I see. You mean kill him—" I pointed to the Frenchman "—just like I killed all the others. Then maybe throw you in for good measure. Is that it?"

He gave me that incredulous, frightened look that people tend to associate with honest men. I nudged the two of them into the living room, pointed them toward the camel-backed couch, then took the plush armchair across from them.

"You still haven't answered the question," I told him. "Which one is it?"

"Which one?" He looked at me like I was totally out of my mind.

"The name, you asshole—the fucking name."

"My name is Christopher Porter if that's any of your business. I've been trying to get them to build a case against you for some time. I guess it came too late. You won't get away with this."

"Wait, wait. Hold it. 'Them,' I guess, meaning the old B of A. Is that what you mean? You've been trying to get them to track down the real criminal, meaning me. OK. I got that. And of course you were only intending on protecting the rights, interest, safety, the general well-being of your client. Of course that's right, isn't it?"

Frenchie had some interest in all of this too. "Who are you?" he asked me. "You haven't told us *your* name." His worried face smiled at me for a second, then turned blank and rigid.

"Why, I'm whoever he is."

Frenchie smiled again. This time the smile stayed. The nerves were tight in his face and he wasn't able to wipe it off.

"You really don't have the faintest idea what I'm talking about, do you?" I told him.

"We are family. Why must we fight?" His eyes believed what he was saying. The smile got sad, then faded, and the face went blank again.

"Sure, except you've got your cousins confused. It's him, not me," I told the kid.

He laughed quickly, nasally. Dapper Dan gave me another questioning look.

"Look," I told him, "try to listen to what I'm telling you. I was close to your cousin Vicky. I don't know how close you were to her. I'm willing to bet you'd never met her before. I don't think you wanted to kill her either. You believed that I was biding my time—I was getting ready to go in for a kill—and that's why you couldn't tell her what you really wanted. You wanted to wise her up to what you thought was going on, but she was so naive you were afraid she'd run and tell me your story, which would only serve to push the button on herself plus tip me off if I wasn't tipped already. Were you trying to warn her while you flushed me out of the woods again? Or did you just want to kill her and botch it like you did when you tried me?"

He laughed. After a moment or so, he looked serious when he said, "You're the one who blew her brains out. Why don't you tell me?"

"I didn't do that," I told him calmly. "Don't say that again." I turned toward Dapper Dan. "Does the B of A administer many tontines?"

"You know an awful lot about something you have nothing to do with," he said.

"I've looked into it. But aren't they illegal or something?"

"I wouldn't know anything about that. Stephen and I are just friends."

"And you only happen to be on the regional board of directors."

"I don't think I've ever handled you. How would you be familiar with me?"

"Leg work. And let's not imply that I've been handled by somebody else."

"You mean you're denying your involvement?"

I laughed. "You're so pitifully innocent, aren't you?"

"And aren't you? Denying a quite substantial source of income, asking me questions about your account as if you don't already know about it."

I decided to ignore the bastard and concentrated on Frenchie. "He's lying about me and he's lying to you completely. I've got nothing to do with all this. Have you met his partner Denise?"

Frenchie looked at Dapper Dan, who shrugged his shoulders in reply. "I know of no Denise," he said. He turned back toward me, looking amused. I could tell now that he was worried, though.

"Well, if I didn't kill her and you didn't kill her, maybe he didn't kill her either. But there's somebody he goes around with that did. If you were following Vicky for any time, you may have seen her with her. About five-nine, five-ten, short dark hair, thin, knockout legs."

"Yes," was all the Frenchman said.

"If you check out the St. Francis, you'll find her there.

I'm not sure which room, but he dropped her off there early this evening about six-thirty. It's taken me two days to figure that out. It's a little hard to tail somebody when you don't have enough change for cab fare. But that's another matter. Just go over there on your way home tonight, say."

"Tell me more," he said.

Dapper Dan barrel-laughed loudly. "Yes, please do, won't you? I never anticipated that you'd have an amusing side to you."

I had the kid's attention now. That was all I cared about. "OK, either you're greedy or you're on a vendetta. Maybe a little of both. I can't completely blame you for it. Right now, I'd place my cards on thinking that you think I killed somebody in your family. I don't have a full list or knowledge of names and dates, but maybe it was somebody you were close to—another cousin. This guy here may have given you a tip on who it was who killed him. He possesses a lot of information and he's the one man, if any, whom you would trust. It wouldn't occur to you that he might be closer to all of this than you think, and it wouldn't have occurred to me either if I hadn't seen the two of them together."

"With the woman, you mean."

"Right. Otherwise, I didn't believe it, but it could have been simple mistaken identity."

"You thought it was more than that."

I nodded yes. "I got called by Arnold Swall who was grandson to either Richard or Stephen Swall—is that right?"

"You seem to know better than us," the pretty boy said calmly.

"Say that he is," the kid said.

"He calls me and wants to talk. I tell Denise. Now, the idea is that Arnold knows something he shouldn't. So Denise tells your dapper friend here, who puts a finger on poor Arnold before I can even speak to him. You didn't kill him, did you?"

"I wouldn't kill anybody for just money," the kid told me. He looked at me hard for a moment, then he said, "I want to protect my life. Everybody wants to live, don't you agree?"

I agreed with him. "Why did you hurt the girl then?" I asked him.

"I didn't really."

"That's not what she said."

"You see, I had no choice."

"But she wouldn't tell you anything."

He nodded.

"That's because maybe she didn't know the first thing about it. Maybe she was too naive. Did you think the two of us were in cahoots working together? Or did you think I was putting one over on her?"

"I didn't know."

"Is that why you pretended to be my buddy?"

"Maybe."

"You were smart at least. There's no doubt about it. The assumption is that if Vicky and I had been in collusion, naturally, each of us would be prone to be suspicious of each other. She didn't turn against me, so from that you decided she didn't know about me. So then you had to push her around some more to make it all look authentic. You couldn't kill her if she hadn't done anything."

"Yes."

"What kind of agreement do you have with this man?"

"He gets a very small percentage because of the risk."

"What risk?"

"He's sheltering the knowledge that I killed you."

"But you haven't killed me."

"This is all a total bunch of nonsense." The tall man stood up.

I leaned forward to poke him back down in place, when all of a sudden there was something in my back. I hadn't heard a thing. I turned around. It was the old man from the Volvo, the pretty boy's driver. He was completely bald without his cap.

"Drop your gun on the floor," he said politely.

I did it, then I sat back in the chair. "We're both real bad amateurs," I told the kid. "We don't know how to use a gun and we sit with our backs to the door. Though you must have seen him waltzing in here. So I guess you didn't believe what I was tellin' you."

"Shut up," the tall man told me.

"People know about this. You kill me and you're not going to—"

"Peter, I do need those pants pressed."

"Yes, sir."

The old guy picked up my gun and handed it to his master. Then he turned around and left the room as quietly as he had come. The pretty boy turned toward me again. He was having a good time playing with the gun, hefting it around, getting a feel for it. I only wished the damn thing were empty. But it wasn't. Six bullets, brand new and shiny.

"Who says I'm going to kill you?"

"Oh, I don't know. I just kind of have this feeling that you'd like to. What I'd like to know, though, is why didn't you just kill the kid instead of getting so complicated?"

"If there's such a thing as reincarnation, maybe you'll come back as a private detective."

"So you do intend to dispense."

"Not with this." He smirked at the gun, patronized me with a kindly smile tailor-made for dunces.

"But you did have to get him here. You couldn't just run all around killing people. So you brought him here, hoping to kill two birds with one stone. And I was the stone, huh?"

"Oh, yes."

"And you had your girl keep an eye on me. Originally, maybe out of paranoia, you weren't completely sure the kid believed you about me. By having Denise befriend me, you could keep tabs on me. Until I told her, maybe you didn't know that the kid had been out for me from the beginning, even before you had her bump Vicky off. You took it hook, line, and sinker from the get-go, didn't you, Stevie?"

The kid didn't answer. He just sat there plowing a furrow across his brow.

"Only the kid couldn't kill us both. You had him believing everything about me, but he couldn't be totally sure about her. For all he knew, she didn't have the slightest idea; so he couldn't go through with it and kill her. That must have pissed you off, having to stick your neck in there and tell your girl to finish the boy's job for him. That kind of thing would make me really angry. We can't predict everything, though. Stupid punk. He was more sensitive and sweet than you thought, wasn't he?"

"Silence," the kid said with a French inflection. He stood up. "What is he saying?" he demanded of the older man.

"This."

The dapper fella calmly fired three shots through the kid's middle. Two in the chest. One that hit him right through the middle of the windpipe. It was pitch black outside the window, and the barrel flared like a microsecond Fourth of July. The window shattered in the center. The kid's eyes turned into glass. His face went slack, listless, thoroughly dead before you could start counting. His lips twisted into a vague frown that hadn't lived long enough to be born. Then he toppled headfirst across the coffee table, sending a crystal decanter onto the carpet. Crème de menthe seeped out of the bottle and soaked into white pile.

The killer turned toward me, smiled congenially. "I would tell you who I am, but I don't want to give you any more ideas than you already have. Though it probably wouldn't matter. There's not a soul who could identify me. Alas. So, what have you? Nothing, really." He looked down at the kid and noticed the green stain and sighed. "I'm going to have to have this damn rug cleaned. I hope it'll come out."

"That's what Lady Macbeth said."

He had a laugh at that, then he said, "Personally, I agree with Shakespeare. I don't believe that people who go around shooting and killing should be allowed to live. We're far too lenient." He took out a monogrammed handkerchief and wiped off the gun as he told me, "I'm afraid I'm going to have to call the police."

I stood up and started to go for him. "You're not gonna get away with this."

"You stay right there. I could shoot you in self-defense."

"But you're afraid to kill me." I slowed down but kept coming.

"Don't tell me you'd like some more wounds." He fired another shot into the window, a couple inches to the side of my head.

I stopped and played statue.

"That's better. Peter!" he called loudly.

The old guy floated back in like a moth, fluttering his hands as if he were surprised and concerned. "What happened, sir?"

"This man's a murderer. Call the police."

The good servant rushed out of the room. I still couldn't hear him.

Chapter Fifty-Three

"I'd plead insanity if I were you."

"But you're not me, are you?"

Recipe for Crooked Ugly Cop Face: Take a big spoiled rump roast. To make sure it's good for cooking, try to find one that's well marbled and fatty on top (if no marbles, just fat will do). Poke some holes in it for eyes, nose, and mouth; then, maybe, if you stick it in the oven at around three-fifty, it'll crack a smile. For now, it was just staring at me from across the table, and I was the one who felt like he was being baked. Ferret Face had been an Adonis next to this guy; and at least if he gave you change for a dollar, he meant to give you all your money back. Oh, well, an unpleasant diversion certainly seemed better than nothing. It made the minutes fly. I was supposed to be in transit to L.A. to face the music there. But it had been two days and I had started thinking that they'd forgotten about me. It was nice to know they hadn't.

"Say we allow that you're not related. That'll just rule out the profiteering aspects. So, I guess that leaves us with what we kinda put together."

"What's that?"

"Just because the French kid killed your girl didn't give you carte blanche to kill him."

"I think you've got this all a little confused."

"OK. Straighten me out."

"I'm not doing any chit-chatting without my lawyer."

"We talked to your lawyer. He said it'd be all right if you answered a few questions for us."

"Really? That's not what he told me."

"We're just trying to find out the truth."

"Then why do you seem to believe Mister Porter's story more than mine? Is it credibility?"

"You said it."

"Well, we'll see how credible his credibility is."

"Let's think this out. If this guy is who you say he is, let's ask ourselves a couple of questions: Number one, according to you, he isn't who he says he is. Is that right?"

"Right."

"He's really a part of the family that stands to benefit from the trust fund. Yes or no?"

"You can answer that for yourself."

"OK. I know you think that's the case. All right, so let's assume it is. Now, if he is this other person and he changes his identity, when everybody else is dead and he's working at the same bank that's administering the fund, how can he possibly change back to his real identity?"

"Why should he have to?"

"Because he can't cash in unless he can prove that he's really still alive."

"Who does he have to prove it to? He's the one who's administering the account. He's two people. He can check, audit, and interview himself without anyone else ever knowing, even suspecting. They don't know that he's really another person. He could hire another person to play himself."

"If he knew that you knew all this stuff, why didn't he just shoot you? Then he could have said it was in self-defense or that the kid did it while you were struggling over the gun."

"Either way, he knew he'd be scrutinized. Lucky for me, I guess he thought he stood a better chance by trying to frame me."

"We've got your reports from L.A. You were involved with a girl who was murdered by a young opportunist. You looked into what happened, found out a little, then you went on a personal manhunt against the whole bunch."

"So that's why I killed all three?"

"I'm counting two."

"Oh, you mean you think the old man was really a heart attack?"

"Sure, it's possible you wanted to kill him too. But I figure he's the guy you got your info from."

"So why wouldn't I kill him once I found out what I wanted to know?"

"You're confessing. Is that what you're saying?"

"I'm only trying to be consistent. A crazed killer doesn't leave any mercy offerings in his wake, does he?"

"You can act like I'm stupid all you want, but you do know that you're got."

"OK. Sure."

"You're so full gone crazy you don't even know it."

"Right."

"In the twentieth century, no high-ranking executive is gonna try to put on a magic show with multiple personalities. If you were in your right mind, I'm sure you'd tip to that."

"Ask his family about it. Did you ask them?"

"He's not the man who's going to be on trial. You are."

"If you wanted to ask them, you wouldn't be able to find them—that is, unless he had them tailor-made and invented."

"You're nuts and you should 'fess up to it."

"And I'd like to tell you what I think of *you*, but I'm not going to."

"I still say you're bug-eyed."

"Are you on some type of take?"

He pegged me with a graceful left hook right in the ear. A man adroitly skilled at administering unnoticeable bruises at the beck and call of synaptic instinct. It jarred my arm and shoulder as much as my head.

"Sensitive, aren't you?" I said to him.

He stood up, bellowed down at me, "I'm no crook!"

His eyes looked funny, so I just nodded and said, "OK."

Like pliers, his hands gripped the edge of the table. "You stink like lies. I just wanted to save taxpayers' time 'cause I know you're guilty. That's the only reason I brought you in here."

He looked like he was going to sock me again, so I summoned up all the restraint I could muster and kept my mouth shut. Then he just leaned across the table and spit a handful of threats in my face. He was a bastard from the old school. It was a giveaway act that obviously had many repeat performances, and I could see it unstrung him that it didn't work. His meaty face was pouring sweat and he misplaced his train of thought a couple times. I let him know that his skulduggery had fallen on deaf ears by staring down at the floor. So he gave up and called for the guard outside the door—but not before warning me how bad this was going to look further down the line. I saved my grin until I got back to the cell.

Chapter Fifty-Four

"Transfer time, huh?"
Handcuffs clicked onto my wrists. A young, well-chiselled, blondish face moved down along the corridors by my side. Four nights and three days. I had caught up on my rest. I wasn't worried about getting off; it was just a matter of when. And if it had to go to trial, then it would. We'd dig up what we had to. Eventually. But then, at other times as of late, it had occurred to me that perhaps I was being cocky without reason. Maybe this Porter fellow had taken every eventuality into account. What if he hadn't left a single track to follow? It was possible, even probable. But it was too early yet to start the serious fretting. That's what I kept telling myself. I was anxious to get back to L.A. and talk to my old pal Ferret Face Steifer. After our last chat, I felt that if I had something to say, now, at least he'd hear me out before he started digging. If I could just get him to do a little scratching into Porter's burrow, then maybe . . .

My escort opened the door and we walked out into the booking area. Ellen was there. She was with my L.A. lawyer, the one that Dr. Brockhurst had gotten for me. I'd talked to him on the phone a couple times from San Francisco and seen one of his Bay Area associates, but I hadn't expected to see him—let alone Ellen—until I was returned to L.A. They stood up from across the room and came over to the desk. The handcuffs were coming off my hands and the lawyer told me that they'd dropped all of the charges. I was free. The desk sergeant gave me my keys and wallet with two dollars and ten cents.

I was in a daze. Ellen put her arm around my waist and

we walked outside and said goodbye to the lawyer. Then we stopped and turned toward each other and just held each other. I gave her a squeeze and lifted her off the ground. She told me to be careful about my arm.

"Why are you here?" I asked her.

"Because you're here."

"That's why I'm asking . . . I mean shouldn't you be cleaning your apartment—you know."

She pulled away from me. "If you're going to get snide—"

"I'm just overwhelmed. You thought we'd changed. You wanted time to think. You—"

"I missed you."

"Me too."

"Well?"

"What?"

"Kiss me, dummy."

Chapter Fifty-Five

"Ben, this is Mrs. Smith—Mrs. Augusta Swall Smith. Mrs. Smith is Chris Porter's grandmother. His real name is Darryl Hutchins."

I scooted around and stood up from the booth. Ellen had made a few phone calls from the hotel while I was in the bath. I knew, of course, that she had something really breathtaking to tell me, but I still hadn't heard it. When somebody gives you two choices—you can hear about the show or go see it—why, of course, you choose the latter if it's something you've been waiting for. And, boy, had I been waiting. On the way to the hotel, she had started to tell me, but she'd been so excited I hadn't been able to understand her. So then, being not a little exasperated, she had said the only way to get it straight would be to get it right from the horse's mouth—except, as she'd said, for the fact that the horse had no mouth.

So that was why I'd been sitting by myself in a booth at Vanessi's in North Beach at three o'clock in the afternoon, nibbling on a piece of sourdough and waiting for Ellen, who had gone to wait for someone out front. And that was why, at this moment, I was daintily, ever, ever so gently shaking hands with an elderly lady who stood before me head held high, her heavily powdered face beaming kindly with a ghostly ectoplasmic sheen. The analogy that sprung to mind was the Great Wall of China: ancient, so old and antiquated, but stately and well maintained. It was a sickening, cheap thought, but she really did smell overflowery, like a funeral parlor. She had as many wrinkles underneath the thick powder as a city does streets. I was surprised to realize that the elegance, the regality was in her face and carriage. Her clothes were actually commonplace. She wore a clean but faded ruffle collared, leaf print green gown, and her shoulders were covered by a thin, ratty, rose-colored sweater drawn together at the neck with a large, heavy silver brooch. My eyes were drawn to the brooch. Scores of pinpoint emeralds and rubies followed the center set pattern of a heart-shaped diamond. It was real, what seemed like the most real thing about her. She was fixing me with a smile that looked like it was never going to end, and her large, lonely, watery eyes twinkled at me as she blinked them. I smiled back and patted her hand and told her that I was very pleased to meet her.

"Mrs. Smith understands everything you're saying, but she can't talk."

"I'm sorry."

"She had a stroke. But you get along, don't you? You don't mind."

The nice old lady nodded her head up and down, blinked her eyes repeatedly, and held onto the same smile.

"If there's something important she has to clarify, she'll write it out."

Mrs. Smith looked down into a small black patent leather pocket bag and took out a small scratch pad. She looked at both of us and nodded happily. Then I moved over to the side and let Ellen help her down into the booth. Mrs. Smith sat in the middle and Ellen and I sat on either side of her. The waiter came and we ordered cocktails. Mrs. Smith picked up her scratch pad and wrote up a Brandy

Alexander. She had beautiful handwriting. Ellen went in for a White Russian and I took J.D. I felt like telling the guy to bring me ice and a bottle.

Ellen patted Mrs. Smith on the arm and told her, "Mrs. Smith, I know I've told you everything about Benjamin, but I haven't told him anything about you. God knows, I haven't had the time to. Ben just got out of jail two hours ago, but he was so anxious to find out about everything I brought him to meet you right away. I thought it would be easier to explain it this way."

The old woman nodded vigorously.

Ellen went on, saying, "I hope you won't mind if I repeat a little of what we've already talked about."

The old lady patted Ellen's arm with a gnarled but steady old hand—a long, delicate, shapely hand. You could tell it had once been lovely.

Ellen turned toward me, her face dead serious. "Let's just say that I was concerned about you after you called me at the office. I went to Daddy and got you bailed out by agreeing to certain conditions."

I started to say something, but she stopped me. "No, let's not talk about that now. So, we got you out. Then you mailed me those papers."

"Sly fox, wasn't I?"

"What?"

"I knew a journalist couldn't resist a hot story."

"You didn't think I'd do it just for you, did you?"

I had asked for it. The waiter came and put down our drinks. Mrs. Smith pointed to the cannelloni on her menu. Ellen went for the scallopine marsala, and I got linguini with clams. The waiter left and Ellen asked me if I had tried to look up the people's names in the trust.

"I didn't have the time to. Is that how we met Mrs. Smith here?"

"That's how I started out. In fact, I talked to . . . Victoria's—"

"Vicky."

"Vicky's grandfather's landlord in Phoenix. But he had already left. I knew he'd come to Vicky's, so I went over there to her house. I found out he had died."

"Mrs. McGinty."

"Right. I spoke with the landlady. He was the last of the original trustors next to Mrs. Smith."

"Is that what Mrs. Smith says?"

"I forget she likes to be called Augusta. Yes."

Ellen and I nodded and smiled at the old lady, then Ellen went on. "That was about as close as I got. I spent three whole days calling Swalls in just about every city you could name, from Miami to Moscow. I didn't dare start with Smith."

The old lady smiled at that, patted Ellen's arm again.

"But one thing I did do was give a cryptic tip to a police reporter friend of mine."

"What'd you tell him?"

"That I knew you and that it would be worth his while to follow the case."

"It's nice to be a case."

"You know what I mean."

"So what'd he do?"

"Not much, but enough. He's got a snitch who told him that the LAPD downtown got a short letter of inquiry."

"And I guess I don't have to guess who that was from."

"You don't."

I turned to the old woman and asked her if she could tell me how the family had been set up. For a moment, I was expecting her to answer me.

Ellen opened up her purse and took out a few folded sheets of notepaper. "Augusta helped me figure it out. Here, let me show you. It's almost like a family tree." She pointed to the top of the list. "Let's take Vicky's branch first. We've got her grandfather, Harold D. Swall. Harold has three children: Harold Junior, Selma, and Robert. Now, their first offspring are the ones who qualify for participation in the tontine agreement. Harold Junior was a Navy pilot. He went down over the Marshall Islands. End of Harold Junior. Selma is childless and Robert has Vicky. The only one who could still be alive in this bunch is Selma. Her married name is Hall. She sends Christmas cards occasionally from various places—the last one was about twelve years ago. We probably wouldn't have been able to find her if we'd wanted to.

"Second branch: Richard L. Swall. Had two children:

Oliver and Marian. Marian's first child was a boy. Augusta can't remember his name. He had rheumatic fever, died before he was a year old. Oliver's first child was Arnold. Arnold had a Tahoe number. I called him but got a no-longer-in-service message."

"He was in Vegas the last time I saw him."

"Did he tell you anything?"

"He was dead."

"I know that."

"How?"

"The police were right behind you. They just didn't have as much information as you did."

"Because I didn't give it to them."

"How'd you find out about Arnold to go see him?"

"He called me."

"What'd he say?"

"He wanted to know what I knew."

"Did you tell him?"

"Sort of. He didn't want to talk on the phone."

"And then you went to see him and he was dead already."

"Yeah."

Ellen looked at Mrs. Smith. "You liked Arnold, didn't you?"

The old lady nodded, her mouth quivering slightly.

Ellen looked back at me. "None of them ever came to visit her."

"Did they know where she was?"

The waiter came back again and put the food down; but the old lady looked so sad all of a sudden, I couldn't pick up my fork.

"Most of them probably thought Augusta was dead."

"But how's that possible?"

Ellen pointed to her papers. "Let me show the rest of this and maybe you'll see why. OK. So, in the second branch, Arnold is the only qualified tontine member. He's killed, leaving only his Aunt Marian, who's still alive and well with a couple of kids in Fort Lauderdale. There was a little problem with her at first. She tried to fake one of them for the one she lost."

"She's no dummy."

"You can't really blame her for it. But the family found

out. So she doesn't have anything to do with anybody. Let's go on to branch number three: Stephen S. Swall had two sons—John and Raymond. They're close, only a couple years apart. One stayed in France after the war. The other one moved over there. They each have sons: James and Stephen. Stephen is the one who was following you."

"He thought that I killed his cousin."

"What?"

"Well, as far as I see it, I may be wrong but I'm speculating that this Porter or Hutchins must have killed Stephen's cousin, then succeeded in sticking the blame onto a fictitious third person—which was me—in order to lure the kid over here. He was hoping to have him murder Vicky, who was supposedly my accomplice; then he was going to murder or frame the boy. And, unless I'm mistaken, then he would have been the last one in the whole pot. Bingo: Grand Prize."

"After I talked to Augusta, I called both brothers. I got in touch with James's father first. He said that Jimmy died in a car accident two years ago while he was vacationing in California. Initially he had come over to see Stephen, who was at NYU. So Jimmy dies in a supposed car wreck. For all we know, it may have actually been a car wreck and had nothing to do with conspiracy, murder plans, anything. Stephen is away from home, studying abroad. He or his parents sends the bank his change of address, then Darryl contacts him and informs him that his life is in danger. Stephen comes to California. Darryl sets him up with the information he needs; and if he associates you with being that real or imaginary killer, then when Vicky is killed he feels he knows for certain."

"He tried to kill Vicky himself." Ellen looked at me like she didn't understand. The old lady's eyes were bugging out. I wasn't sure whether it was glaucoma or fright. "He was made to think Vicky and I were working together, but for some reason it didn't quite fit and he couldn't go through with it."

"Are you sure?"

"Of course not. But it's the only thing that seems to make sense. I don't believe the kid was a natural-born deliberate or premeditated killer, if that's what you mean."

"I asked the uncle if there had been any recent rumors or cause for alarm."

"And?"

"He had no idea what I was getting at, so I told him every theory I could think of. This was a week ago. He said he'd get in touch with Stephen's parents immediately. They called me and I told them the same thing. First, they went to New York, then they came out here. By the time the police sent out an all-points bulletin, you'd been arrested—"

"And their son was dead. The kid must have thought he was being a hero."

"Besides, he believed his own life was at stake."

"If it had all worked out, he probably would have been well rewarded. How much you think?"

"Let me finish the family tree first." Ellen turned to Augusta and said, "I hope this isn't too much." The old lady tried to smile and patted Ellen's arm. "Augusta married a Mister Charles Smith. Mister Smith was a judge on the California Supreme Court."

Mrs. Charles Smith lifted her chin with the proud memory.

"They had three wonderful daughters together. Darryl's mother's name was Cecilia. She was the oldest. The other girls were named Deborah and Elizabeth. Darryl's mother and father and both sisters died in a house fire. It was during the summer and Deborah and Elizabeth were visiting Cecilia, who'd just moved back East."

"So Augusta and her husband raised Darryl."

The old woman started shaking. Ellen held her and talked to her quietly. Then, after a few moments, Ellen said that we should eat. But the old lady wanted to finish the thing. She gestured and made soundless syllables.

So Ellen said, "Darryl put Augusta in the home ten years ago. That was after her stroke. Mister Smith died eleven years ago. He was eighty-seven."

"When you say nobody came to visit, does that mean Darryl too?"

"He came once the first year and that was it. Augusta couldn't write at first, but the administrators there tried to do something. By the time she could communicate, she'd lost the desire to do so. She felt abandoned."

"She was like his own mother and he literally forsook her. Yet he fronted for her keep."

"It was probably too much for him."

"Either that or there's some guilt only he knows about."

"That's possible. Let me tell you: I found out about Augusta and I went to see her. No one else had been out. She lives in a rest home in San Bernardino, not too bad a place. We talked, and I learned about the grandson. After you got arrested in San Francisco, I took her out for the afternoon. Guess where we went?"

"To see Darryl."

"That's right."

"Wait a minute. What made you so sure? Did Augusta know he was using a different name?"

"She told me she had a grandson in business whom she hadn't seen for about ten years. I asked her if she knew about the tontine arrangement and she said that was why she had written her letter. She was worried that something might be wrong, that something might affect him. She felt hurt by his neglect, but she still cared about what might happen to him."

"How did you know that Augusta's grandson was Porter, who was really Darryl Hutchins?"

"I didn't know that Porter was Darryl. I just knew there was something fishy about him."

"How?"

"Don't be silly. A man was killed. Either he shot himself or the other man shot him. What else was there to consider—you? Besides, the old trust papers were affiliated with the Bank of America. Porter was an officer of the bank."

"What happened when you saw him?"

"We went to the bank. His office is in the large tower adjoining, but he wasn't there. His secretary said he was taking care of something in the bank. She didn't know how long he would be, so we decided to drop over and see if we could find him. He was on the second floor talking to an accountant. Augusta went up to him."

"What did he say?"

"Granmama. He was quiet for a moment, then he started chirping away like everything was normal and wonderful.

Asked her how she was, said he had meant to visit but hadn't had the time lately. Things like that. I don't have to tell you how Mrs. Smith felt. Darryl's voice kept getting louder. Finally, he screamed at her to let him alone. It was horrible."

"So what finally happened?"

"It got quiet as a church. People were looking at us. Then Darryl ran out of the bank. After that, I didn't have any trouble talking to a few other people. With Augusta's help, we confirmed his identity. Then we called in some auditors to go over his accounts. And that was it."

I looked over toward the old lady. She was neither happy nor sad. Her face was masklike, and the wrinkles in her brow and down the sides of her cheeks were moving around like a puzzle that kept changing its pieces.

"I'm very sorry this had to happen," I told her.

She lifted up her beautiful old hand and patted my arm. Then she patted Ellen's arm. She took my hand and put it on top of Ellen's. Then she pulled over her cannelloni and started eating.

Chapter Fifty-Six

Darryl's plan, a life's dream. He had probably spent twenty years trying to think of a way. And he had almost found one except for one wilting, nice, eighty-one-year-old woman whom he had disregarded as either boon or threat. She had just been trying to help. She had still cared. She had still remembered. But what she had remembered was a little boy, probably a somewhat sad little boy, but nevertheless a child who had been kind, affectionate, considerate in his own way.

Mrs. Smith had conveyed to Ellen that her three brothers had been partners in a construction company, and when the oldest, Stephen, had died, the other two had gone bankrupt. Stephen had been the brains. The tontine had been something that her brothers had thought would have a binding effect on the family circle. A friend of the family had done the same for his brood and he had been proud of it. This man had been in the insurance game where, as I found out later, phony tontine "policies" had been issued as enticing freebies in conjunction with selling life insurance policies. Big rivals like the Insurance Company of North America, Mutual Life, and Equitable Life had used this ploy in their client-recruiting campaigns. This was banned in most states before 1910. But as a private trust, the Swall Family Tontine had been completely on the up and up.

As far as the sharing, there could have been a lot of it. The original principal had grown from two hundred thousand in 1932 to a cool half million in 1950. That was when the Swalls had optioned out a certain portion of principal and interest for recommended investments controlled by the bank. With diversified investments in real estate, municipal bonds, and other marketable securities, the original principal had mushroomed to eight million by 1960. In 1965, Darryl had come to the Bank of America in San Jose. He had worked two years there, then had requested and received transfer to San Francisco in 1967. From the beginning, of course, he had been known as Christopher Porter. Ellen told me all of this and more—more than I really cared to know.

There had been ten potential members, but only five first offspring had survived to maturity. Four out of five of them were now dead. Unnaturally so. Crummy, very crummy odds. With close to twenty million sitting in the kitty. They were going to have an awfully hard time deciding who that dough belonged to. I assumed they'd probably divvy it up with what remained of the family.

I was lying back against six fat pillows waiting for Ellen to come back from shopping. I thought about the last night. We'd taken Mrs. Smith and the hired nurse out to dinner—an alternately sad and happy occasion. The old lady hadn't had a vacation in over ten years. She hadn't been able to see enough. Her features had taken on a childlike cast. We went to the latest Burt Reynolds movie and she kissed both of us afterward when the lights went up in the theater. Ellen had promised her that we'd come visit.

I looked at the new dressing on my shoulder. The first thing Ellen had done after lunch yesterday was to get a doctor to our hotel—a colleague of Daddy's. We were staying in this quaint little five-room Victorian place on Union Street. It was modeled on the English Bed and Breakfast. Our room was called the Pines, and pine cones had been placed on the dressers and nightstands. The air gave off a fresh, hear·y bouquet.

I sat up and spread some marmalade over my buttered English muffin, took a few bites, then leaned back again. I felt like some more orange juice, but I wasn't about to bother ordering. Ellen had told me she was going to do an article on everything for her magazine. Her editor was really excited. He thought there was a movie in it. But they'd probably buy the police reporter's story from the paper, then take a meeting with Sterling Silliphant on the screenplay. Dino De Laurentis would produce. *Sex, Money, and Blood:* Read the Bantam paperback! Maybe I could get them to take a meeting with me before they took one with somebody else. After all, it was my story.

"Big deal. What's his track record. What's the kid done anyway?"

I could feel a tic starting in my right eye. I put my hand up and rubbed it. I felt my face. It was as smooth as a baby's bottom. Ellen had shaved me with her leg razor in the morning. It took her twenty minutes. By the time she finished, she had shaving cream in her hair, all over her robe. She told me that I'd better not get into the habit of being pampered. I offered to pay her back by shaving her legs. When she got into the bath, she called me in, handed me the razor, and stuck out her leg. So I stroked it. Gently. I took my time, doing a good job, but found myself distracted.

I was at a definite disadvantage because of my shoulder, but it hadn't mattered. The sun fell across the bed. Her breasts were ripely swollen, slightly pendulous. I was only one who could tell she was just a couple days away from her period. I'd missed them. They were so soft in my hand. I brushed her silky pageboy back off the rich and dusky olive skin. Then I just looked up at her face. After a few minutes. Her dark eyes grew darker, then stopped seeing me. Her mouth looked like it was sleeping with a good dream, and then she must have called my name about fifty times.

I could hear her again. It was a song. Just for me.

"Ben, Ben . . ."

Ellen's song.

Chapter Fifty-Seven

"Benjamin, wake up!"

"Hey, Ben."

The first voice was part of the dream. The second wasn't. I opened my eyes and Ellen was standing by the side of the bed with her arm around Petey. I couldn't believe it.

"What the hell are you doing here?"

"It's Friday. Thought I'd just take a vacation—for the weekend."

"Sonofabitch."

Petey looked uncomfortable. His hands were in his back pockets and he was flapping his elbows around like an ostrich. "If you'd a called me, maybe I coulda helped or somethin'."

"Maybe I should have."

Ellen let go of Petey and walked toward the bathroom. "Peter called me because he was worried about you."

"That's what I told him he should do if he didn't hear from me."

Ellen closed the bathroom door. Petey became solemn and stood there quietly, staring at my shoulder dressing. His mouth was open just a little. I felt like a decorated war hero, which made me laugh.

"What are you laughin' at?"

"You, 'cause I missed you."

"Is your arm OK?"

"Good enough so I can give you a bear hug."

He came to me and let me hug him. I felt like I wanted to say something, but I didn't know what it was.

Chapter Fifty-Eight

"This area was called Cellblock D—otherwise known as Isolation. You were sent here if you were black or if your life was being threatened by other prisoners or if you disobeyed a guard. Those who were brought here for the last reason might spend time in one of the six Dark Holes along this bottom tier. In these cells, the men were at the mercy of the guards. If a guard thought you needed it, you could be stripped of your clothes and forced to survive on bread and water. You would have no bed or mattress, so you'd have to sleep on your knees and elbows to avoid contact with the cold steel floor. There was virtually no light in these cells. If a guard wished to, he could leave open the small grate covering the meshed screen in the door. Or he could shut it, blocking out all light. Many men lost their minds here. More than we probably know. If you want to see what it was like, step right ahead and I'll lock you in— just for a minute."

We were on the Alcatraz tour. The kid was having the time of his life. He was absolutely spellbound with the likes of Machine Gun Kelly, Capone, the Birdman of Alcatraz, and all the other Hollywood dash and glamour that goes along with the territory. He grabbed Ellen by the arm and took her with him into one of the Black Holes. I didn't want to go in, so I stayed out and watched. Almost everybody else in our twenty-five-man tour was in one of the cells. Our guide walked along the row of six cells and shut all the doors and grates. You couldn't hear any of the squealing and chattering once the doors were shut. It was just me, a couple of old folks, and the young guide, who was done up like a Canadian Mounty in the park ranger's uniform. He looked like he belonged in a forest. The guide and I talked about the weather for a minute, then he swung open hell's doors and men and women wearing matching ensembles came out carrying their cameras and purses, babbling excitedly as they blinked their eyes and squinted into the light. Petey scooted away from Ellen and ran up on the guide's tail so he wouldn't miss a word as we headed toward the exercise yard.

The wind picked up as soon as we got outside. Ellen was upset because she was wearing a summery linen dress. It was a beautiful day on shore, but it could still get nasty out on the Rock. She had goose bumps all over her bare arms. I put my arm around her and held her close. We watched Petey following the guide and looked out across the bay at the city. It was quiet enough to hear a little traffic noise. Or maybe it was just the mechanical sound of the choppy waves as they washed up against the rocks all around the island. If you looked straight up over the middle of the bay, the sky was brilliantly blue, shimmering. When you looked out over the city, the sky went gray white like an old man's hair. Down around the rock, the sea, the recreation yard, everything was dull and dark gray. It gave you a frightening, isolated, singled-out feeling, enough so to make you believe in divine retribution if there ever could be such a thing.

"I know it's not very liberal of me, but I'd like to see Darryl and Denise put up in a place like this."

Ellen frowned. "Forget about them."

"I will, eventually."

"Where did you say she was holed up?"

"In the St. Francis. For a week, I guess."

"That's right. One of the cops told me she'd charged enough at Macy's to open her own dress shop."

"Really? You didn't tell me that."

"I also didn't tell you what she said when they took her."

"Something sweet?"

"Oh, yes."

"What was it?"

"Something like she should have killed you herself."

"Me?"

"'That cocksucker friend a hers' I think were her words, to be exact."

"Nice."

Ellen smiled. Then she started to say something and stopped, a habit of hers. Her mouth opened, her lips formed a vowel, then no sound emanated and the cavity closed on a thought.

"What?"

"Nothing."

"Something. What is it?"

"I don't know how to ask, but did you love Vicky?"

"In some ways."

"Change the subject?"

"Yeah."

"What should we talk about?"

"Let's talk about how sexy you are when you shiver." I swallowed hard, then I said, "You're everything to me. Do you love me?"

She laughed right in my face. Her eyes were watery and so were mine. She nuzzled in closer and put her cold hands in up under my shirt. "You're so corny. That's what I love about you."

"Thanks. Thanks a lot."

I looked down at our tour. They were moving out of the recreation yard and up the long stairs by a rubble of old buildings. Petey was waving at us to catch up.

"Look."

Ellen looked over and saw Petey. "You're not mad I had him come up here?"

"No."

"Peter told me you shared yourself with him."

"So were you surprised?"

"Yes. It meant a lot to him—and to me."

"He didn't say anything at the time."

"Ben, you of all people should know how he is."

I agreed with her.

"He was really concerned about you."

"He was, was he?"

"Of course he was."

"What the hell am I going to do with him?"

We were walking down toward the recreation yard. Petey was waiting for us and Ellen said, "That's up to you."

We came up to Petey and I said, "I bet you were scared when I had you deliver that message."

He looked absolutely disgusted. "Are you kidding?"

I laughed at him, which made him look angry. "You're a pretty tough guy, aren't ya?"

He didn't know what to say, so he started to walk back toward the tour.

"Tough enough for this place?"

"Maybe," he called back over his shoulder.

"Hey, Petey, wait a minute. I wanna ask you something." He turned around. "What?"

"Are you tough enough to empty the garbage when it's your turn, wash dishes, stuff like that?"

"What?"

"Don't you understand what I'm saying?"

"If you're going to say it, say it," Ellen told me.

"What I'm trying to say is that I'm gonna adopt you, you little bastard!"

Petey stood still. He was frozen and so was I. Then, the next thing I knew, I had him up off the ground. He was in my arms and I was crying like a baby.

"I'm sorry, kid. I just got a little overemotional."

I wiped my eyes and put him down. He had rivers running down his cheeks. Ellen was working on an ocean.

"Is it OK with you if we have an extra roommate?" I asked her.

"I think so."

"You knew this would happen, didn't you?"

"Yep."

"That makes you even cornier than I am."

"I guess it does."

Petey had finished crying. He wiped his tears off with the sleeve of his Levi jacket. "Come on, you guys. Stop bein' mushy."

"OK."

By the time we caught up with our tour, it was already over. But we didn't care. On the way back, we were sitting on the upper deck on the ferry. It was getting sunny again. The wind was pushing at my face, making my scalp tingle as it tugged on my hair. Ellen was rubbing my neck and Petey was standing by us looking over the water. I had my hand on the rail and a seagull came by overhead and took a crap on it.

Petey saw it all happen. I felt my hand, looked at it, and looked over at Ellen. The two of them were laughing their heads off as though it were the funniest thing they'd ever seen.

I wiped it off underneath the seat. Life will do that. Come along and take a crap on you. But as long as you're still around to appreciate it, I guess it's OK. I joined in laughing, leaned back, and stared straight up at the sky. It's big out there, and what can you do about it? Not much. But you can try. You can try.

BLACK LIZARD BOOKS

JIM THOMPSON
AFTER DARK, MY SWEET $3.95
THE ALCOHOLICS $3.95
THE CRIMINAL $3.95
CROPPER'S CABIN $3.95
THE GETAWAY $3.95
THE GRIFTERS $3.95
A HELL OF A WOMAN $3.95
NOTHING MORE THAN MURDER $3.95
POP. 1280 $3.95
RECOIL $3.95
SAVAGE NIGHT $3.95
A SWELL LOOKING BABE $3.95
WILD TOWN $3.95

HARRY WHITTINGTON
THE DEVIL WEARS WINGS $3.95
FIRES THAT DESTROY $4.95
FORGIVE ME, KILLER $3.95
A MOMENT TO PREY $4.95
A TICKET TO HELL $3.95
WEB OF MURDER $3.95

CHARLES WILLEFORD
THE BURNT ORANGE HERESY $3.95
COCKFIGHTER $3.95
PICK-UP $3.95

ROBERT EDMOND ALTER
CARNY KILL $3.95
SWAMP SISTER $3.95

W.L. HEATH
ILL WIND $3.95
VIOLENT SATURDAY $3.95

PAUL CAIN
FAST ONE $3.95
SEVEN SLAYERS $3.95

FREDRIC BROWN
HIS NAME WAS DEATH $3.95
THE FAR CRY $3.95

DAVID GOODIS
BLACK FRIDAY $3.95
CASSIDY'S GIRL $3.95
NIGHTFALL $3.95
SHOOT THE PIANO PLAYER $3.95
STREET OF NO RETURN $3.95

HELEN NIELSEN
DETOUR $4.95
SING ME A MURDER $4.95

DAN J. MARLOWE
THE NAME OF THE GAME
IS DEATH $4.95
NEVER LIVE TWICE $4.95

MURRAY SINCLAIR
ONLY IN L.A. $4.95
TOUGH LUCK L.A. $4.95

AND OTHERS . . .
FRANCIS CARCO • PERVERSITY $3.95
BARRY GIFFORD • PORT TROPIQUE $3.95
NJAMI SIMON • COFFIN & CO. $3.95
ERIC KNIGHT (RICHARD HALLAS) • YOU PLAY THE BLACK
AND THE RED COMES UP $3.95
GERTRUDE STEIN • BLOOD ON THE DINING ROOM FLOOR $6.95
KENT NELSON • THE STRAIGHT MAN $3.50
JIM NISBET • THE DAMNED DON'T DIE $3.95
STEVE FISHER • I WAKE UP SCREAMING $4.95
LIONEL WHITE • THE KILLING $4.95
THE BLACK LIZARD ANTHOLOGY OF CRIME FICTION
Edited by EDWARD GORMAN $8.95

HARDCOVER ORIGINALS:
LETHAL INJECTION by JIM NISBET $15.95
GOODBYE L.A. by MURRAY SINCLAIR $15.95

Black Lizard Books are available at most bookstores or directly from the publisher. In addition to list price, please send $1.00/postage for the first book and $.50 for each additional book to **Black Lizard Books, 833 Bancroft Way, Berkeley, CA 94710.** California residents please include sales tax.